Sandm

By

Tammy Bird

First Publication 2018
Flashpoint Publications

ISBN 978-1-949096-03-3

Cover Design by AcornGraphics

Editors: Patty Schramm and Nann Dunne

Acknowledgements

"What you need to remember is you are good enough, momma." One of my grown children told me that on one of my darkest writing days. "You have a story to tell, and your words may be just the words that someone somewhere needs to read." He probably doesn't even remember saying the words, but I will never forget them. His siblings said similar things over the years as I struggled to refine my writing voice. For those words and for their love and understanding, I am grateful. Thank you for being you, Sarah, Katie, Angela, Roscoe, Crystal, Nic, and Eli. I am a better writer and a better person because of you.

To my closest friends, my grandkids, and my extended family, thank you for sharing in my happiness and my frustration as I traversed this new land. Thank you, too, for your encouragement when it seemed too difficult to continue and for bragging about me when I wasn't strong enough to brag about myself.

Thanks to my writing academy crew, both instructors and peers, but especially to Ona Marae, whose extensive guidance and friendship taught me a great deal about writing and about commitment to our words and to each other.

To those who showed support through the revision process and into production, thank you. A special nod to Ann McMan who not only designed my phenomenal cover but guided me through the first attempt to put this story into words, to my daughter-in-law, Jen Seha who somehow convinced me I could trust her to read my first revised draft when I was afraid to let anyone in, and to Patty Schramm who wrote the words that every writer wants to hear: "I want to publish your work." Thank you for believing in me and for believing in *Sandman*.

A special thank you, as well, to Aimee Young who named the small café that plays a small role in the story but a big role in my heart and to the man in the ice cream parlor on Buxton Beach who answered my comment about how quiet the strip of sand was at the end of October with, "Yep. So quiet you could bury a body in a dune and no one would notice."

And finally, my Dear Lisa. You are the best friend I have in the world. Thank you for loving me, for marrying me, and for taking this journey with me. From reading early drafts to giving me advice on the cover to spending countless hours in the bookstore while I wrote, you were as important to the completion of this book as I. No words can express the gratitude and love I have for you.

Dedication

This book is dedicated to my mom, who lived a life of pain and determination like none I have ever known, yet continued to thrive. From her I learned drive and perseverance, both qualities I have needed in my own life's journey.

Thank you mom, for being my advocate when I was not my own. Thank you for telling anyone who would listen, "My daughter is writing a book." Thank you for our last years together and all of the laughter and card games and love.

If you are listening, mom, "I did it. I really wrote a book."

Chapter One

Sunday, November 18, 2018, 4:00 AM

The Outer Banks, North Carolina

"Looks like a fucking war zone," Katia Billings-Castillo said, her voice barely audible.

Glimpses of the cluttered beach appeared along the headlight beams after each swish of the windshield wipers. Hurricane Anna, off the coast, had spawned a couple of tornadoes, and one had touched down on Buxton Beach.

Several volunteer EMS workers littered the small strip of sand in response to the mass casualty incident. Additional help might not arrive for days, and Katia found solace in their presence.

She saw a pink object wedged between the narrow slats of a sun-faded fence. A child's toy. "It's going to be a long morning."

"No rest for the weary." Elliot Palmer, her partner of four years, gave her a small smile.

Katia reached into the console and pulled out a handful of light-blue, disposable gloves. She wiggled her left hand and then the right into a pair and shoved the rest into one of the deep pockets of her windbreaker. She ticked off items in her head they would need: triage kit, airway bags, tags. "Let's go." She breathed a grateful "thank-you" into the sky when a string of spotlights came on and banished the darkness.

They grabbed their triage gear and pushed out of the vehicle against the relentless rain.

The downpour pelted Katia's face despite the bright-yellow hardhat and matching jacket she wore. A shiver moved up her spine and landed at the base of her neck. "Fuck, El." She pitched her voice an octave above the wind. "The Clark place."

Elliot nodded to the right. His chin moved forward slightly, and his Adam's apple bobbed in his throat.

Katia turned and followed Elliot's direction. "Aiden," she whispered. She bent down on one knee next to the tiny form in turquoise pajamas. Keep your head on straight, she thought. No breath. No pulse. Black tag. Move on. The air and rain absorbed the sounds of the sirens and brought them focused and screaming into her head. Moving in for a closer look, she put her face near the cheek of the five-year-old and placed her finger against his neck. She shook her head.

"No pulse." She breathed deeply before pulling a black triage tag out of the windbreaker pocket that didn't hold the extra gloves. She secured the tag to the arm of the small frame.

Katia stood up. They would come back for him. Right now, it was about finding the living.

Neighbors grouped into twos and threes. Side by side, the rescue workers searched through the scattered debris looking for people and tending to the injured who were emerging.

"Over here," a man yelled. He made a sweeping motion with arm and hand. "She's breathing. Hurry. Come on." Katia moved through the remains of a living room and into what was left of the bathroom. The woman's arm hung across the side of an old clawfoot tub. Other than the appendage, her body was fully on the outside of the cast iron, porcelain-lined focal point of the room. Katia knelt in front of the woman. She didn't recognize her, perhaps a visitor. She eased her to the ground and felt for a pulse. The woman was alive. She had no visual injuries outside of a large, raised bump on the side of her head.

Katia attached a yellow tag to the woman's wrist. "Stay with her."

Katia moved away from the destroyed beach house. Steady drops of rain fell from the rim of her hat and onto her chest and shoulders. The beach was strewn with boards: pale-blue, green, pink, and yellow-stained pieces of wood stuck out of sand and dunes at weird angles. Looking to her left, she considered the best route to take from where she stood. She sidestepped a pack of cigarettes and a cell phone. Glass crunched against the soles of her steel-toed ankle boots. A table sat eerily upright as if waiting for the family to sit down to breakfast. A baby's crib lay on its side several feet away, the youngest of the Clark family tangled in its mosquito netting.

Two tears broke free and mixed with the rain on her face. There was little she could do to stop them. These were her neighbors. People she grew up with. She reached into her pocket. Assess. Tag. Move on.

At its widest point, Hatteras Island stretched three-and-a-half miles between water and dunes and was fifty miles long from end to end. But on this day, the water pushed its foam directly onto the lower dunes—at times making its way to the flattened beach grass—before beginning its retreat to the sea. Chatter on the radio indicated that Hurricane Anna continued to spin offshore but was making slow and steady progress out to sea. Here in Buxton, the downpour had subsided, but the air was still thick with condensation.

Katia nodded to one worker and then another as she moved through the tangled web of wood and steel. Everyone remained intent on tasks at hand. They were quiet until words were needed to ask a question or to guide someone toward the triage area.

Katia spotted Elliot to the left of a dune. He squatted, leaning forward on his toes. Two men stood slightly behind and to either side of him. She quickly identified the first as Brent Grainger. He and Elliot became friends in preschool and remained inseparable. The other, Andrew Hunter, was new to the island, a woodser from Virginia somewhere.

Katia noticed Andrew's stance. His typically squared shoulders were rolled forward. His face looked like it was being pulled by an invisible string toward the dune.

She quickened her pace. As she neared the trio, she noticed the pale blue of Elliot's gloved hands. They appeared to glide back and forth across the wet sand like an eraser being moved back and forth across a whiteboard.

Katia tried to move faster, but her tired legs and the rough terrain worked against her. The hard, water-soaked sand sent tiny shockwaves through the soles of her boots and into her feet with each step.

Watch the wires. Stay close to the fence. Her eyes looked down quickly and then back up. What does Elliot see? Her gaze moved up and down. She caught sight of something in the sand. A kid's plastic riding toy. She moved around the swaying red seat that was now barely attached to a set of bright-yellow handlebars.

She felt the tension of the men from a hundred feet away. She could sense it in their bodies. She rounded the edge of the dune. Her eyes met Brent's and followed them to where Elliot's blue-gloved hands moved across the sand.

"Holy fucking shit." Katia nearly lost her balance as she came to a stop right behind Elliot.

She had been with the Outer Banks Emergency Medical Services Station for four years. She was used to pulling broken and bloody bodies from the brink of death, breathing life into the dying, facing untimely deaths. People sobbing. Begging. Screaming. The lullaby of the survivors her constant companion. But this?

She could now see what she'd sensed from a hundred yards out. Brent's body was shaking. It was most noticeable in the movement of his hands, which hung at his sides.

The grotesque scent of rot filtered through the ambient smell of sea and sand. It filled her nostrils. Breathe anyway. She forced the air in and out of her lungs. She moved her gaze to take in the partial bit of human sticking out of the dune. She wanted to move closer, but her lead-filled legs held her feet against the wet sand. Breathe.

Her body was on full alert; every one of her senses was heightened. The rain became slivers of glass that poked her skin repeatedly. The wind filled her ears, all the way into her neck. The smell. Oh my fucking God. Her head pounded. Breathe. Just keep breathing. The world was moving in slow motion. For the first time in her twenty-five years, Katia faced a version of death that made her stomach churn and her throat burn.

Through her peripheral vision, she was vaguely aware of the actions of the others as each moved without speaking to form a line. The horror of death like this wasn't something an untrained person should witness. She didn't want to see it, but she couldn't look away from it. It was a nightmare she was unable to stop.

Katia looked to Brent. His face gave nothing away—except for his lip, which was clenched between his teeth, his chin white from the pressure.

Elliot pulled a radio out of its holster on his belt. "Who's taking the lead on this?" He paused and listened to the response. "Send him over to the Clark's lot. We have a body." Another pause. "No. Not a fatality of the storm."

Katia noticed one shoe. Even covered with pebbles of sand, she knew the shiny multi-inch heel was expensive. The purple of the heel melted into the swollen, purple foot from which it hung. Her eyes moved up past skin swollen to the verge of popping. The matte purple swirled with green on the leg of the woman in the dune. The body was mostly buried. Mounds of sand made the woman appear disjointed—like Katia's thoughts. She tried to stay in EMS mode.

One leg, from the thigh down, was exposed. She looked farther along the dune's edge to where the fingers of one hand poked from the sand. Like the exposed lower limb, the hand was swollen purple and black. She wondered how the steady rain hadn't punctured the outer layer of flesh. She rolled her head from side to side. The gray-green of the early morning turned a muted yellow as the sun tried desperately to shine some light through the rain and fog.

"The storm is slowing," Katia said.

The others nodded in unison.

Andrew motioned with his hand toward the sea. "Someone needs to tell the ocean. It still seems angry."

As if on cue, the waves roared and churned up a new wall of liquid blues and greens topped with foamy white. The ocean's offering left a wide dirty-white fringe along the edge of a possible crime scene. It pooled around their boots.

Katia found herself repeatedly returning her gaze to the hand of the woman in the dune. In the increasing light, she saw it. A ring. Sudden awareness pummeled her gut. Her chest felt tight, her head foggy. Her vision became tunneled. She could see her team members, but they were moving farther away and becoming smaller. She could hear Elliot talking to Brent, and Brent's response.

"What a fucked up way to wrap up a shift," Elliot said.

"Seriously," Brent replied. "At least the weather report says the storm's headed out. Slowly. But out."

"At least."

Katia heard Andrew say something about the children. An unknown voice responded, and it all faded. She was alone in the dark tunnel, mimicking her brother's verbal coping mechanism of repetition. The body. The body. The body. She blinked several times in rapid succession and popped her jaw. Words uttered in her direction were making their way in. At least she thought they were directed at her.

"Let's head in. Get dry. We can regroup and figure this shit out."

It was Elliot's voice. She tried to focus on his words, but her mind refused. Visions of the ring and of the purple shoe zoomed in and out of focus. Her stomach seized. A brassy taste filled the back of her mouth. Her head throbbed. She collapsed to her knees on the wet sand like a rag doll. She waited while the foam chewed at her knees, ankles, and hands. She closed her eyes and listened to the sound of the waves as they splashed against her skin. She heard her mom's muted voice in the distance: Smell the flowers. Blow out the candles. Employing the childhood trick, taught to her by her mom before she died, helped steady her breathing. She waited until the sand crystals were no longer spinning and she could stand.

She leaned into Elliot for the brief moment it took to gain full control of her legs and then fled. She ran hard and fast away from the decaying flesh, past the houses crumpled in the sand, and past remnants of what used to be and what would never be again.

****

For two weeks, he watched the storm gain strength east-northeast of Puerto Rico.

It was a poorly organized mass of weather. He jotted, "Likely of very little consequence." in his notebook on a page titled "November 9, 2018."

On November 10, conditions changed.

The local weatherman reported that the inconsequential cyclone strengthened into the first named storm of the season. Anna.

Within the day, Anna was peaking at 115 MPH, a category three hurricane, and she was stalled off the coast of Hatteras Island.

"Anna has settled in, folks," the six AM weatherman said. "The center of the storm is twenty-nine miles east of Hatteras Island. Peak winds of 115 MPH and rainfall at 7.51 inches have been reported. There's severe flooding along the Pamlico Sound. Everyone who opted to stay behind has been told to remain indoors. Two confirmed tornadoes have been reported in Buxton, where peak storm surges of 10.2 feet continue."

As he listened, he turned to a previous page in the notebook and neatly marked through item after item. He was prepared.

1) ~~Jugs from garage. Fill~~.
2) ~~Flashlight batteries.~~
3) ~~Radio batteries.~~
4) ~~Check generator~~.

Reports of high winds and storm surges were commonplace on the islands along the east coast of North Carolina. Until two hours ago, television reporters droned on about suggested evacuation. Perfect smiles parted to release words that no one heard. Full-time residents rarely traveled Highway 12 to get away from a storm, and this time was no different. Except it was, and two hours ago, everyone listened.

He looked again at the screen. He loved storms. The bigger the better. They made his heart pump and his insides tickle. Anna was big. And she was just sitting there, exerting her power like a lioness. He closed his eyes and pictured himself on the beach when the tornadoes touched down. He took a deep breath, filling his lungs with air until they could hold no more. He exhaled slowly and opened his eyes.

He listened to the woman's voice. "We have crews en route and will—"

A different woman's voice interrupted the calm weatherperson. "Breaking News" flashed on the screen. "We interrupt this broadcast to bring you breaking news from Buxton Beach. Authorities have confirmed at least five people have been killed."

His senses came alive as he watched reporters and rescue workers converge on the scene.

The announcer enunciated every word. Slow. Methodical. To him, it sounded like chalk on a chalkboard. "With us now is Dennis Clancy, owner of one of the houses left untouched here in Buxton. Dennis, can you tell us what happened?"

He leaned forward and squinted, trying to look past the man and the reporter holding the mic to his face.

"The sound was excruciating. We could hear it. We ran out and jumped in the car. We were, we were driving. God. I saw it in my rearview mirror. Told my wife and kids to get on the floorboard. Drove for our lives. Literally. Drove for our lives. And now Alex is dead. And Ashley. And the boys."

The watcher opened his mouth wide and stuck his tongue out. He flattened it and turned it until the sides touched the upper and lower lip. His tongue was sore on each side from pressing it hard against his teeth as he strained to see what was happening on the beach.

The reporter on the scene held the edge of the hood on her navy-blue poncho. The body of the garment hugged her hourglass figure. She tried to look composed, but lost, as she fought the strength of the wind and rain. "Homes have been leveled, just wiped clean. It's hard to put into words." Her voice wavered. "Just piles of debris."

Behind her, first responders and neighbors combed through rubble. Her cameraman scanned the area. Cars were tossed around, flipped over. They were close to the Dune Café. He could see it in the background, securely rooted above the dunes and beach where water pounded relentlessly. It appeared untouched. This made him happy. The Dune Café was his place, the place his family lunched, tired from hours of kiteboarding and castle building. He loved the way his feet dangled from the lime-colored bar stools and the way the booths squeaked when he slid across the colors of pineapple and mango and lime. As a child, he used the long mirror behind the counter to assess the offerings of freshly baked pies. As an adult, he found the mirror gave him a multidimensional glimpse into the lives of the other patrons. From child to adult, he loved the mirror the most.

He knew this strip of sand just as he knew the inside of his own home. These were his dunes, his special burial ground. He rarely worried that his work would be discovered. Each time a storm neared the area he watched the news a little more closely, felt his mortality a little more keenly. But each time since his first gift to the dunes, Mother Nature left intact the area of the beach where he kept those who deserved to die, those who thought children were objects to be toyed with, and those who couldn't be saved.

His eyes went back to the reporter.

"At least four children are among those dead…"

Her voice crawled under his skin. Women like her always kept secrets. The slick, navy-blue material that cut into her dark hair and the sway of her body against the elements made her look vulnerable and kind. That's what the television station manager wanted the viewers to feel. Look at me. I won't hurt you. How could I hurt you? I love you. Don't be afraid.

He was afraid of a woman once, too afraid to tell, and too afraid to run. He would never be afraid of one again. Never. Now he was always on the lookout, always listening, always ready.

Again, he panned the beach behind the deceitful, dark-haired woman. His heart thudded in his chest as she talked about the children. The area around the tornado's aftermath had changed since his own childhood. The dunes regularly changed shape, growing when sand was piped in and shrinking when storms came to call. Buildings were constructed and torn down. People came and went. Each summer brought new visitors, new children to play with when he was young, new women to watch as he grew into a man.

Through every season of change, every time he returned to his dunes, his treasures remained safe.

Will they find them all now? One kick of sand. One wind gust hitting a dune just so. His breath quickened. His jeans tightened around his arousal. He let his hand drop to his bulge. The thrill of potential capture was something he hadn't anticipated. He stepped closer, something between awakening and agitation growing in his gut. He knew he would soon strike again.

Chapter Two

Katia sat silently in Elliot's SUV. She and Elliot were twenty-one hours into a twenty-four-hour shift when the call came in for the mass casualty incident. That was seven hours ago. Her mind churned to the rhythm of the storm. Death at the hands of a killer doesn't happen in Buxton. She felt nauseous. Outside the windows and in her head, fury reigned. Thoughts pinged against her cerebral cortex, like hail against street signs, until every part of her body throbbed. She tasted the salt of her tears and the salt of the sea that blended together on her cheeks before sliding between her lips and onto her tongue.

The years of laughter she shared with Elizabeth and her mom rang in her head. The three of them spent hours together in Gina's living room. It was where she learned to dance and where she felt safe enough to cry. It was where she learned about menstruation and sex and protection against unwanted pregnancy and disease. It was where she fell in love with Elizabeth.

Memories of her first real kiss flooded Katia's mind. She and Elizabeth stood in front of a full-length mirror. They watched their own reflection as their lips met and tongues touched. Elizabeth giggled mid kiss and Katia stepped away. Katia recalled the conversation.

"What's so funny?" Elizabeth said. "Am I doing it wrong?"

"Nothing," Katia said. "It's just. Well, it's weird, I guess. I don't know."

"Which? Kissing or just kissing me?"

"Watching us kissing."

There was more laughter.

They told their parents on Katia's eighteenth birthday.

Katia's father yelled at the top of his lungs until Katia and Elizabeth rushed out of the house in fear. Within moments, Katia's father chased them down in his car.

"Get in the street!" he said. His head was hanging out of the driver's side window, moving back and forth to look between the narrow road and the two girls. "I brought you into this world, and I'll take you out of it."

"Papi," Katia said. "Please stop. We can talk when you calm down. I'm not getting in the street." Katia was afraid to go any farther, so Elizabeth stood with her and waited. Eventually, Katia's father left them standing on the sidewalk.

Gina's reaction was the opposite of Katia's father. She knew it would be. Gina never made either girl feel bad or different. Now Gina was dead.

How could this be happening? What fucking monster has invaded our world?

A tear formed at the corner of her eye and spilled over, cutting a tiny new stream through the sandy grit. That one tear opened a dam and the tears flowed freely. As her cries turned to sobs, she began to rock back and forth rhythmically. No. No. No!

Elliot's large hand grasped her shoulder. His silent attempt to create a sense of stability was appreciated. She knew he meant well. He knew her, at least the EMS her. Katia couldn't have asked for a better partner or friend. Katia also appreciated that. She didn't have a lot of friends. After her mom died, she closed herself off to everyone other than her dad and her brother. Elizabeth and Gina were the only other people she let in. And look where that got me, she thought. Katia leaned back, head against the seat, and closed her eyes.

She heard her father's words echoing in her head: "Get hold of yourself, Katia Pilar Mercedes Billings-Castillo." She hated it when he used her full name. The only way to the other side is through. Where was her dad now? She hoped at home with Marco. Her brother wouldn't be afraid. He would be in his room with his weather magazines and his weather board. Children on the autism spectrum could have any number of obsessions. Weather was one of Marco's.

Marco wouldn't be afraid, but she was afraid for him. Katia worried that Marco would one day get so excited about the rain and wind that he would wander away from the house with his camera. Taking pictures was another of Marco's obsessions, and it often led to eloping. That's what they called it when a child with autism spectrum disorder wandered or bolted to get to or away from something without forethought.

"Katia." Elliot bent toward her across the console. "Katia, look at me." His face was inches from her own. "Who is it?"

Katia took another deep breath, opened her eyes, and looked at her partner. She trusted him. He was her brother-in-arms. Smell the flowers. She gave herself the same instructions she had used since she was three when her best friend pushed her off a swing and she couldn't catch her breath. Blow out the birthday candles. Her mom said the act of inhaling and exhaling while picturing the items would take her mind off the scraped knee and bruised ego.

Elliot was chewing on his bottom lip, his chest rising and falling rhythmically. "It's her, isn't it? Elizabeth's mom?"

Katia counted her own breaths and matched them to his.

"Yes. And I have to—"

"You have to do nothing. Not right now. We need food and rest."

She hoped he knew how much she appreciated him. In the upcoming days, she was going to have to talk about this day, and about her past, over and over again. She wanted to, but not yet.

"Elliot, I'll do whatever. Whatever it takes. I just need a minute."

"I told you," Elliot said. "I got you."

She was not one to back down from responsibility. One minute. Just one minute. She closed her eyes. "El." She rubbed her palms down her thighs, drying the sweat on the rough fabric.

"I know," he said. "It's okay. In your own time." His voice was deep and slow. The sound and southern rhythm felt like sweet tea tasted on a hot summer day. Katia drifted into a half-asleep state. It was the kind of sleep where you feel awake, but you know you're sleeping. Her dad was there. And Marco.

"Make a wish before you burn down the house with those flames." She heard her dad, but she didn't see him.

She felt the pain of her first birthday without her mom.

Wish? She didn't have a wish. What could she possibly wish for? I wish I could erase these stupid fucking thoughts. That's what I wish.

She read the pink-and-yellow words on the cake: Happy Sweet 16.

Mom is dead. Dad hates me. Marco lives in an autism-governed world. And Elizabeth is too busy to be here to eat cake. Fuck sixteen.

Katia watched Marco.

"Cake? Cake, Ka-tee-ah? Cake? Cake?" Marco's words were full of six-year-old excitement.

She tousled the dark waves of thick hair on her little brother's head. It wasn't him she hated. It was autism. She loved him a *lottle*. The word made Marco laugh. He knew he was the only one she loved a lottle.

"Yes, Marco. Cake." His fawn-colored eyes sparkled.

Katia gave him her best smile.

"Thank you, Papi," she said. "It's been a wonderful birthday."

She continued to watch the memory unfold.

There was her father pouring his first two fingers of Kentucky Bourbon.

There was dream Katia cleaning away the last remnants of a pretend happy birthday, tucking Marco into his pajamas, putting him to bed, and reading a text message from Elizabeth.

There was Katia sitting cross-legged on her childhood bed and hearing a knock on her bedroom window.

Her half-asleep self knew that wasn't right, but her dream self turned, expecting to see denim-blue eyes and pale, freckled skin. Instead, Gina was staring at her through a translucent sand dune, eyes unblinking, a gaping hole where her smile should have been. Katia's throat tightened and her heart picked up speed. Another knock. The pull toward consciousness increased. The knock was real. She blinked herself fully awake.

Zahra Knox, a police officer trained in forensic crime scene investigations, stared through the window. Her soft, black curls, dense but yielding, filled the upper half of the glass, and her bright-yellow windbreaker filled the rest of the opening. Katia knew Zahra years ago in primary and high school and more recently from The Pink Clover, a bar both women frequented during their time away from work.

Elliot pushed the button to lower the window an inch. "Zahra."

"Elliot. Katia." Zahra gave a slight nod at each in turn. "The high school gym has been made available. Dr. Webb is ready to begin transport."

"I can help," Elliot said. He turned and looked at Katia. "Unless you need me to stay."

"No need," Katia said. "I'm okay." She tried to sound better than she felt. The thought of people she knew and loved being housed on the floor of the gym until they could be moved to the mainland didn't sit well in her already aching gut.

Elliot slid out and Zahra slid in.

An awkward silence hung in the air between them. The last time they spoke, Katia was leaving Zahra's bed in the wee hours of the morning. Zahra sent a text message the next day. Katia didn't respond.

"Are you okay?" Zahra asked, finally breaking the silence. "I wish I didn't have to, but I need to take a statement for the record." Zahra's voice was soft and soothing. There was no indication of animosity or bitterness.

Katia began to relax. "Sure. Close the window." She reached into the bag that rested on the floorboard in front of her and pulled out a T-shirt. She handed it to Zahra to use as a towel.

"Chivalrous, even here." Zahra met Katia's gaze with her own.

Katia smiled at the words.

The women had connected in August after a chance meeting at The Pink Clover. Katia wasn't interested in a full-fledged relationship, but the electricity between them was unquestionable. Three times in as many months, beers had turned into sex. Each time, Katia avoided follow-up conversation. Each time, it freaked her out a bit more. Since the breakup with Elizabeth, Zahra was the only person Katia spent more than one night with.

"You need to tell me what happened down there." Zahra inclined her head in the direction of the beach.

"Not much to tell," Katia said.

"Here or at the station?" Zahra's voice stayed low and kind.

Katia shrugged. "Here's cool." She stared straight ahead and recalled out loud the movements she made that took her to the dune. "Something bright, out of place, caught my eye. It was purple. Shiny. It was Gina Dahl's shoe…" Katia's voice trailed off.

Zahra pulled a pen and a small pad of paper out of her shirt pocket. She scribbled a few words on the pad before looking back at Katia.

Katia added, "And her ring."

"ID hasn't been confirmed."

"For me it has." Katia's voice cracked.

"I know." Zahra laid her hand on Katia's leg and moved her thumb back and forth.

Katia watched Zahra's thumb. The dark-brown digit blurred against the navy khaki fabric of her pants. She looked at the woman whose touch could set off a reaction of wetness and warmth. She tried to focus on the movement. Her throat burned. An increasing stickiness arose just under the outer layer of her skin.

"Katia? Hey. Put your head back."

Circles formed around Zahra's figure. The circles pulsed to the sound of Zahra's voice. Katia swallowed hard.

Zahra put her hand on Katia's forehead and eased it back until her head rested against the tan headrest of the SUV.

The wave of nausea subsided. "I'm okay."

Zahra was quiet.

"It's her, Zahr."

"Tell me about your relationship with Elizabeth." Zahra pressed forward with the interview.

"Why Elizabeth? She doesn't even live…" Katia's eyes widened as she realized where Zahra's line of questioning was leading. "You can't think… Fuck, Zahra. Come on."

Katia's relationship with Elizabeth was beautiful. Until it wasn't. Then it was toxic. They were as bad for each other as they were good—on again off again for the last three of the five years. When they were off, Katia spent whole weekends at The Pink Clover in Manteo picking up women who were willing to fill her emptiness with reckless sex. Elizabeth used those weekends to prove Katia didn't really love her. She could still see her face as the red crept up her neck and settled in her cheeks while she screamed, "If you loved me, you wouldn't be able to just fuck anyone, Katia. Do I look stupid? Do you see me fucking other women because we're fighting? No. That's the answer. Fucking, no."

How much should Katia tell Zahra? In the end, she decided to give a condensed version and answer whatever questions followed. Let the police figure out what was important and what wasn't.

"Elizabeth moved down the street from me when we were in high school," Katia said. "We were lovers. Then we fought. A lot. Finally, we couldn't work through the bullshit and she left to go find herself. The end." Katia put the palm of one hand on each side of her head and pushed against the throbbing of her temples. Gina was dead, and Katia didn't even have Elizabeth's fucking number. "Has anyone called Elizabeth?"

"No," Zahra said. "The identity hasn't been confirmed."

"Fuck you." Katia's voice sounded as tired as she felt. She knew Zahra was asking legitimate questions and providing the appropriate responses to Katia's statements.

The Hatteras Island coroner, Dr. Stewart Webb, was a few hundred feet away picking through the skin and bones of the woman who was the closest thing Katia had to a mom. She had to give Zahra whatever information she could to help her figure out how Gina ended up under several feet of packed sand. She knew that. It just seemed wrong to be doing any of this without Elizabeth.

"I know you're tired, Katia. We all are." The soft tone in Zahra's voice never wavered.

"Elizabeth and I were best friends, Zahr. Before we were lovers."

"That's why I need you to tell me everything you can," Zahra said. "Even if I don't want to hear it as your… Whatever we are. I have a job to do. And I need your help."

Katia tried to think of what might help an investigation. She began spouting off information. "Elizabeth's dad bailed when she was three. It was always just her and her mom. Until me. Gina called us three peas in a pod." Katia paused as the tears threatened an encore appearance. Katia hated weakness, especially her own. She bit down hard on her bottom lip for several seconds, wiped sand from her drying pant legs, and continued. "She went on a date here and there. And there was Mr. Easton off and on one summer, but it didn't work out. She said he was too into ice cream. That was her way of saying he was fat. He wasn't. She worried about appearance—a lot. Had to as a real estate agent, you know?"

Zahra made a few notes on a new page in her small flip tablet. "Anyone else? Anyone lately?"

"Not that I know of," Katia said. She tried to see what Zahra was writing, but she was turned slightly in her seat, and it was impossible to read the curved scribble. Katia used her finger to follow a drop of water as it ran down the window. "Since Elizabeth left, I wasn't around her place as much. She broke up with me in a text message. Elizabeth, that is. Pissed me the fuck off. I went to her house. We argued. I told her to call me when she got her head out of her fucking ass…"

Katia's last few words trailed off and hung in the air until they faded into silence. She turned to look at Zahra. "Those were the last words we exchanged."

She hoped Zahra wouldn't hear the hurt in her voice. "She moved to Virginia. I stayed here. I do see her mom sometimes. She cooks out. Did, did cook out. Always invited me. Sometimes I went. Sometimes not. Mostly not."

Behind them, new activity surged. A flurry of reporters and police officers had gathered nearby.

"What the…" Katia turned toward the noise that came from the edge of the beach. A voice, male, but unrecognizable, sounded. Soon a cacophony of voices arose. Cameramen were setting up their equipment, fighting each other for the best angle. Katia assumed it was to get shots of the body as it was moved from the dune to the waiting transport unit.

An officer who was standing near Dr. Webb moved up the beach. Katia recognized him. He was one of the few who had already arrived from Manteo to help with the aftermath of the storm. He looked anxious.

"You Zahra?" His eyes locked on Katia for a moment and then moved to Zahra. "You?" Zahra pointed her index finger back on herself. "I'm Zahra."

****

He knew the beach, knew storms, and knew how the elements affected decaying flesh. No DNA evidence would implicate him in the crimes. He was certain of this. Sand dunes held water, water invaded orifices, and invading water killed DNA.

He thought about the first time he felt the sand rub his own skin. His aunt asked him to walk with her. It was late. He was ten.

"Come on, Little Man. Walk with me."

She winked when she said it, as if they shared a secret they both enjoyed keeping. He hated their secret. He hated the sweet smell of her skin and the warmth of her breath against his mouth that got softer and faster when she made his body react in ways he told it not to react. He didn't want to go, to walk with her, to listen to her, to feel her. He didn't want to, but he did. He always did.

It started with a touch through his pajamas as he lay motionless in the quiet dark of his room. When she wanted more, they moved to the beach. No one heard the sounds of her as she pressed herself against him behind a hard, wave-beaten dune.

"Here, Little Man. And here. Let me teach you. You're old enough to learn."

He tried at first to argue, to tell her someone might see. But they both knew no one would. It was November in Buxton on a section of beach that was hidden from the world. But at least he tried.

"Auntie, please," he begged her. "I'm cold. Can we go back?"

"Not yet, Little Man. You know you don't really want to, do you? Relax. You know I would never hurt you. I love you. I love you so much. So much."

Her breath increased against his mouth with each word. With each touch, with each movement, his resistance waned until he gave in, again.

He tried to bring his mind back to the present and refocus on the reports, but she was always there, just as she was when he was a weak boy of nine, of twelve, of fourteen. But I wasn't weak when I was fifteen, was I, Auntie? That walk didn't turn out the way you intended, did it? His thoughts drifted back to the sand, erosion, old DNA, and her.

"Dad, please. I'm fifteen." He and his father stood face-to-face in the kitchen. But for a one-inch height difference and his own gangly limbs, it was like looking into a slightly skewed mirror. He spoke to the reflection of himself. "Let me stay, Dad, please. She doesn't need to come, and I'm old enough. All of my friends stay home alone. Seriously."

"It's not just a day, son. It's a week." His father never broke eye contact.

"But—"

"No buts. Not for a week." His father's voice was firm.

He lost, and he felt sick to his stomach. After six months of avoidance, she won. "Fuck my life," he mumbled as he stormed off to his room.

His plan of retaliation started on that day.

He had imagined it more than once: The tip of a sharp hunting knife meeting her soft, white skin. One push of the blade, the dent inward, the pop that would release the tension around the blade. He dreamed of the thick, red blood oozing, coating the silver as pain formed on her face. He would breathe his warm breath against her lips, as his pulse quickened. He wanted to feel the life slipping away, body to body, skin to skin. Only then would he find relief. He even had the knife he wanted to do it with hidden in a shoebox deep in his closet.

At fifteen, she was coming. At fifteen, he was ready.

The wooden walkway creaked under their footsteps. He concentrated on the sound and on the way the waves of heat still lingered just above each weather-beaten slat. It was November. The heat would disappear with the sunset. He smiled. The rentals along the beach stood empty. There wasn't another human in sight. It was the perfect place.

He let his free hand rest along the top of the rail, the other hand in hers. Together, they descended five wooden stairs and stepped in unison onto the soft sand. The sun was almost gone. He pointed above the ocean where the soft yellow-orange was turning a crimson pink. "It's the perfect night, Auntie."

"It's beautiful, Little Man." Her voice was a whisper against the crashing waves. The two of them stood perfectly still. "You were right. Earlier is better."

He didn't respond. If he did, his voice would betray him. For the first time in the history of their secret relationship, he felt excited to be alone on the beach with her.

When he couldn't contain his excitement any longer, he stepped toward the dune to the right. He had chosen it for its size and position. The fence, which ran parallel to the ocean for ten feet, was built by a restoration company to fight erosion long before he was born. It did its job well, trapping tons of wind-blown sand. And now, it was guarding one side of his chosen death nest. He tugged gently on his aunt's hand, leading her to the smallest part of the beach-grass-covered dune. "I've found the perfect place, Auntie. Come on. Let me show you."

She smiled and touched his face with her free hand. "My sweet Little Man. So grown. So beautiful. Show me."

He licked his lips and swallowed hard. So this is what it feels like to want someone completely. The tingling in his stomach built and sent signals downward to his growing manliness. His breath quickened.

He slipped the backpack from his shoulders and pulled out a blanket. Without a word, he put one end of the blanket into her hands. When the blanket was taut, each of them piled sand onto their respective corners. He moved to the middle of the black-and-red-checkered cloth and patted the spot next to him.

Tonight he would not have to be coaxed. Tonight he would become a man.

"Little Man," she said, breathing into his mouth, "you have missed me, haven't you? I can feel it." Her fingers toyed with his lips and touched his skin.

"I've been waiting to get you alone, Auntie," he said. He reached around to her back. She had taught him well. He eased her down onto the blanket.

He did what he was taught to do, what she wanted. He did what would take her out of this world and into a world where there was nothing but their bodies and their breathing. "Is that good, Auntie?"

She moaned. "You know where. Come on. Please. You know where."

"I do. I do." He straddled her like a fervent lover. "You look beautiful." His breathing was coming too fast. He had to slow down. Come on. Can't lose control. Focus. Focus. Focus. He calmed his body, ran his fingers over her cheek, down her neck, over her hard nipples. He couldn't risk her opening her eyes or questioning his movements.

He moved his hand up and into her short, blonde hair. With the other hand, he reached into the open backpack and withdrew the hunting blade. With a single fluid motion, he yanked her head back and slashed through the soft skin of her neck. He hadn't expected to see the gristle of her windpipe or hear the thin sharp sound that escaped her lips. He hadn't anticipated the flailing arms or the hands clawing at the gaping hole. He loved her completely in that moment. Like a man.

Her words echoed in his head: "Auntie needs you close. You love me, don't you? Doesn't that feel nice? Never tell, Little Man. Okay? Promise your Auntie."

"I promise, Auntie," he whispered against her lips. He leaned back and slashed again. This time the sharp blade connected with the jugular. Blood sprayed his hand, his chest, and his face. Warm lines and dots of bright-red liquid. He pressed himself hard against her body until she was completely still, and then he pressed for a moment more.

He was exhausted. He wanted to sleep here at her bosom like a little boy, against her warmth, but he was now a man and there was much to be done, more than he anticipated. The red splotches that colored his body also colored the sand around him, and a pool was forming under the cooling corpse. He discovered that night that murder is harder than it appears.

Years after his first taste of sweet, sticky death, he studied the reporter who was describing the scene where a body was just discovered. His mind clung only to the phrases that were important to him. The rest was just white noise.

"We must warn you. The details of this discovery are disturbing…"

"A woman's body…"

"Discovered partially buried…"

"Large dune."

The words filtered into his mind in chunks and filled the spaces between the growing rage. He wanted to hit something, to let the fury control him. It felt good to let it control him, to not think or feel until the moment of release. He took a deep breath.

Too many people. It's too risky. Just breathe. Focus. He stared forward, every nerve in his body on alert. He listened carefully now.

"An emergency medical responder for Buxton was working with other first responders to search for possible survivors where an E-3 tornado touched down on the ocean side of Buxton when he says he noticed something out of the corner of his eye. The EMS worker didn't want to speak on camera…"

The cameraman panned the area.

His heart beat faster. From his side of the television set, he strained to see what the cameraman was seeing. His blood warmed as the man behind the camera continued.

"The body is badly decomposed and harmed from the storm. No word on sex or age at this time. We will continue to bring you updates as we get them."

Too much movement at the beach prevented him from seeing which of his gifts had been returned to him. He thought about the redhead named Megan. She came into a store where he stopped for coffee on his drive back to Buxton. She smelled like apple juice and shampoo. Sweet and clean.

His draw to her was immediate as he contemplated speaking to her only seconds before he noticed her keeping an eye on a young girl who stood near the alcohol. He instantly knew what was happening, and it infuriated him. The woman nodded to the young girl then moved toward the store clerk. As she threw her hair over her shoulder and questioned the clerk about whether or not they carried an obscure item, the girl lifted the six-pack and walked out the door, unnoticed by anyone but him.

Megan was so easy. Outside her apartment at seven forty-five the next morning, he watched the girl get on the school bus and sit, head down, alone. His heart ached for her. Five minutes later, he walked right into the front door, placed the needle in Megan's neck, and folded her into a large, rolling suitcase. No one even glanced his way when he lifted the bag and placed it in his truck.

He buried her deep into the dune when the sand was soft and malleable. But he pulled her closer to the surface when he returned, wanting to see her when he brought other offerings. It took him several hours to settle her in and fill in the sand after each visit. He didn't mind, though. He liked her, despite her refusal to do good rather than evil. Perhaps it was her age, which the papers listed as thirty-one, or the way she refused to scream or flail when he pulled her hair back and laid the blade against her neck.

"Do you understand what you did wrong, Megan?"

"Fuck you." She looked him right in the eye as she spoke, the words coming from low in her throat. She looked almost pleased to be leaving this world. "Little slut likes to steal. She likes to fuck, too. Want to fuck her? Let me go, and you can fuck her for free."

Oh how good it felt to hear the sound of Megan's flesh splitting, knowing that little girl would be free.

It might also be Ulma, the worn-out blonde. She was a feisty one. He watched her for months in the diner, as she ran her fingers through the hair of the local boys. He heard her flirt with them. He saw her long, skinny fingers and unkempt nails as they twirled in and out. She lived alone. Babysat when she wasn't at the restaurant, gave music lessons.

Right. Music lessons. Even now, he cringed at the picture he developed in his mind of the creepy blonde pulling the little boys tight against her at the piano and running her bony fingers up their backs as they pounded away nervously at the keys.

He respected the ones who didn't scream. He also enjoyed carefully digging out the slender, flowing, Ammophila grass after each kill. The low-tide stench, funky but evocative, built from the merger of ocean and sound, always took him back to the first time. He enjoyed the burn in his muscles as he dug, as he arranged their bodies in the sand. He enjoyed replacing the grass safely on the dune after each visit, each new burial. It was like a puzzle to be solved.

"Female," the reporter droned, returning him to the present. "Adult. More details as news arrives."

What they didn't know yet was that whichever dune they were exploring, digging would reveal more, so many more.

He listened throughout the morning to the Barbie-perfect, twenty-something repeat the words she was being fed from somewhere in the distance:

"Name withheld until next of kin can be notified."

"Found by EMS workers who were searching for survivors from last night's tornado that destroyed a row of homes on the ocean side of Buxton."

"Large area taped off."

He stood close to the television set and tried to pick out markers that would tell him exactly which body the storm had delivered from its grave. There were so many. For years, he continued to give his gifts to the ocean by way of the dunes. He liked the idea of each one being absorbed through the earth from which they came, continually pushed down by the shifting crystals and pulled down by the hungry sea.

The ground, sea, and air kept his secret, until now. Until now, he felt as though it was the earth's way of thanking him for ridding the world of women who would otherwise be allowed to continue hurting children. Had the elements disagreed with a choice? His mind churned in time with the raging sea on the screen.

All of the debris, all of the townspeople and rescue workers trampling about made it hard to tell which body was found. Then he saw it. The snarled tree with burnt branches, black limbs, and thick trunk poked defiantly out of the pale yellows and blues. The coroner and an assistant were to the left of the restaurant, down the beach and down a few dunes.

Soft Gina. A smile formed on his lips as he recalled the feel of her skin in his rough hands. It was harder to get her alone. She had a daughter that was always in tow, a daughter that was a lesbian. He watched her flaunt her daughter's choice, heard her talk about freedom to marry and freedom to adopt. It enraged him. What does a mother do to her child to convince her it's okay to follow through on such evil? He watched her for months. She was rarely alone.

He waited.

Finally, her daughter moved away. Still, he waited. When he found his moment, she fought him. Oh how she fought. He rubbed his hands along his biceps where Gina had dug her nails deep into his skin. She was barely a week dead, and the punctures were almost healed. He found a remaining scab, pulled it free of the wound, and pushed his own nail into the lesion to keep the feeling alive.

He smiled at the television set, a smile of dark anticipation, being thankful for technology. He knew what he had to do.

****

Katia stood as close as the crime scene tape allowed to the woman who was now only purple, onyx, and stench protruding from the dune at the edge of Buxton Beach. The rain was no longer consuming their world. The sun shone straight up in the noon sky, and the surf rolled with less force. Under different circumstances, the sea would be littered with locals on their boards. She looked out at the empty waterscape. No celebration of the end of the storm would occur today.

Zahra's round sprigs of hair fell like a dark cloud around her face as she took pictures from every angle of the sandy grave. Her special training in forensic crime scene investigations was evident in her synchronized movements with Dr. Webb. Katia begged them to let her help, even though she wasn't trained and would never be allowed past the barricade that separated her and the other onlookers from the immediate scene.

From where she stood, she found it hard to make out exactly what was happening. Gina's body was being prepared for removal. Katia recognized the growing collection of evidence, which included a clear jar filled with beach creatures taken from various body crevices. They squirmed and slithered. Her stomach did the same.

After what seemed like hours but was in fact less than thirty minutes, Dr. Webb zipped closed the black body bag and looped the plastic security tag through the zipper and metal ring. He nodded toward two men who stood just inside the yellow barrier. They would take the body to the staging area until it was safe to transport it to the closest morgue in Raleigh.

Katia intended to accompany the unit to the morgue when the time came. Until then, she considered her options. She had nothing else to do at the scene. All of the neighbors whose homes were affected by the touchdown of the tornado were accounted for. She wasn't a police officer or crime scene investigator—a CSI. Zahra made that clear. She wasn't hungry, but she decided to force herself to put something in her stomach and was ready to head back up to the asphalt when she caught sight of Dr. Webb. His posture was off. She looked in the direction he faced. She couldn't see what he saw, but she heard the angst in his voice when he spoke.

"Zahra," Dr. Webb said. He motioned for her to join him. "Bring the camera."

Zahra moved with purpose toward him. Within moments, the shutter on her camera was opening and closing at rapid speed.

Katia hated being sidelined while others moved with purpose. A man, whose badge read, "Levine," snapped orders to the officers who arrived with him only moments before. "We'll set a second perimeter here. Vitkus, grab the stakes and tape. Doc? How far?"

"All the way down," Dr. Webb said.

Vitkus grabbed the roll of crime scene tape and began defining the new perimeter. The area now included a series of connected dunes that ran for several hundred feet perpendicular to the Atlantic Ocean. Others went to work inside the perimeter, dividing the dunes into smaller sections in preparation for Dr. Webb's tedious job of brushing away sand and gathering clues.

Katia edged her way closer to the newly sequestered area. She fought her urge to duck under the yellow tape. From her vantage point, she saw what looked like small twigs pushing up through the sand. Instinctively, she knew they were bones, though she couldn't tell from what body part. A foot, maybe. Or a hand. Fuck. Her eyes slowly took in the area around the twig shapes. Smooth, rounded beach. A board. A backpack. And more bones. A lot of them. Please be animal bones. She took a deep breath. The CSI people wouldn't be so frantic if they were animal bones.

Webb put his hand on Zahra's shoulder, stopping her. "Wait." He moved his gaze to Vitkus. "I'm going to need buckets from the van. And the screen. Will you?"

Vitkus looked toward Detective Levine, who nodded his approval. "Sure, Doc. On it."

The buckets would be lettered to match the tiny flags placed in each quadrant of the sequestered dunes. The screen would be placed close by to sift particles. Clothing, metal, wood chips, everything would be catalogued. Dr. Webb, who was often called to assist in cases along the East Coast where evidence seemed minimal to nonexistent, would work tirelessly and methodically. If this were a burial ground for a monster, if even a small trace of evidence existed, he would find it.

With his reputation and talent, Dr. Webb could have gone anywhere through the years, places that would have been much more exciting, places that would have lined his pockets and uplifted his name, but he chose to stay here on Hatteras Island, the place of his birth.

Total respect. Katia knew how good Dr. Webb was. She was happy he was here. Total respect and gratitude for his presence no doubt was shared by every person on this beach today.

Zahra hung the camera around her neck, its bulk resting against her full, curvy frame. She stepped over a board and squatted down next to Dr. Webb. Katia watched the two, following Dr. Webb's gloved fingertip with her eyes. He was brushing gently at the sand.

"It's a bone," he said. "A pelvis." He finished wiping away the sand and held it up for inspection.

Zahra raised the camera and captured a few pictures.

Katia's gaze moved between the blue-gloved hands holding the camera and the off-white-and-tan protrusion in the sand.

Dr. Webb took a measuring tape from a black-leather bag that sat open next to his left leg. He carefully avoided contact with an Adirondack beach chair that was wedged against the small dune.

Katia noted the angle of the chair's seat and thought it might be nice to sit and feel the waves and sand crabs roll over her feet. She wished it were yesterday morning when the world was right side up.

The doctor tapped the Record button on a device in his shirt pocket and said, "Second victim. Dry remains. Bone size indicates female." He paused the recorder and took measurements. He pressed Record again and continued. "Sub-pubic angle of 78." He laid the bone gently on the sand, stood, took out his phone, and dialed.

"Hi, Paige," Dr. Webb said. A pause. "Listen. I'm out in Buxton. Close to the…" Another pause. "Yes. Worse. Do you have an available dog?" Dr. Webb waited. "It's complicated. Not directly storm related. We need your help."

Dr. Webb hung up the phone and placed it in his pocket. He turned to Zahra, and the two of them engaged in a deep conversation with Detective Levine, discussing calls that needed to be made, what they each needed to do, how far out the search should be.

"At least a half mile in each direction," Dr. Webb said. His arms gestured wildly to the left then the right. "I'm not sure what we have here, but we need to be thorough."

Afternoon faded into evening. Neighbors who helped through the morning and early afternoon were replaced with emergency personnel from all along the coast. People returned to their homes to feed their families and get their children ready for bed. The injured were being tended to in the high school gym and either released or made as comfortable as possible until they could be moved to proper care facilities. Katia should be at the high school tending to the injured, but she couldn't leave.

Zahra turned from the huddle and faced her. "Are you okay to be here? Why don't you go home? You don't need to be a part of this. I can drop by tomorrow."

"I'm not leaving," Katia said. "This is my beach. Our beach. Some son-of-a-bitch killed one of our own. I want to be here." Sweat trickled from her armpits and curled down around the underside of her small breasts. Her heart pounded. She studied Zahra's expression.

Zahra held her gaze. "There's nothing else to do here. It's up to Dr. Webb and our team and the nose of the dog Paige brings. She's good, Katia. You know she is."

"I know. Still staying." Katia crossed her arms over her chest.

Paige owned Johnston's Training Facility with her brother, Bob Johnston. They trained and honed the skills of cadaver dogs and those who handled them in the field. Paige and Bob worked with Zahra and Dr. Webb on a missing child case several years ago. Katia was a part of the search team, along with many others. When Dr. Webb suggested the division bring in the SAR trainer, some questioned the ability of the dog to tell one scent of death from another. Dr. Webb was patient but stern. He schooled residents on this type of search and on the idea that one should never dismiss any type of help that may bring peace to a family missing a loved one.

In that specific case, Johnston's German shepherd, using his more than 220 million olfactory receptors, intelligence, and training, was able to pick up the scent of the seven-year-old girl's remains buried fifteen feet underground.

Katia found the process of the search dogs fascinating and even visited the training facility to watch the dogs in motion. During her tour of the facility, she learned that with patience, and repetitive behaviors, the dogs could be trained to recognize and discover remains as small as a human tooth or single drop of blood. It was nothing short of amazing. Paige and Bob Johnston were heroic in her eyes, and she was glad they were here.

Just as it was last year, the nature of the current scene was going to require complex strategies, cooperation, and understanding. Katia felt certain this was exactly what they had with Paige and Bob.

"The Johnstons' ETA?" Katia asked. She turned away from the sound of the water and the smell of the dune.

"About twenty minutes out," Zahra said. She glanced at her watch. "They'll start about a mile up and look for other sites while we work here. I'm going to stay to help the doc start the collection of additional samples from the dune and surrounding area of this site. See what else we can come up with that might help us put this puzzle together."

"I'll call El," Katia said. "Let him know what we found. I'll hang out up top." She pointed toward the parking area. "Let you guys do your thing." Hearing Dr. Webb talking into his recorder behind them, she paused to listen.

"Victim is female. Clothing present but disintegrating. Decedent in putrefaction decomp. Throat slashed. Approximately 1.7 meters in length. From on-site visuals of pubic area and skull, victim is Caucasian, adult…"

"Zahra?" Katia looked at the full, well-shaped lips, deep dimples, and almond-shaped eyes with pupils so dark they were barely distinguishable from the iris. What she wanted to say was, "I wish we were anywhere but here. I wish I wasn't a paramedic and you weren't a cop. I wish I could wrap my fingers in that kinky, untamed hair you hate, get lost in the curves of you." She couldn't say any of that. She still didn't know Zahra well enough to know if she would understand her sense of coping with pain. Sex was Katia's escape. She didn't think it was Zahra's.

"Yeah?" Zahra's tone was soft but hurried.

"Nothing. I'm—I'm just glad you're here. On this."

"Me, too."

Chapter Three

Andrew spoke into the recording app on his phone. "Name: Andrew Hunter. Time of incident: Four o'clock AM. Incident type: Tornado stemming from Hurricane Anna. Rescue and recovery. Location: Buxton Beach. Tower Circle Rd. Multiple injured transported to Buxton High School. Six casualties…"

He hit Pause when he heard someone enter the station. Exhaustion was competing with nerve endings that pulsed after more than thirteen hours of constant movement and discovery. He needed to talk about the day with another human. He hit Record and finished his brief: "Released from the scene at five twenty-eight PM. All patients taken to high school to await further transport." He hit Stop on the recorder and slid his phone into his shirt pocket.

He hoped it was Katia who entered from the rear of the station, nearest the showers. He wanted to know why she ran away from the woman with the purple shoe. As an outsider, he didn't know everyone the way the others did, and hard as he tried, no one seemed willing to change that. Right now, he would settle for a targeted conversation about every glorious, adrenaline-pumping moment of the day.

It wasn't Katia. He guessed she was still on the beach where they left her when they transported the last of the bodies to the school. It was Brent.

"Thought I heard someone." Andrew watched Brent peel the wet work shirt off. "I was just finishing up my report."

"What a day, huh?" Brent was looking toward his open locker and not toward Andrew. His T-shirt, the same shade of blue as the shirt he just removed, hung on a hook on the open door. Underneath, Andrew knew, was a picture of his daughter, who was, according to Brent, his favorite human on the planet.

"It was that. Katia didn't come with you?" Andrew glanced around the empty room.

"Nah. Elliot headed home to hug the wife and kids. She stayed to travel with the body from the dune. It hasn't been identified as such, but it's definitely a local real estate agent. The mom of Katia's ex."

Andrew didn't respond right away. He tried to judge whether or not Brent was open to discussing the full scope of the death of the day.

"Everything okay, Andrew?"

"Oh. Sorry. Yeah. Just thinking about the corpse we found. So Katia knew her well?" Andrew took a deep breath. His brain registered the smells of sea and rain, salt and sand, and the life and death that hung on the windbreakers, button-up shirts, and pants of both men. It was a smell he enjoyed more than he cared to admit.

"Name's Gina Dahl. Her daughter, Elizabeth, and Katia were a thing in high school and until a couple of years ago. It ended badly. Elizabeth moved to Virginia to work in some art gallery. And maybe to get away from Katia."

"That's harsh. Katia doesn't seem like that big of an asshole." Andrew didn't want to say too much. This was the most any of them had opened up to him since he arrived. The catastrophic event might be his way in.

Brent slid the T-shirt over his head and closed the locker. "I don't think so, but I don't date her. Who really knows anyone?"

Andrew decided it best to move away from Katia and edge toward the aftermath of the tornado. "The Clark family. You know them, too?"

"Pretty well. Yeah. My kid is in the same class as the oldest one. It's hard to fathom that all four kids and their parents are gone just like that."

"The baby was still in the crib. That was some creepy shit."

Andrew's tone must have set something off in Brent. His facial features changed and his body tensed. He ran his fingers through his hair as he spoke. "I didn't see the baby. I transported the middle two boys. They didn't look creepy. They looked sweet. And dead. And I'm beat. I better go."

"You headed home?" Andrew wasn't ready to let Brent off the hook quite so fast. "Shift has me wired."

Brent looked at Andrew. "I'm thinking a shower, a beer, and bed."

Andrew shrugged. Obviously Brent was finished and Andrew remained an outsider. "Whatever. I'm out, too."

Andrew started home on Highway 12. *One way in. One way out. That describes the Outer Banks.* His dad's voice was in his head. *Not a big deal in the summer, but those winter months... Just remember, I warned you.*

Andrew glanced at the cars parked alongside the highway. Rescue workers weren't easily shocked, but little could have prepared them for the amount of death and destruction they uncovered today. He drove slowly to avoid patches of high-standing water and swirls of sand that spilled over onto the road.

He meant to drive past the disaster-site-turned-crime-scene. With no reason to stop, he could say he was there to check on Katia, but he knew no one would believe him. Better to wait until there was a legitimate reason to return to the dunes. Still, the draw was too great. He turned his wheel to the left, and the car drifted into a crowded parking lot. It seemed the men and women who earlier went home to tend to dinner and families were back.

Andrew stood away from the crowds that formed on the blacktop. They were close enough to get a glimpse of any gruesome dune find and far enough away to keep a decaying or decayed body out of their nightmares. About five feet to the left of him, Andrew noticed two women. The duo appeared to be the nexus of knowledge. Everyone around them listened to their words, shook their heads, and asked questions while they pointed this way and that.

Andrew moved closer. They were oblivious to him. He watched one and then the other as each answered questions. Both women wore flip-flops and sweats, a combination often seen in the lonely winter months on the Outer Banks, known locally as the OBX.

"Girl, they're bringing a dog," the thinner, older woman said as she crossed her arms over her chest.

"A dog?" The rounder woman looked perplexed. "For what?"

They probably think it's a regular dog—a little home mutt with no training or manners. Andrew hated pet dogs. He simply couldn't understand the draw to having a creature in your house that served absolutely no purpose other than to bark and shed.

"Said there's probably more bodies." The older woman shook her head and sighed. "Ain't safe anywhere these days. Told Hank we need to just sell the house and live on the boat. Ain't likely to get to ya in a boat."

Andrew snickered. Stupid bitch. If someone wants to kill you, a boat isn't going to save your ass. He started to walk away, but the older woman said something that stopped him in his tracks.

"Think they'll go back and question the ones from the teacher mess a few years back?" Her voice had a tone of worry. "I bet they do. Did ya live here then?"

"No." The round woman paused a moment before continuing. "Heard about it, though. Some say that kid what went missing was with her. Seventeen, I think. Never did find any proof, though, did they?"

"None I know of, and I been here since right about the time. Questioned a bunch of locals. Some married guy. Said something about an affair."

The women fell into silence. The larger woman bit her nails and cracked her knuckles. He knew exactly the time they were talking about. The teacher and student had achieved ghost story status around here. It was common to hear locals weaving a tall ghostly tale around the two when a beach fire and beer were involved.

The older woman pointed toward the area where the white tents that were placed on the police-dotted beach had begun to multiply. "Guessing whatever they're finding down there will be telling, though. Heard along the way that several women gone missing over the years, but nothing found to show they didn't just get in a car and leave."

Andrew endured a few more minutes of babbling from the women and then walked away.

As he moved, he carefully stayed to the far edge of the crowd. He made his way to where the sand met the blacktop. As he did, he alternated between listening, observing, and watching the news on his cell phone. He got a kick out of seeing his surroundings flash on the tiny screen in his hand. He looked at the growing number of reporters and picked out the one who stood at the center of his screen. He glanced at the dark-haired lovely in the blue windbreaker, seeing her first on the blacktop and then on the tiny screen, one an echo of the other.

The echo game grew old. Andrew clicked the button on the side of the phone and watched the screen go dark. He looked out over the beach. Images of Frisbee in the sand when he was a child meshed together with time in the US Marines when he watched a twenty-year-old blonde recruit explode less than a foot away. Two beaches. Opposite ends of the world.

After his parents sold his childhood home last year, it made sense for Andrew to come back to the Outer Banks. His parents told him they needed to move forward. He needed to move forward. He knew they were tired of taking care of him. He was a grown man in the home where they cheered his first steps, not once, but twice: first as an infant and second as a broken shell of a man honorably discharged from the only life he thought worth living.

At twenty, while driving a Humvee emergency vehicle overseas, an IED almost ended his life. When he was released from the Walter Reed National Military Medical Center in Bethesda, MD, his parents welcomed him home with open arms. And now, at twenty-nine, with a Purple Heart hanging in a frame above his childhood bed, he was living in the same place where he returned to heal.

After the incident, the Internet became Andrew's life, his means of socialization. He learned to code, learned the dark web, learned to troll. He loved all aspects of it—the good, the bad, and the ugly. He discovered the dark web in the days after he wished he were dead but couldn't die, when his mom fed him soup and told him how much she loved him, how much she needed him to live. Slowly he had lived and relearned to walk and talk. When he started school, he incorporated what he learned inside Tor's dark web with what he learned in class, and soon he was making money offering his services under the cover of invisibility. Hacking, researching, coding. People paid a lot for his ability to reach the unreachable, for his ability to keep them invisible. He could no longer be a paramedic with the US Marines, but he could apply the fierce dedication and precision he had learned and reinvent himself.

In the cavernous corners of the deep web where the outlaws and misfits go to play late into the night, Andrew made more connections with like-minded computer blips on the screen. Every day he trained harder, hacked deeper, and became more valuable to those who sought him out. Soon there was no limit to what a person would give in exchange for his services. He thrived on reaching into the anonymous, hidden-onion domains, accessible only through the Tor network.

His ability to communicate in innuendos and code did nothing to help him reenter the face-to-face world of his peers. He didn't care. He liked his anonymous world and the jobs that allowed him to work long into the night until he was numb enough to fall asleep in his childhood bed.

Andrew Hunter thought he had the best of both worlds: A place to live that left him behind a wall of childhood safety, and a job that let him feel important and needed behind the wall of adulthood logic. And then his mom told him he had to leave.

In those early morning hours, long after most of the world was sleeping, he brought up Tor on his homemade workstation. Maybe a job will help me stop thinking about my mother's announcement, he thought.

His search in the predawn hours of that day led him to Gerald and ultimately to Buxton. So in a way, all of this was his mother's fault.

Andrew thought about Katia back on the sand. He pictured her surrounded by rubble. The muscles in her back pushed hard against the blue of her uniform as she moved pieces of a boat with her rubber-gloved hands. When she was in the zone, she appeared invincible. He thought of her later, at the dune, the way the invisible torment pulled her to her knees. Her vulnerable side was new to him. In her moment of weakness, he wanted desperately to put his hand on her shoulder, to comfort her. He didn't. And right now, he hated himself for that. It was yet another missed opportunity to connect with a woman he admired. Being despised by the fairer sex was the fate of the socially awkward, and Andrew was an expert in awkward.

He looked across the pavement and across the sand. He felt the heat rise from his chest to his cheeks. Katia was just like the rest.

Chapter Four

Katia saw the Companion Animal Mobile Equipment Trailer pull into the far side of the parking lot and made her way over. Bob was taking a German shepherd dog from the back. Paige waved her over to the side where she prepped for the job ahead. Katia placed her hand in Paige's and pulled her in for a brief shoulder-to-shoulder hug.

"You look like shit, Katia." Paige leaned back slightly without breaking contact.

Katia nodded, attempted a smile. "You know. Just another day in the twenty-four-on, forty-eight-off roller coaster."

"Hm." Paige looked toward the horizon and the setting sun. "What's that mean for you? Thirty-five on, zero off?" Paige let go of Katia and took a step back.

"Something like that. We were twenty-one in when the call came through. I'm off now, though. Don't imagine I'll go back before the mandatory psych eval, at least."

"So why're you here? You have to be out of spoons. Seriously."

Katia was both aggravated at the insinuation she was unable to cope and impressed that Paige used the spoon reference. It was a reference used throughout the autism community. Obviously, it was now more mainstream. Paige was right. She rubbed her temples and gave a weak smile. "It's okay. I borrowed from tomorrow's."

Paige didn't smile in return.

"Zahra texted you, didn't she?" Katia asked.

"She said you would meet us up here."

Katia knew from Paige's tone there was more. "And?"

"And that you preliminarily ID'ed the body."

Katia turned her attention to Paige's brother. She shook his hand briefly. "Hi, Bob."

"Hey there." His handshake was no nonsense. "Nietzsche's ready to get on with this." He wrapped the leash around his hand several times before he spoke to his sister. "We don't have much light left."

Paige nodded and started to move toward the scene.

Bob and the shepherd stayed several steps ahead of the two women.

"It's Gina Dahl, Paige."

"I'm so sorry." Paige looked at the ground as they talked. There were too many obstacles, too much water, to look away for more than a second or two.

Katia was thankful Paige didn't remind her that the ID wasn't confirmed.

"She cares about you. Zahra, that is."

Katia's boot sunk several inches into the soft sand. She paused to pull it free and took several quick paces to fall back in step with Paige. "She cares about preserving the scene and maybe thinks I'm a bit of a distraction. But seriously care about me?" She furrowed her brow and tilted her head. "That's a stretch."

"Seriously, chica?" Paige stopped and looked squarely at Katia. "She had the biggest crush on you in high school. If you ask me, it hasn't changed much in the last seven years."

"Zahra? Seriously? She didn't even know me."

"Yeah, Zahra." Paige resumed dodging debris as they crossed the beach. "And no one knew you, Katia. If your name wasn't Elizabeth Grace Dahl, you didn't exist in your world."

Her words hit home and stung Katia's pride. "Bullshit." Her toe hit the corner of a steel rod, and she lost her balance.

Paige grabbed Katia's elbow to steady her. "Bullshit?"

In front of them, Bob led Nietzsche around a concrete block that housed other steel rods. Paige continued. "You sure are dense for being so smart. Name one person from high school you developed a friendship with that lasted beyond an occasional hook-up or party. Not someone you run into at The Pink Clover and maybe fuck."

Katia opened her mouth to speak, but Paige cut her off.

"And not someone who you reconnected with at a crime scene and friended on social media because you're in love with her fantabulous fluffers." Paige winked, clearly trying to lighten the mood.

Katia let the words sink in. She did focus a lot of her energy on Elizabeth in high school. An introvert by nature, she didn't need many friends. She never understood those who craved attention. Even before the death of her mother left her angry at the world, she craved alone time. After her mother's death, she buried deep into her own skin as a way to deflect the callousness of her classmates, some of whom took joy in her new pain. Elizabeth was different. She never teased her about being a boy or a no-boob wonder or a motherless freak.

Elliot was her friend. Brent, too. But not in high school.

Three years ahead of her, Elliot and Brent were more work friends than friend friends. She decided to use them, anyway.

"Elliot and Brent went to school with us. We're friends."

Paige shook her head. "They married sisters right out of high school. The sisters were friends of Elizabeth, not you."

Paige was right. After she started studying to become an EMT, she and Elizabeth went to Elliot's many times for cookouts and poker, but the four weren't her friends in school. The guys were several years her senior.

"Elizabeth liked people more than I did."

"And you liked Elizabeth."

"Of course I did."

Elizabeth was her first love. Truth be told, she was her only love. Feminine to her masculine. Soft to her rough. Her girl. Elizabeth had dragged her along to beach parties, football games, kiteboarding events. They had friends. Elizabeth's friends. When Elizabeth moved away, her friends stopped reaching out to Katia, and Katia didn't reach out to them.

"And just what's wrong with making friends because of a fantabulous dog?" Katia asked. "I like dogs. They're loyal. They don't give a flying fuck if you don't call them to meet for dinner or gossip or giggle at some stupid thing that happened at work. They like to work. They like to sit quietly. Dogs. A girl's best friend."

"You're incorrigible. And you don't even have a dog."

"But you do. And here we are. Talking just like friends." Katia made a two-thumbs-up motion with her hands and smiled. "Poof. Friendship secured."

The two fell into silence as they maneuvered across the rest of the sand between the blacktop and the sea. As they walked, Katia saw snippets of herself, as a child, on the path they were walking now. She was holding a kite string, running, her long, black hair swishing back and forth, tickling her bare shoulder blades. Her mother loved being here. She called it her happy place. "Run, Katia. Run like the wind." Her mother's laughter-filled voice followed her, her feet kicking up puffs of sand as she ran. "Not too far, stay on the beach."

The Point was her parents' favorite part of the beach. Even with its location a mile from any paved parking spots, the Point continued to be a popular area both for tourists in the warmer months and for locals the rest of the year when it remained fairly deserted. Katia supposed this was part of the draw for her parents. She saw the two of them holding hands, talking, watching her. Their voices were lively in her memory. She could almost feel the strength in her father's hands as he swung her onto his shoulders and headed in the direction of her home.

The safety she felt on her father's shoulders, in her mother's laughter, was dead, just as dead as the Katia of those years. When her mom died, half of her heritage died, leaving her with a hole as dark, as deep, and as wide as the one they maneuvered around now.

Katia tried to stop thinking about the past as she led the two-person, cadaver-dog-handler team past scattered wreckage and toward the carnage that still rested partially buried in sand and murky water. She was tired deep in her bones. All she wanted to do was remove her soggy clothes and rest, but rest was a long time away.

Bob was several steps ahead of the women. He turned and waited for them to reach his side. "At least the rain and wind have finally subsided."

Paige and Katia nodded.

The water was slowly seeping back out to sea. Soon, all that would be left of the horror Anna produced was the heavy stillness that hung in the air, absorbing the sights, smells, and sounds of death.

Katia pointed to Dr. Webb, who squatted on the far side of the yellow-tape barrier at the opposite edge of the large dune where the first two victims were discovered. He held a bone close to his face, studying the slight curves and dips that would set it apart from other bones in the sand. Close by, two men in blue were preparing the second set of remains for careful transport to the staging area.

"What is it, Doc?" Katia asked. She wrapped her fingers around the yellow police tape that isolated the area, pulling it up just high enough to allow Bob and Paige to slip underneath.

"An ulna bone," Dr. Webb replied. "Not our original victim's and not victim number two's."

"Paige and Bob are here with Nietzsche and the equipment." Katia motioned to the trio. She remained separated by the strip of yellow, but she didn't leave the scene. She felt stronger than she did an hour ago and wanted to help if she could. There weren't a lot of police officers on the scene, and most of the neighbors who stood by earlier were gone.

Dr. Webb faced the group. "Looks like we have multiple victims. One in active decay. Two others in the skeletonization stage."

Katia watched Paige's chest rise and fall as she took a deep breath. Active decay. Active decomp. Putrefaction. She hated those words. Putrefaction meant maggots, flies, and stench. And that meant nightmares.

Paige reached for Dr. Webb's hand and helped him stand. "I have the preliminary report, sir. Tornado destroyed three homes. Seven confirmed bodies, with others possible. Anything else we need to know?"

"Six confirmed from the tornado. One here." He motioned behind with a slight flick of his head. "Three here, now. Not tornado related. Just found remains of a third victim in the same dune. They've been here for a while, years likely for two of them, based on preliminary observations. Just started processing."

"It never gets any easier, does it?"

"No. It doesn't," Dr. Webb said slowly as he reached down to scratch the head of the German shepherd standing at attention at Paige's side. "With you and Nietzsche, here, I know it will at least be thorough."

Katia shifted her weight slightly so as to position herself where she could watch Zahra as she worked over victims two and three. From her vantage point, the two sets of remains looked intertwined. The leg bones, if that was what they were, crisscrossed. She counted three long bones. Three legs? Her mind cataloged the snaps of Zahra's camera. No sign of clothing. Bones more condensed than with victim number one, as if they were piled together as they decomposed, or maybe they were put here after decomp. Why would one victim be buried right after death and others buried sometime later? Could the shifting sand have pushed the bones together? Fascinating. She looked away from the bones, stopped counting the clicks of the camera, and gazed directly at Zahra, whose black khakis and black T-shirt blended into her dark hair and even darker skin. Katia was drawn to her dark intensity even here in the middle of so much pain.

"Katia." Dr. Webb motioned toward the white tents a few feet away from the dune. "Do you mind taking them to Levine."

"No, sir." Katia was thankful for something to do. She looked in the direction of Paige and Bob.

Dr. Webb spoke to the handlers. "Levine will show you where to set up. Introduce you around. Fill you in on plans for the arrival of the SAR team from Charlotte."

****

Paige Johnston felt the heaviness of everyone in the tent. She'd been in this position before. The people with her in the tent wanted her to take Nietzsche and get things done immediately. The truth was, that wasn't going to happen. It was dusk. She needed to fully understand the topography. That was critical in terms of the directionality of scent. Depending on the conditions when the bodies were buried and the amount of vegetation present, it could be a challenge for Nietzsche to track an exact location. They had to take their time.

"I'll take Nietzsche farther down. Work our way back," Paige said. "I think it's best if we start a little outside of our mile mark. Give him a fresh scent."

Bob nodded. His position on this job would be to stand by at command post. He'd listen to the radio as Paige talked through exactly what was happening in the field. He would take notes not only on what was being said but also on the changes in weather, in wind direction, even in Paige's voice intonation. Nothing was too small to note. If he located remains, Nietzsche would go down on his belly and wait for his handler. He would not dig, circle, or in any other way compromise the scene. Paige would tell Bob. Bob would tell Zahra. She and Dr. Webb, along with appropriate officials, would take it from there.

"I've got a bad feeling about this one, Paige. A very bad feeling," Bob said. He looked both ways down the long strip of mostly isolated beach. "There are a lot of places where a sick fuck can hide a body out here."

"Well, let's hope this sick fuck hasn't been at it too long."

"Hmph." Bob's guttural sound said exactly what Paige knew they were both thinking. The differences in decomp among the bodies discovered in dune number one didn't point to a killer who was new to the killing game.

Paige took hold of Nietzsche's collar. She moved him away from the perfume of death that hung in the air, to a position where he could begin trekking back and forth until he picked up the edge of a new scent. They started a mile from the original crime scene and away from the destruction caused by the tornado. Doing so removed many distractions.

"Come on, boy. We have work to do." The third-generation cadaver dog's ears perked up at the mention of work. He was beautiful with his black-and-gold markings against a silky tan coat. He stood, a glint in his eyes, bubblegum-pink tongue lying over his white teeth, anticipation apparent. "My little nose artist," Paige said scratching Nietzsche's ears.

Nietzsche didn't take a step. He stood, haunches against her leg, sniffing the air.

Paige licked her lips, breathed deeply, and gave the command. "Nietzsche, search."

They worked their way from the dunes closest to the roadway to those closer to the beach. Back and forth, Nietzsche trotted. Back and forth, Paige moved with him. They were like a well-oiled machine. He was one of the best cadaver dogs she'd ever trained. Once he was given his command to search, he worked through heat and cold. Hills, rocks, and water were minor inconveniences. He knew exactly where his body was in space, could work in rubble or sand, collapsed buildings or deep woods. He was trained to pick up the scent of any number of volatile compounds that make up human remains, be they dried bones or the recent dead.

****

Paige spoke into the mic attached to her shirt collar. "Nietzsche is in scent." She looked down at Nietzsche. He was in the zone, moving slowly, tail high and head up, the concentration visible. She watched as he worked his nose in the air and to the ground.

"I'll tell Zahra. They're cataloging and bagging the remains up here. I can send an officer your way," Bob said.

"Okay." Paige returned her full attention to the task at hand. Her heart rate quickened.

Nietzsche came to a stop next to a dune not quite one-half mile away from the location where Dr. Webb and Zahra worked on their earlier find. The coordinates told Paige the comfort zone of the killer was between one-half and one full mile of Buxton Beach.

Paige knew Nietzsche's final alert, or indication of a find, would depend on where the body was on the scent spectrum of active decay and decomposition. The passive lying down was the trained sign for Nietzsche when he found a cadaver, but if the remains were fresh, his response may well be a bark and return, also the indication for a live find.

Paige wondered how anyone could come back to the same place, time after time, bury bodies, and never get caught. He would have to have a beach-approved vehicle, which indicated a local. She shivered at the thought that someone she passed in a store or on the beach or at the Putt Putt Golf Course outside of the local ice cream parlor could commit this type of crime.

In the few seconds it took Paige to reach Nietzsche, he assumed the passive down stance. His tail thumped softly against the sand.

"You did good, boy. You did good."

Into the mic attached to her shirt, she said, "He found something."

Chapter Five

Elizabeth awoke, groggy and disoriented, as if from a stunted sleep after too much alcohol. Except she didn't drink much—and never to the point of complete absence of memory. She wasn't in her bed, which was the only place she slept since leaving Buxton for Virginia Beach months ago.

What the… She rubbed at her eyes with her thumb and forefinger, trying to clear the filmy goop that formed during her sleep. Was it sleep? Where? What is this place? Small. Dingy. What? 5x10 feet, maybe? She looked up through the dim, single-bulb light. She felt as if her 5'4" build would have to crouch slightly to stand. Maybe slightly crouch or slightly clear. Hard to tell. Concrete? A door to the right. No. No door. A doorway. A way out?

She tried to stand in the dim room.

She made it upright, glanced up. The ceiling was inches away.

Her legs felt heavy, like lead, and the right one caught as she tried to gain her balance. She looked down and saw the metal links strung five or so feet across the small room, ending right outside the doorway. The rusty exterior of each link blended into the color of the air in the room. Her eyes traced the shadowy outline from her ankle to the large, round loop sticking out of the wall next to the opening. A five-foot tether? Chains?

She grabbed the chain and yanked.

Panic overtook her.

She strained to see through the murky light. When she could see nothing to use to break free, she dropped the chain, knelt down, and put both hands flat on the lumpy surface. A mattress? She pushed her body from side-to-side. Each movement pushed the thinly stuffed material to the hard floor below. She stretched and rubbed and patted as far as she could reach. Every stroke of her palm brought closer the reality of the moment.

The drugs slowly wore away at the adrenaline, and Elizabeth closed her eyes. This was happening. The dizziness from her rapid movements across the mattress caused the bile to rise in her throat. She pushed both hands tight against the mattress, but it was too late. Everything was black, swirling. She eased herself safely into a lying position and waited for the blackness to clear.

The soft swish of a door caught her attention. She rolled her body toward the sound, careful to keep her head in synchronization with the movement. The sliver of light that met her eyes brought her close to unconsciousness again. She swallowed the bile. The dimness returned, and with it came her ability to open her eyes without increased pain. For the moment, she was thankful for the rusty-yellow light. Thoughts came to her like sound bites. She couldn't remember how she got here. She could smell a man.

A moment later, a shadow moved into the room. The door pushed inward again. Light moved into the room. She flinched but forced herself to keep her eyes open.

The man pushed the door to its fully open position.

She watched. Not a door really. Too small. A square. A piece of concrete coming away from the wall. But he pushed it so easily, so quietly. The size of the opening doesn't matter.

If he got in, I can get out.

She blinked to adjust to the entering light. She kept her head still as she pulled herself to a sitting position.

"Hello, Elizabeth." His voice was both soft and rough, like a lover who was saying good morning after a night of sweet slumber. "You're awake. Good."

"What the hell? Who—" Some faraway moment of recognition cut off her words. "Why—" None of this makes sense.

He stepped closer, finishing her question. "Why are you here?"

Elizabeth scooted toward him, arms moving in front of her, ready for battle. She stopped before the tether pulled taut. Her eyes fixed on the blade. Chills filled her entire being. A scream pushed against her closed lips.

"Let me tell you, Elizabeth. Let me tell you why we're here." He stayed slightly back, as if he both wanted to touch her and felt compelled to avoid it.

She knew the fear showed in her blue eyes. She wondered whether he could see it. She watched him, watched the knife.

He licked his lips and closed his eyes briefly.

Every muscle in her body tightened, stretched in anticipation of the moment when he would push the knife slowly through her skin.

"They found your mom yesterday, Elizabeth."

My mom, Elizabeth thought, her mind still trying to focus. What did her mom have to do with this? When had she seen her last? Talked to her? She couldn't remember. Last week? Last month? She was so involved with the new art exhibit.

"My work is getting noticed," she told her. "They want twenty pieces. Twenty, Mom."

There was indisputable happiness in her mom's voice. "I'll tell Katia the good news for you."

"No need, Mom."

Elizabeth was an only child; her mom a single parent after a messy divorce. And then Katia was in their life, and they became a world of three. She could see her, so young, so mad at the world, so darkly beautiful.

Elizabeth's thoughts were jumbled. She remembered Katia's first tattoo and her mom's laughter. Then she was in her room, and Katia was sobbing, screaming, begging her not to leave. But she had to. The relationship was too volatile.

The two women loved her too tight, too hard. Mom. What day is it? I loved Katia. Still love Katia. I'm not in love with her. Mom, don't share my news with her. It will only make her angry. She hates me. Have you seen my mom? Katia? Tell her I'll call soon.

Everything mixed together in her mind. Were they together, now? What was the shadow talking about? What did he mean, found her? Where's my phone? Maybe I can text her. She stretched her neck, her head heavy against the muscles. Stay awake, Elizabeth. Her thoughts were all over the place. My mom. He said something about my mom…

"Elizabeth? Elizabeth. We have so much to talk about." He kept his distance, remained only a shadow in her drug-induced stupor.

"Why are you doing this? Who are you? What do you want? Money? My mom sells real estate in Buxton. Buxton, North Carolina. She can't pay—"

"Shut up, E-liz-a-beth." He cut off her words with his sharp tone.

She hated the sound of her name on his lips. Why did he keep saying it, making it sound vulgar, ugly?

"Want to know a secret, a secret about this room, about me, about the women who taught me something new every time, something to make this space more secure, something to help me determine best lengths for the chains, safest lighting choices?"

His voice was low, distorted, with a hint of a lilt, as if he was trying to alter it so she didn't remember it or know how happy he was to be telling her his secrets. She looked above her head, strained to see the light. Some sort of wire covering, she thought. To prevent his prisoner from breaking it, using it against him, perhaps? That voice. Something familiar. What is it? She couldn't quite place it. Still too foggy. What did he give me? Why?

"So many women have been in this small room over the years." His low chatter broke into her thoughts. "They've tested the lead you're on. It's five feet, by the way. Perfect for getting exactly as far as you need to go. Soon I'll allow you to stay awake long enough to go through the opening into the tiny area two feet to your left. There's a toilet, a shower. Would you like to wash the stench away, Elizabeth?"

Her heartbeat quickened. He intended to make her shower. Then what? Bile in her throat—gagging. She bent forward from her sitting position, wrapped the chains around her hands and yanked the chains tight. There was no give from the concrete walls. Instead, the chains cut into her skin, causing immediate welts. What's on the wall? Come on. You need as many details as possible for later. Smooth. Clear. Seems to be sealed with varnish. She tried to focus. She had to regain self-control, wait for the right opportunity, and wait until she could think more clearly. Smell the flowers. Blow out the candles. Smell the flowers. Blow out the candles. Katia. Where are you? I need you to find my mom. Had she been in this room? Did she die at the hands of this man?

The man appeared to ignore Elizabeth's anxiety attack. She sat back after a few minutes and concentrated on the movements of his mouth, bringing his words back into focus.

"Over the years, women of all sizes and ages have yanked at their chains until wrists and ankles were raw and bleeding, attempted to pull the showerhead from the concrete wall. Many banged their heads against the round porcelain circle built to hold waste. And you will try, too, Elizabeth. To no avail."

"Why are you doing this?" Elizabeth could smell the blood of the other women. She could hear their screams. Her fear was theirs. "I did nothing to you."

"I like the beach. I'd love to take you there, to lie with you on a blanket, skin to skin."

He squatted close enough for her to smell his sweat mix with the blood and urine of her prison. She didn't respond.

"I feel your fear. Fear comes through your pores. Did you know that?" He leaned forward on his haunches, taking the weight off of his heels for a moment, and rolled his head all the way to the left and then all the way to the right. He positioned the backs of his arms against the concrete wall behind him and pushed to propel himself to a standing position. "There will be no beach for us, Elizabeth. No sand to hold the warmth of the day, no sand to muffle your screams as the sharp blade finds its way through skin and muscle and tendons. The elements have chosen a different path for us." He stopped talking and took a step forward and sideways. He didn't get close enough to touch her, didn't get close enough for her to see his face in the faint light. He backed out of the small opening in the wall. "Good-bye for now, Elizabeth. The drug will soon wear off, and you'll know exactly who I am."

"No. Please Don't leave. Tell me why you're doing this to me." She was begging now. "What are you going to do to me? I'll fight you. I'm not going to die. Do you hear me?" She screamed and beat her fists against the mattress. "Do you fucking hear me?"

The door slid into place.

Loud.

Solid.

And then silence.

Chapter Six

Paige noted her exact coordinates and physical surroundings. She waited for Zahra, who was on her way with another police investigator she said was from Charlotte. Walking toward the spot where the dog lay, she continued to record: "The sand has washed away quite significant portions of the dune. Much of the normal grass is gone, leaving whole sections bare." Paige reached Nietzsche, hit Pause, made eye contact, and spoke directly to the dog. "Heel, boy."

Nietzsche rose and returned to her side. Paige shone a flashlight on the spot where his prints remained as a wraithlike reminder of his presence. Farther down the beach, spotlights lit up the scene. Soon they would here, as well. She hit Play on the recorder. "Nietzsche assumed cadaver stance at 7:00 PM, November 18, 2018. There appears to be a faint outline of a body, barely visible against the underside of the sand. Noted position is west side of the dune, facing houses. Houses are intact in this location." She pushed a loose strand of hair out of her face. It was going to be a long night, and she was thankful they were working in November and not in the heat of summer.

Before today, this strip of sand with its old wooden-plank sidewalk was central to many a postcard purchased in the restaurant a few thousand feet away. Debris from the three houses, smashed as a small boy would smash a carefully constructed house of blocks, now lay scattered on this section of the beach. Planks—maybe part of the sidewalk—stuck out of a nearby dune, and a filthy, soaked mattress stood against the boards. Everywhere she looked was destruction.

What will today mean for the economy of little Buxton?

Paige felt a stab of guilt for wondering such a trivial thing in the middle of such devastation and death, but the Outer Banks was home to many people she loved who depended on tourism to survive. As sick as it was, traffic possibly would increase, maybe all year round. Morbidity is a motivator.

Paige looked past the row of intact rentals to the paved area beyond. One solitary policeman stood stationed between two sections of wood fencing to keep onlookers and reporters at bay. None of them, not the rescue workers nor the onlookers, knew what they were up against. But they must know it was going to be bad.

Paige moved carefully, with Nietzsche in perfect step, to the board walkway. She stood on the bottom step of five, her hand resting lightly on the weathered rail. The blue-green water continued to push waves of seafoam onto the shore under the darkening sky. It would soon be solid night in Buxton, North Carolina. She wanted to walk back to the truck and drive, but she pushed on, continuing her assessment. There was no one at the scene at this spot except for her and her dog. Gawkers were on the blacktop above and farther down where the first scene was secured.

Paige squinted in the direction of the original dune. She noticed an increased number of blue uniforms dotting the beach, as well as an increased number of people in and out of the white tents like little worker ants. The tents would provide some realm of privacy from the prying eyes of the reporters, both on the ground and in the air. She couldn't tell how many tents were erected, but it was definitely more than one.

"More than one means multiple bodies, doesn't it, Nietzsche?" she said, patting his side. She tilted her head back slightly in response to a noise overhead. A helicopter with a local news emblem whirled in place. "And multiple hidden remains mean multiple vultures." She brought her eyes back to the beach just as Zahra and a team of homicide investigators from Charlotte reached her and Nietzsche. This area would soon resemble the beach less than a half mile away, complete with crime scene techs at every dune. Multiple homicides spanning years of victims motivated everyone.

Paige inhaled deeply. She was raised on the smell of sandy seaweed that filled the air. What would a killer have been thinking as he stood here? And how in the hell did he carry out such a laborious task unseen and unheard? She again breathed in the air, trying to calm her heart rate and her nerves with the salty smells. Every day, she was thankful humans didn't have the more than 220 million olfactory receptors in their nose that canines did. As far as she was concerned, depending on the stage of decomp at a scene, the five million she had were too many.

Zahra arrived with a detective she said was from Charlotte.

Without acknowledging Paige, the man said, "We'll set up here."

Zahra nodded toward a small group of cops who were making their way to the dune with stakes and tape to cordon off the new square.

Paige was antsy to continue her movements down the beach. She looked at Zahra. "Nietzsche and I are ready to release the scene if you are."

"Of course," Zahra said. "Yes. Let's get you two back out in the field."

Paige hit the Record button and began speaking. "1935. Scene released to Officer Zahra Knox."

****

Katia was exhausted when she got home—mentally, physically, and emotionally. She was sure that by morning the first body found on the beach would be positively identified as that of Gina Dahl, mother of Elizabeth Dahl.

Where are you, Elizabeth? Katia was so angry when Elizabeth left. What'd she say? She tried to remember Elizabeth's words as she held her hands and looked directly into her eyes, but all she remembered clearly was Elizabeth's breath as she spoke. It held the slight smell of sweet coffee and cream. She still missed that.

She pulled into the driveway, guilt still riding shotgun. She didn't have Elizabeth's phone number. She didn't know where she settled in Virginia or if she was still there. She was sure Zahra thought ill of her because of it. She reached for the door handle with what felt like a hundred-pound hand. Push, she told herself. She felt almost ethereal. Her shift started at seven last night. Other than a brief nap in Elliot's SUV, she had been awake and full of adrenaline for slightly more than twenty-five hours.

"Kahteeah!"

Barely through the front door, Katia heard the sweet voice of her little brother. Two seconds later, he rounded the corner of the hall.

"Hi, mister." She put her fist out to meet his. It was their version of a hug.

"Two, zero, zero M. P. H." He smiled.

"I know. Did you put it on the board?"

Her brother nodded, and she smiled. "Marco?"

He glanced at her face and looked to the side.

"Did you eat?" He nodded again and rubbed his stomach, sticking it out so it created a little pouch.

"Hey, kiddo." Her father's voice came from the living room. "Left you a plate on the stove. Marco's favorite."

"Frozen pizza?"

"You know it."

"Thanks, Papi," Katia said, using the term of endearment her mom left behind as a part of her idiolect. Idiolect. Katia loved that word and words in general, really. She got that from her mom. Kind of ironic, since the central being in all of their worlds had almost no words in his arsenal. "Going to shower first." She tousled her brother's hair and gave him a slight nudge toward the living room. Over the years, Katia learned this was one mode of touch that didn't send Marco into panic mode. He actually appeared to like it. It was a win-win. She was able to show her little brother she was connected to him, and he got to show her he accepted that connection.

"Not really hungry." She threw the words toward her father who sat in his recliner in the living room. He looked tired, too. She studied the tan face so different from her own. She and Marco had the coloring of their Spanish mother. Marco had inherited his father's green eyes and the curl of his hair, though his father's hair was blond, and Marco's was jet black. She, in turn, had her mom's almost black orbs and straight black hair, though not as jet black as Marco's. Funny thing, genetics. I hope he's okay. Katia didn't have the energy today to actually ask. She turned from her little family. She didn't want to say much in front of Marco, and her father, whom she texted all afternoon, would understand.

Katia peeled away the layers of her navy-blue uniform and her still-damp bra and panties and stepped into the hot shower. She stood, numb, and watched as the sand and dirt rolled down her body. There were no explainable thoughts, no way to make sense of the day. She carried the lifeless bodies of children and friends through rubble and saw the partially eaten remains of the woman she loved as much as any child loved a parent.

Katia pulled out of her driveway twenty-five hours and twenty minutes ago with a life that was less than perfect, but predictable. She worked. She took care of brother and father. She read. She drew images of death and talked to her mother in the dark. Occasionally she danced and fucked. This was her normal. She had no idea that this was the day her world would be changed forever. But it was, and she didn't know how to respond.

She slid down the side of the shower wall until her rear made contact with the warm tile floor. She pulled her knees against her chest, wrapped her tattooed arms around them tight, and let her emotions take over. When no tears were left, she reached up for the soap and scrubbed her skin until it was red and sore. She sat on the floor of the shower until the water ran cold and anger tore through her, smothering the numbness of fear.

****

RU there? Katia typed the message to Zahra and then stared at the white letters in the bright green bubble. It was after midnight, but she still couldn't sleep.

She liked Zahra, a lot. The first time she saw her in The Pink Clover, she didn't recognize her as someone she went to school with. She watched her dance for hours, mesmerized by the way her body melted into the words of each song. The woman twirled in time to her partner's movements. With arms outstretched and her head back, she bared a long, dark neck that begged to be bitten. The pale-blue peasant top flared out as she spun, revealing a beautiful dark pudge of skin. On a typical night, Katia walked up and talked to a woman who caught her attention. Not with this one. She didn't want to ruin the moment for either of them. It took three chance meetings for Katia to approach her. Now she fought with herself constantly to stay neutral in the relationship. Zahra deserved more than Katia's dark moods and hateful outbursts. Elizabeth stayed as long as she could. Katia knew that now. She was the one who screamed first, she who couldn't trust, she who blamed.

"You said you would never give up on me. You're just like everyone else. You used me to get what you wanted. Fuck you. Go. I don't need your lying, cheating ass in my life. I hope you fucking die." Katia remembered pieces of the last conversation. She didn't stop there. Her rant had gone on for many minutes.

Elizabeth stood quietly, letting her go until she was spent. She looked at her with a deep sadness. "You need help, Katia. Help I sure as fuck can't give you, and help you sure as fuck can't give yourself."

"What I need," she responded, "is to quit letting people like you into my life. What I need is for you to get the fuck out and never come back. What I need is to Be. The. Fuck. Alone."

Elizabeth left that day. The next week, Katia received the text saying she was leaving town, going to Virginia Beach to try to get her art career off the ground.

No contact. Please. Her words were followed by three emoticons: a cat, an easel, and a paintbrush.

Katia respected the request—until yesterday. "I'm trying to reach Elizabeth Dahl," she said to the strange female voice on the other end of the phone. "It's an emergency."

"This is Felicia Grant. I've had this number for a month. I don't know an Elizabeth Dahl. Sorry."

Katia's stomach turned somersaults thinking about it. Not only had she now lost two moms, she had no idea how to reach the only person who needed to know Gina was gone. Her phone buzzed in her hand. Zahra.

Still on scene.

How many? Her fingers tapped out the message.

Five so far. Unreal.

Katia's eyes misted, her stomach knotted even further, and her face burned with anger. *So far?*

Four in the dune with the first find. Zahra didn't say a name in her text, but Katia knew they both understood. *Widening search.*

Paige still on site? Katia knew she needed to leave Zahra alone, but her fingers wouldn't cooperate with her brain.

No. Had to take Nietzsche in. Start again tomorrow. Headed in soon.

Talk to you tomorrow. Katia signed off.

Zahra, Dr. Webb, and the many others who swarmed the scene would work long into the night. Zahra could tell her nothing more now, probably nothing more for days. She needed to work with what she knew. She pushed the button to turn her phone dark and laid it on her nightstand. Exhausted, she reached up, turned out her light, and slept a fitful sleep filled with the foam of the ocean coming up around her dead body.

Chapter Seven

"There's always a trail," he whispered. "Always." Looking toward the ceiling, he stretched, elbows out, back arched, head sunk deep into the pillow. The day was filled with dark, ugly swirls that filled every corner of his mind. Such exhilaration. Such doom. He had no desire to keep the ugliness tucked away in the dark. He was proud of it. His gaze searched the darkness of his bedroom, resting briefly on each corner, the closed door, and the opening to the adjoining bathroom. He repeated the ritual several times a night, more often following the procuring of one of them.

Corner. Corner. Corner. Corner. Door. Bathroom.

This was his safe space.

Don't let them in your safe space. If they get in, it will never be safe again.

Sometimes he woke from a black sleep, and she was there, looming over him. His aunt. He had let her into his safe space, and now she could come and go as she pleased. Even in death.

Corner. Corner. Corner. Corner. Door. Bathroom. He closed his eyes tight.

Elizabeth's apartment hadn't been hard to locate. He was a very resourceful man with an exceptional memory. Gina bragged all over town that her daughter heard from several exhibition halls regarding her artwork. Later she bragged about the one Elizabeth chose. She didn't mention a state, but she did mention the name. That was all he needed.

There was also the whole town's knowledge of the resident-lesbian break-up between Katia and Elizabeth that sent Elizabeth away. Rumor had it she was just a state up. He heard two women months ago discussing an art gallery exhibit coming up that was going to include a local. The dots almost connected themselves. He knew her address months ago, immediately after killing Gina, and he kept it tucked in his wallet just in case.

He didn't like to be rushed. He liked to plan his steps carefully and methodically, sometimes taking months to plan. "Not this time," he mouthed into the darkness. He could feel his aunt's presence seeping in like an unwanted spirit.

"Good job, Little Man. Are you proud of yourself?" Her voice was always there. No amount of planning and ritual made it stop. Killing calmed it, if only for a moment. The rest of the time, he tried to talk over it.

He lay perfectly still. He opened his eyes and stared upward. The slight movement of the covers from his steady breathing calmed him. He had won when he was fifteen, and he would not give into her presence now. It had taken him three hours to drive to Virginia Beach and three hours to drive back. Add to that thirty minutes in the apartment and thirty minutes to unload and assess. He was proud of himself.

Now he wanted Elizabeth to feel what her mom felt. He blamed them both for the imperfections of Buxton native, Katia Billings-Castillo, who would have been just fine had the pair of transplanted woodsers not intervened. He blamed Gina for her loose household rules and her demands to have Elizabeth close to her all of the time. It's unnatural. Completely sick and twisted. When he saw them on the streets of town, touching, walking too close to one another, laughing at something no one else could hear, he wondered what Gina did to her daughter when they were alone. He knew Gina didn't have a boyfriend, hadn't since she and her daughter moved to Buxton. He kept a close watch on all of them, and he made it his mission to know about them—everything about them. Women are more dangerous than men. His aunt taught him that. More dangerous and more deceitful.

His original plan wasn't to go to Virginia Beach so soon. Two days ago, he didn't know if he would ever go. Elizabeth left Buxton. She was no longer a threat to his beach. He eliminated Gina a week ago, buried her deep within the dune alongside his other secrets. It was Gina's fault he made the trip this morning.

He didn't need or want the kill that was coming. Kills were like food to him, nourishment after a long period of starvation. Like holding your piss as long as you can before you go to the bathroom, so long you feel like you're going to explode if there's no release.

Have you pissed yourself, Elizabeth?

He knew Elizabeth wasn't conscious enough to pull her pants down or to move away from the mattress to find a comfortable place for release. He was sure she had pissed herself by now. The thought pleased him.

That was what he needed, that moment of pure euphoric release. But he remained perfectly still except for his eyes and the movement of his chest. He focused now on the up-and-down movement of the sheet, barely visible in the dark. He didn't offer himself release to get away from his aunt, just as he didn't kill for the sake of killing. To do so would be barbaric.

He allowed himself thoughts of Elizabeth as he lay in bed. His aunt's spirit recoiled as he did. She wanted to be the one he pictured. He thought of Elizabeth's lips—like her mother's—curved just right, slightly parted, and pink. He would taste them as he tasted her mother's, gently and with purpose. Elizabeth needed to know men were powerful and gentle.

Elizabeth was wearing faded jeans and a white, paint-spattered T-shirt when he arrived this afternoon. Retrieval was easy. She was so lost in her brushstrokes she hadn't heard the light buzz or tap as he cut a small hole in the glass and popped out a circle just large enough for his hand. The window slid open silently, and he removed his feet from his shoes so as to approach without a sound. He was bold. He was secure in his ability to subdue her without being noticed until the needle found its mark, so much so he stood just outside the doorframe and watched as Elizabeth continued to move the brush across the canvas in front of her, the starkness of white giving way to the muted grays tinged with pale pinks and blues. A face took shape as he watched. No solid outline. Just curves of barely-there color. Darker toward the hairline, where gray turned into a soft, unchallenging shade of black. It looks like Katia, he mused as he took the final steps into the room.

In one swift motion, he put his left arm around Elizabeth's body and jabbed the sharp end of the needle deep into her neck. He felt himself harden at the memory. Elizabeth was light, maybe one hundred and five pounds and maybe five feet two. He preferred long blonde hair. It afforded him the power to decide the final length. Elizabeth's hair brushed her shoulders. Not the preferred length, but not bad.

When he sliced the throat of his aunt all those years ago, he wanted to cut her hair. He gave into fear back then, but never since. He still regretted his haste to shove the body into the grave he dug in the side of the dune. Such a waste.

When his folks returned from their trip, he explained that he and his aunt played a long game of Frisbee along the beach and his aunt decided to head out immediately after. They bought the story. It wasn't unlike his aunt, at all. She always left before they returned.

"Time's a wastin'," she used to say. "Can't let the grass grow under my feet, Little Man."

I have learned so much, Auntie.

He picked up the phone from his bedside table. Within seconds, Elizabeth's form came into view. He stroked her lifeless form on the screen. She was his now, and she would not leave alive. The thought made him warm inside, and he wiggled under the covers, his bare skin heating the inside of the cool sheets. After laying the phone back on the table, he rolled over, pulled the covers up under his chin, and drifted into a sweet slumber.

****

Katia's father was already gone when she came downstairs the next morning. Through still-tired eyes, she read a note on the counter.

Business in Kitty Hawk. Home late. Message on the machine from the station. Papi.

She walked over and hit the button on the old answering machine her father refused to toss out.

"Katia. Garett's taking your next shift. See you Sunday."

She wasn't sure whether she wanted to be thankful or ticked off. She chose thankful. That gave her six days.

She wasn't at all hungry, but she needed to eat. Cabinet. Cereal. Milk. Robotically, she checked off the steps. Spoon. Sit. She looked into the living room. Marco was sitting cross-legged on the floor watching cartoons, cereal bowl in hand. "Morning, little brother," she whispered in his direction, knowing he would get agitated if she interrupted his ritual with normal-volume words. This morning, she couldn't take them either. She rubbed her temples with the middle finger of each hand, elbows on either side of her bowl. The marshmallows smelled sickly sweet.

One point of contention between Katia and Elizabeth was Marco. Elizabeth agreed with Katia's father that the growing boy should be placed in a group home where he could get round-the-clock care. Katia didn't agree, not then and not now. "We already lost our mother," she argued every time. "Now you want him to lose his father and sister, too?"

She glanced at her brother as she chewed her first bite of Lucky Charms. His dark, unruly curls that sprouted from his head in every direction always made her grin. She couldn't imagine not seeing them every morning.

She often thought it unfair that he was such a beautiful mix of Latina and Anglo with his dark-caramel skin, black curls, and perfectly shaped golden-green eyes. She watched his long, black eyelashes bob up and down. With every down motion, they seemed to lie atop his cheek. Mami's lashes. Katia inherited only two things from her father. One was short eyelashes. The other was freckles. A freckle-faced, masculine-leaning, lesbian Latina with glasses. That's perfect.

She put another bite of the sugary cereal into her mouth.

It saddened her to think that her brother's beauty would likely never be shared with anyone but her and Papi. How many people would still find him beautiful in his silence and in his screaming? How many would understand the ticks and the flapping?

Katia stirred the floating marshmallows and toasted-oat pieces in her bowl and watched Marco. His body was shaking with silent laughter. His smile as wide as his face.

A smile like Elizabeth's smile. A full-face smile.

Katia told Elizabeth two weeks after they met that her smile was like Marco's smile. Elizabeth seemed happy with the comparison early in the relationship. Not so much as Marco aged and became harder to control.

Where the fuck are you, Elizabeth?

Katia took the last bite of cereal, stood, and made her way to the sink to rinse her bowl. She looked out the window as the water ran the milk down the drain. The sand and ocean that served as her backyard her whole life felt different today, menacing, uninviting. It made her heart hurt deeper, more completely. The water ran. She waited. Three. Two. One.

Right on cue, Marco slid his bowl between her arm and waist and into the sink and headed to the bathroom to brush his teeth. Marco was nothing if not predictable. Today was Monday. Monday was a school day. School days, Marco left the house at eight o'clock with his sister or his dad. At eight thirty sharp, he exited the car, waved, and walked into the building where he would stay until four fifteen when he would open the door of his dad's car for the ride home. Life would be a lot easier if everyone were more like Marco. She glanced at the hall clock. Eight o'clock. Marco appeared dressed in his favorite Science is Awesome T-shirt and black jeans. Katia opened the door and the two walked out together.

****

Katia pulled into the drive behind Gina's red Mini Cooper. The car was Gina's pride and joy. She wouldn't have left it here if she were going to the beach. And yet she's dead on the beach. No. In the beach. She swallowed hard. Her goal was to find Elizabeth. She let herself in the front door. Gina's pale-blue jacket hung on the first hook in the hall. Pictures of Gina and Elizabeth, of Elizabeth as a baby, a toddler, and as a graduate, lined the wall up the stairs. On the small round stand by the door, a copy of *Real Estate Weekly* lay folded open, the car keys tossed on top.

Katia ran her finger across the ad on the page. It was Gina smiling her famous real estate smile in front of a beautiful beach house. "Call me for all of your real estate needs," the print read.

How can you be dead? Katia realized she was touching the page without a glove and pulled her hand away. She wiped a tear with the hand that still held the key to the front door. Gina gave it to her when the girls were in high school. She never asked for it back.

Katia could still feel Gina's arms wrap around her. She smelled like foundation and mascara with a hint of Estée Lauder Pleasure perfume and cinnamon gum. Katia didn't like makeup or perfume for herself, but she loved the smell of Gina—loved the way the smells mixed perfectly to calm her as she laid her cheek against her shoulder, pressed her young-adult breasts against Gina's larger motherly breasts, and breathed deep her mixture of smells.

Gina was one of the prettiest, kindest, and smartest women she had ever known. Katia loved her. And then she died. Katia sighed and clenched her fists so hard her short nails managed to find flesh. Ouch. Fuck.

She heard Gina's voice. "Take your shoes off, girls. I don't need sandy tracks on my clean wood floors." Katia slid her feet out of her tennis shoes and moved deeper into the house until she stood in the living room where the three of them used to eat popcorn and watch horror movies.

As Katia slipped on a pair of latex gloves, she spoke aloud, weirded out by the silence. "I don't know where to start, Momma

G," she said. "Help me. Where is she? There has to be a clue here somewhere. A number. An address. Something." Katia knew this place like her own, but she never paid attention to where Gina kept her personal items. There was no need. Now she wished she had.

Opening drawers in the distressed white end tables, Katia was careful to not touch or move anything that might be important in an investigation later. She was aware she shouldn't be here at all, but that wasn't an option. Instead, she carefully and repeatedly lifted and replaced items, using only a fingertip or two on each one. She repeated her pattern of sleuthing throughout the other rooms. She didn't find anything of importance until she entered Gina's bedroom.

The room was just as Katia remembered it. She repeated her practice of the two-fingertip, lift-and-replace in the nightstands. She always wondered why Gina had two. Balance, she supposed, though she didn't understand it. Older people have weird habits. Two lamps, matching. Pain-in-the-ass bed ruffle that always matched the spread on the always-made bed. Her slippers tucked neatly under the edge of the bed. The bottle of water, half-empty, next to her thyroid medicine and vitamin B supplement.

Katia's stomach turned, pulled at her insides, and sent a sound up through her throat and out into the air of the room. It was a deep mewing sound, a sound like a wounded animal. How. Can. You. Be. Dead? How? Pain manifested as anger, and anger spewed from every pore. Katia reached for the pillows and flung them across the room, two at a time, until all six soft, fluffy, pink-covered rectangles were on the floor. The muscles in her face tightened and twitched. Fuck a made bed. She was sobbing now, her shoulders lifting and falling to the rhythm of the pain inside. She yanked at the comforter and sheets, balled them up, and threw them after the pillows. Fuck you, Gina. Fuck you, Elizabeth. Fuck you for leaving me to figure this out. I wish you had never moved onto this street.

She screamed until the words came out as air. She beat her fists against the bare mattress, twirled sideways, knocked the water bottle and pills to the floor. The crying had stopped. Now there was only the quick breathing in and out and the hiccups that come after a hard cry. And anger. She recalled the day they lowered her mom into the ground. She had tried to fall into the hole. She hated her dad for not letting her. Just like she hated Gina right now. Just like she hated Elizabeth. Fuck you all. I hate you. I hate you. I fucking, fucking, hate you.

A whimper brought Katia's movements to an abrupt halt. Whatever it was, it was in the bathroom. She listened between hiccups. It came again. And then she remembered. Frankie. She walked slowly to the door, forgetting the anger and hatred of the previous moment. "Frankie," she said. Katia did her best to offer a calming voice. "It's okay, boy." She opened the door slowly. "Hi, boy. It's okay."

The dog was lying in the corner of the bathroom floor. It was obvious from the dry water and food bowls and from the smell of urine and feces that he was there for a few days, at least. She turned the water on in the sink and let the cool liquid fill her hand. "Here, boy. Just a little to start. I'll get you some food." Frankie's tail wagged, tapping out his thanks on the linoleum floor, but he didn't make any move to stand. "Come on, boy. You're okay." She continued to coax the little brown fluff-ball mutt out of hiding. Frankie whimpered, wanting the water but obviously still spooked. Slowly he started toward Katia, shimmying on his belly, until he was close enough to lick the water from her palm. "That's it, Frankie. That's it. What happened, boy? What did you see?"

****

It took Katia thirty minutes to calm Frankie and put the room back in order. Now she sat at her kitchen table stroking the furry ball of fluff snuggled hard against her lap.

"Papi is not going to be happy." She ran her fingers down the curve of the dog's back. "We don't do animals." She gently pulled one of Frankie's ears and then the other. "Well, Papi doesn't do animals. Of any kind."

Katia and Elizabeth were ecstatic when Gina brought the small dog home five years ago. He was the runt in a box of matted, sickly looking puppies that a young boy was selling for twenty dollars apiece in front of the local grocery store. She remembered the question Gina asked her and Elizabeth, grinning from ear to ear. "You girls up for a challenge?"

"She spoiled you rotten, didn't she, little guy?"

Frankie wagged his whole body.

With her free hand, Katia opened the lid on her laptop and entered her password.

"Settle down, mister." Katia found herself actually smiling for the first time in two days. "Glad you're feeling better." She put her fingers on the keyboard and typed "Elizabeth Grace Dahl" into the search bar. There wasn't much to go on. Elizabeth packed a yellow-and-black mini Cooper named "Bee," a graduation gift from her mom, and drove off into the sunset. Katia wished she hadn't been dedicated to honoring Elizabeth's wish to be left alone.

Frankie looked up at her. "I know. I should know. But Elizabeth swore your mom to secrecy." She felt like the little wire-haired mutt understood. His tail tapped methodically against her leg. "She didn't want me to know where she was. I was evidently a hindrance to her future."

Over the next thirty minutes, the search revealed few useful results. Elizabeth deactivated her Facebook page. She no longer retained a North Carolina phone number. Elizabeth Dahl appears thirty-one times in a public record site called Checkmate, but none with the middle name Grace. But there is an Elizabeth Grace Dahl who teaches biology at a college in Ireland.

Katia had texts out to every friend in the area who might have a new number. Most responded within seconds to tell her they no longer kept in contact. One indicated she received a tweet shortly after Elizabeth moved that said only that she missed the smell of the ocean but not the noisiness of the residents. It was from Elizabeth's old number. Katia felt helpless. The soft patting of Frankie's tail against her leg only served to make the feeling of helplessness greater.

The investigators would begin searching for Elizabeth as soon as a positive ID of Gina was made. Emotionally, that didn't matter to Katia. She knew in her heart Elizabeth needed her right now. Right. Fucking. Now. She glanced at her phone and tapped the screen. Three fifteen. Still no text from Zahra. What was taking so long? Zahra had promised to give Katia an update as soon as they had positively identified Gina's body and any of the others they had discovered. Katia pulled Frankie close with one hand and wrapped her fingers of her other hand around her coffee mug. "Might as well get a refill."

Chapter Eight

Wednesday, November 21, 2018, 9:00 AM

"The lucky five?" Zahra slid the door shut behind her.

Dr. Webb acknowledged her presence with a nod. "I wouldn't say lucky." He paused. "And good morning. I hope you were able to get a bit of rest. It's going to be a long day."

"More than you, evidently," she said.

Five of those retrieved from the dunes now lay in the main lab. In front of Dr. Webb, on a shiny silver table, were the remains presumed to be Gina Dahl. As Zahra approached Dr. Webb, his low-spoken words became clearer.

"I know it's you," Dr. Webb said to the discolored female corpse. "I don't know who all of these other folks are, but I know you." He looked right and then left, making a sweeping motion with his arm around the room filled with more silver tables. Tags were attached on the recovered bodies, wherever tags could be attached.

Zahra took in the work already accomplished. "Did you go home last night, Doc?"

Dr. Webb didn't answer until he finished removing the sharp edge of silver between nail and nail bed of the woman on the table. "I did, indeed."

Zahra reached for a petri dish and held it under the tweezers-like instrument in Dr. Webb's right hand. Pinched between the two silver prongs was a tiny piece of evidence.

The doctor held it up to the light and then placed it in the dish. "I woke up thinking about this." Dr. Webb looked around the sterile room. "So many waiting to tell us their stories. These five obviously offer us the most hope for positive IDs, so we'll focus here this morning." He pointed to Gina Dahl. "This one is underway. External examination and sample collection started about an hour ago."

Zahra placed the lid on the dish and set it next to the computer. She would begin cataloging as soon as Dr. Webb brought her up to speed on the current decedent. She looked over to the corpse-laden table attached to the far wall and back at Dr. Webb.

She'd be cataloging data until her fingers fell off, or until exhaustion took over the doc's body and he called it a day. First more likely than the second.

"The rest are next door." Dr. Webb motioned toward a sliding door that led to a room much like the sterile one they stood in now. "They're sending an additional forensic anthropologist from Richmond to help with the bones of the oldest. Should be here first thing tomorrow."

Zahra said, "I'll get prelim pics so I can get her cleaned up for round two. Unless you would rather I start elsewhere." She pulled two blue gloves out of the box labeled "Small."

"No. You're right as rain, Zahra, dear. Get her gussied up for me. I'm going to step out momentarily."

Her mentor and friend moved toward the door. His steps weren't as long, and his back wasn't as straight as it was when she started working with him. She wondered if he would retire after this case. She knew she would if she could. "Take a deep breath for me, Doc."

The banter between her and Dr. Webb would seem harsh to outsiders, but considering the surroundings and the fact that there was a makeshift grave in the dunes of their hometown, it was the only way she knew to withstand the smell of death and rot that invaded their current workspace.

"Looks like we have all female adults except one, a young male. Teen likely. Perhaps early twenties. All Caucasian." Dr. Webb threw the words her way as he hung his lab coat on a hook next to the door and reached for his government-issued navy-blue jacket. "We'll know more in the upcoming days, but that much is clear."

Three days ago, fourteen bodies in various stages of decomp were retrieved from a one-mile stretch of Buxton Beach. Dr. Webb and Zahra worked to collect evidence in a makeshift retrieval and containment center at the local high school until yesterday afternoon when the roads cleared enough for the remains to be transported to Greenville, NC. Here, autopsies would be performed by forensic pathologists and anthropologists.

Zahra and the doctor volunteered to travel the two-and-a-half hours each day to aid the others in the continued collection of evidence until all remains were identified and catalogued.

Ultimately, Zahra would like to be a medical examiner. She was enthralled with the human body and the tales it could tell about a person's last hours, days, years. Since graduating from the academy as an officer specially trained in forensic crime scene investigations, she took pictures at most crime scenes Dr. Webb was called to assess, often traveling with him to other counties and states to do so. A few years shy of thirty, with several duty years behind her, Zahra was used to collecting evidence from scenes and bodies, taking fingerprints, gathering hair, blood, and statements. She was even getting pretty good at performing accident reconstructions that mimicked the worst scenes imaginable.

This case was different. Nothing in her training prepared her for the last four days. There were so many bodies and so many bones. She looked around the room and the steel tables. She thought about Katia's friend, buried face-up in the dune, her naked legs exposed by the wind of the disastrous tornado—some mother's child, some daughter's mother. Her mind filled with images of the child's body, buried with an older woman. None of this made sense. It was so much to take in. Maybe too much.

****

Katia felt helpless. After the volunteers were replaced with law enforcement on the beach, there was nothing for her to do but wait. She paced her living room. She looked out the picture window in the kitchen at the now calm ocean waves.

Zahra was in Greenville today. They would officially identify Gina, and Elizabeth would be contacted. Her mind spun thoughts of Elizabeth happily painting, oblivious to the fact that her mom was dead.

The ringing doorbell jolted Katia back to her current surroundings. She didn't have the kind of friends who showed up unannounced. Her father often invited his customers to the workshop to look at building-related material, but the workshop had an outside door. Her father never gave a person permission to ring when he wasn't at home.

The person at the door wasn't there for her father. It was Andrew. Katia hadn't expected him. His tan jacket created an illusion of sand against the blue of the ocean in the background, and his long neck made her think of a turtle stretching toward the sea.

She cracked the door. "What are you doing here?"

"Elliot said you wouldn't be back 'til Sunday. You okay?"

"Yah. Just, you know. Weirded out a bit."

"Understandable."

Andrew fidgeted and shifted his weight left to right and right to left. At work, Andrew was confident but quiet, alert to his surroundings but apt to stay in one space until a call came in. As he stood in front of her, he looked like a young schoolboy unsure of his next move. There is no move, Andrew. Not even if you grew a pussy and boobs.

"Can I come in?" Andrew looked over her shoulder into the hallway. "You alone?"

The hair on the back of Katia's neck stood up at his words, and a chill ran through her body. Gina is dead. You said you've been coming to Avon all of your life to vacation. Who are you really? Why are you here? She didn't really think Andrew was a murderer, but she also didn't think she would ever be witness to a sandy mile of beach turned into a graveyard. Someone killed them. "I'm not really up for company."

"Up for talking about what happened to you on the beach? I'm a good listener." His voice was an octave above normal. She wondered if he was trying too hard or if the days were catching up with him. Either way, Katia wasn't comfortable with him being this close. She pushed the door forward and moved her foot closer to hold it in place.

Andrew put his tennis shoe in between the door and jamb. "Come on. Really?" His voice sounded irritated. "We work together, Katia. I am not the bogeyman."

Katia tilted her head and stared at Andrew, her forehead creasing. "It isn't like that. I'm tired. My dad and brother will be home soon. I just want quiet to process."

"I watched them dig out the other bodies."

"And? Why are you telling me this?" Katia felt uncomfortable continuing the conversation and uncomfortable closing the door in his face.

"Pretty fascinating to watch everyone play their roles, don't you think?"

Katia didn't like the way his voice lowered and his face softened when he said the words. "My best friend's mother was one of the victims. What the fuck, man? You should go." She looked down at his foot, wondering what she was going to do if he tried to come in farther. Punch to the throat, Katia. Knee up. Fingers in the eyes. She remembered the self-defense classes she took with

Elizabeth. Gina would stand on the sidelines, laughing when they couldn't get it right, but making sure they tried until they did. "You have to punch harder than that, Elizabeth. Foot forward, Katia." Laughter. Oh how she missed the laughter.

"Best friend? Are you being serious? Weren't you two lovers?" Andrew wasn't letting up.

His persistence annoyed her. "You should leave."

Katia noticed that Frankie was now poised close to her feet, at attention. It would have been humorous if she wasn't so tired and if she wasn't unsure as to what Andrew's visit was really about. Katia reached down and scratched the top of his head. What she would not do is show fear.

Andrew stood unmoving, as if trying to decide if he should push in or leave.

As if on cue, Frankie stood on his hind legs. Katia heard a guttural sound coming from his throat. She knew Andrew could hear it, too. "You're not coming in, Andrew." Katia kept her voice even. Inside, her heart pounded a little too fast. She wished she had carried her phone to the door.

"I don't understand you. I just want to talk about the incident," Andrew said.

Katia could hear the frustration in his words. She stood her ground.

"What do you think is going to happen? You think I'm going to rape a woman I work with every day? Murder you, maybe?" His voice sounded even higher than before, a little boy's voice. "Fuck it." Andrew removed his foot from between the door and jamb. "Just thought you might like to hear about what I saw. Guess not."

****

Once completely uncovered, Gina's body was easily identified, even if additional information was needed before Zahra and the others could make a positive ID. Gina Dahl sold and managed rentals all along the Outer Banks, and her face was on more than one Seaside Real Estate billboard and ad.

"Why were you the least decomposed, Gina?" Zahra said. "Fourteen deaths. You were last. The most recent. Why? Why you?" She touched the small infinity symbol tattooed on the top of the woman's left wrist. "Katia showed me her tattoo. She told me you took her and Elizabeth on their eighteenth birthdays. Pretty smart not to let them get each other's names. Moms always know best, don't they?"

Zahra pulled up the camera and pointed it at the small symbol. She adjusted the zoom on the high-powered lens. "Thank you for being there for her. She is pretty great, you know." The shutter clicked as she captured another image. She moved the wrist slightly to get a different angle. "She's also stubborn as hell. Deep. Fucking dark and intense, even." Zahra took several more shots. "But I don't think you could have helped with that." She laid the arm back in a more normal position and allowed the camera to fall back against her breasts.

"Actually, I don't know if anyone will ever be enough for her, though Lord knows I want to be." The corner of Zahra's mouth moved upward slightly. She couldn't remember a time when she hadn't been in lust with Katia's slender, tight, boyish self. Her unapproachable demeanor was made more prominent by her choppy, black hair that hung in strands across the top rim of her glasses. Her contrasting sense of duty to family and community only served to make her more alluring.

Zahra sighed and reached for the sheet that lay folded neatly at the end of the table. "Anyway, thanks for being there for her. She loved you." Zahra pulled the sheet up over Gina's body, leaving her face exposed for one more moment. She hated this part. It was so final.

Gina was now clean and photographed from every angle for the third time. Zahra ran through the stages as she did every time in her head, as they were ingrained in her from school. Pictures at the crime scene before anything is touched. Photos in the light of the lab where the decedent can be turned and analyzed. Pictures after the body is rinsed of all debris. Same body. Different stories every time. I am so sorry, Ms. Dahl. So sorry. She pulled the sheet over the woman's face and turned back to her circle of five.

Another female lay on the next sterile table. She was a Jane Doe. Too decomposed to identify by sight, assuming they would have known her, and left in the dune with nothing to help them figure out who she was. "I'm going to leave you for now, Ms. Doe." Zahra used her most polite voice. "Your friends here have a bit more story to tell." Just like Dr. Webb had taught her, she talked to the bodies on the table as a way to remain calm. When people asked, she aligned it with a person talking to her cat or dog. You know they aren't going to answer you, but you're looking for clues as to what they want while you talk. "Right, Ms. Doe?"

The two others, Lacey O'Donnell and Nadia Grey, were identified easily at the scene. As of yet, there was no official ID, but each was buried with a purse and each purse held the owner's driver's license. The lab results, she suspected, would confirm the names soon enough.

Running the license numbers through the database brought forth old case files on both women.

Lacey O'Donnell. Missing from Manteo, North Carolina, since 2014. Reported missing by her husband when she failed to return from a work conference. The conference was across the state line in Virginia. Because of proximity and reported marital problems, the husband was a prime suspect. Friends and neighbors reported the woman as dedicated to her children above all else. Both children, a boy, age ten, and a girl, age eight, were currently with their father. The case was ongoing, though leads had long since dried up, and the case was stale.

Nadia Grey. A local teacher. Abducted in 2001. Presumably with a boy. Seventeen.

Zahra swallowed hard and looked between the computer screen at the two remaining decedents, one of whom was a male presumed to be in his late teens to early twenties. "Are you that boy?"

The boy and Nadia Grey were found buried at opposite ends of the defined kill zone. "If you are Roger Townsend," she said in the direction of the only male victim in the room, "Why in the hell did he bury the two of you so far apart?"

Each of the five in her current circle were photographed from every possible angle while still on the beach with the sea lapping against the dunes around them. Now they waited to provide their own set of clues through samples. They waited for their turn to pose for pictures in the bright light of the lab, for their turn to be cleaned, and for their turn under the scalpel of Dr. Webb.

Zahra picked Lacey next. She'd been working on collecting samples and entering information into the database for close to an hour when Dr. Webb joined her from wherever he had gone. He was a private man. She knew he would tell her what he thought she needed to know and nothing more. "Anything promising out there, Doc?"

"Meetings," he replied. "Everyone is a bit whopperjawed, you know? They want miracles. We need to provide them. We told them to get us some more help. Sooner, not later."

Zahra felt like he was staring right through her. He looked exhausted, old suddenly, which was a word she would not have applied to him until today. "Dahl is ready for you. O'Donnell will be shortly." She motioned toward the as-of-yet officially unidentified woman. She waited. He should have corrected her. Dr. Webb was proper, by the book. Facts, Zahra. Our job is not to guess. No matter how likely we are to be correct in those assumptions. But the words didn't come. She held her tongue. Turned back to the job at hand.

They spent the next few hours working side by side, the silence broken only occasionally by a question or a beep from a machine. Every fiber of Zahra's being hurt. Together they processed four of the five decedents, completed sample collecting from the fifth, and learned from the beeping machines somewhere along the way they indeed had Gina Dahl and Lacey O'Donnell in the room.

"These two are interesting," Dr. Webb said. He pointed to the remains of the decedent assumed to be Nadia Grey and then to the one presumed to be Roger Townsend. Zahra nodded. "The boy especially. Appears he was wrapped carefully before burial and placed center of the dune so as to slow decay immensely. I'll begin with him again tomorrow." He made eye contact with her and nodded down to the table. "While you finish processing Jane Doe."

The day had just ended, and Zahra was being released. "It's only three o'clock, Doc. Do you need anything else from me before I leave?" She met his tired eyes with her own.

"No. You did well today, Zahra. This is a tough one."

Zahra watched for a moment as he turned the woman's right hand palm up. His movements were gentle and fluid, like the man. She started to argue, to insist on staying, but she knew she would lose in the end anyway. Besides, every muscle ached. They had begun processing bodies at five o'clock this morning and had even ordered in their lunch to keep an eye on the computer for lab results and updates. She reached behind her back and pulled the string that would allow her to slip from the pale blue gown. "Thank you, sir. It is. It is indeed."

Before she even reached the sliding door that separated her and the stench of death from the fresh air of the rest of the world,

Zahra decided to take a ride over to talk to Katia. She had learned a great deal today and she wanted to share with her.

Elizabeth's address in Virginia had been located, and patrol cars were headed to her apartment. This would be a relief to Katia but might also bring additional pain. Telling Katia face-to-face was much better than sending text messages. Selfishly, Zahra also knew seeing Katia would make her happy at the end of a very unhappy day.

The drive over was filled with thoughts that swung like Newton's Cradle in her head. On one end of the five-ball structure was the morgue filled with dead bodies. Pull back and release. Gina, Nadia, Lacey, Roger, and Jane Doe. *Clack.*

The names hit the balls at rest in the middle of the Cradle. The beach, life before the Sandman. Sandman. That's what the media was calling him. It didn't seem right to grant such a horrific person a name that conjured up pictures of children snuggled tight under their covers waiting for sleepy dust to be sprinkled in their eyes. She could feel the momentum and energy heading for the other side, the colliding surfaces, the variables in play.

On the other end of the cradle was her relationship with Katia. The silky, caramel-colored skin and pouty lips of an adorable but angry boi covered in tattoos. A white crescent moon and four stars outlined in black ran the length of her long torso, and a tiny red heart nestled on the inside of her right thigh. She presumed the heart was for Elizabeth. *Clack.*

Elizabeth. Her mom, dead, poking out from the dune, her purple shoe a reminder of what was. *Clack.*

A watercolor owl resting on a small white breast. Katia's mom loved owls. She learned this the first time they fucked, half toasted from a night at the bar. The silver ball arching out and back toward the center. Like Katia's back when she climaxed. The future unknowable. *Clack.*

Katia's three-story, pale-yellow beach house came into view. In the driveway, there was a vehicle Zahra didn't recognize. Maybe I should have called. She slowed down, trying to decide what to do. She didn't want to interrupt Katia's time unannounced if she was busy. There was the pendulum again, swinging to the side that wanted what wasn't hers to have.

That's dumb, Zahra Kate. You are an investigator doing your job, not some stupid love-sick kid trying to get closer to a crush. This is your job.

She cracked her knuckles, a nervous habit her mom said would make her knuckles huge. It didn't. Her hands were small, her knuckles proportionate. She straightened in her seat and eased her car around the curve and into the driveway of Katia's home.

Zahra's brain immediately started processing the scene on the porch. Andrew? What's he doing here? His posture was off. Katia looked annoyed. There was a small dog at Katia's feet, just behind her right leg, poking forward, at an attack stance. Zahra knew from their late-night conversations that Andrew gave Katia the creeps. She also knew Katia would say that about most men who gave her more than a passing glance, especially if they were outsiders. But something was definitely not right with the situation in front of her. Her cop senses were on fire.

She pushed the car door open and looked up at the lemon-sherbet-colored house with white trim. Two raspberry-colored flower troughs hung perfectly spaced between white, square pillars on the porch. Katia's father built it for his bride thirty years ago. It was one of the biggest single-family homes on the beach and one of the beachiest and most beautiful with its two-level, wraparound porch and white, scalloped trim.

"That house is what would happen if you crossed an old, wooden, beach house with a big, old, southern, Savannah, Georgia, Queen Anne," her dad used to say. As a kid of a Buxton native, Zahra often heard her dad tell stories of how Mr. Billings spent months making everything perfect for a wife he loved desperately. "He would have done anything for Rosario," her dad said. "Pity that drunk boy killed her before her time." After Rosario died, Mr. Billings used the home as a show house for clients who needed design ideas for their own homes. Katia hated that, too.

Zahra stepped out of the car without taking her eyes off of what was going on at the door to the house. Andrew pulled his leg backward and strode away, eyes looking at the ground, toward his car. He turned back for a brief moment. Did he expect her to call him back? Zahra watched him closely and nodded when he looked over and caught her gaze. He quickly got into his car, slammed the door, and turned over the engine. Their eyes met again as he backed past her. He's creepy as hell. She looked at Katia and tried to give her a reassuring smile.

"Fuck. I'm glad you're here," Katia said. "That dickhead was trying to push his way into the house."

"You want to file a report?" Zahra asked. "I know an investigator who isn't afraid to throw her weight around." She did her best to lighten the mood a little. "At least talk to El on Sunday. See what he thinks. It's probably nothing. He freakin' works with you. Certainly, he wouldn't be stupid enough to try anything."

"I guess." Katia made a gesture with her hand and pulled the door fully open. "Said something about me wanting to know what he knew. Guess he watched the extraction of the remains."

Zahra put her hand on Katia's face as she crossed the threshold. "More importantly, how are you?"

Katia didn't move.

Zahra let her hand linger for the briefest moment, let it slide gently forward toward Katia's mouth and down across her chin. Tenderness was not what she and this woman were about. Their encounters were anything but, and yet, in that moment, it was what she wanted more than anything else. Zahra let out a breath that lasted a full five seconds, not wanting to say too much or too little. "I can come back and stay tonight if you'd like."

"Not that I wouldn't mind the company, Zee. I would like it. You know that. But we'll be fine."

Zee. I love it when she calls me that, Zahra thought. Her heart beat against her temple. The woman created a physical reaction with a smile and a word. Her heart hurt for Katia, for Gina, for Elizabeth, and selfishly, for herself.

"Don't look at me like that." Katia rotated the door lock and peeked out the window. "As much as I would like to fuck this away, I just need to process. You know?"

Zahra kept her voice low to match Katia's. "Okay. Brave heart. But don't say I didn't offer. And I said nothing about fucking, though that's certainly on the table if you need it."

Frankie followed the two down the wide hall and into the large kitchen. Zahra decided turning the attention to him might lessen the tension in the room. "Where'd the mutt come from? Thought your dad didn't allow them."

"El and Brent seem to think Andrew's okay." Katia glanced slightly back over her shoulder. "Just socially awkward as a bitch. I was a bit thrown by the whole foot-in-the-door shit. I'll admit that."

"Got it. You didn't answer the mutt question." It took a second, but Zahra realized why. "Katia. That's Gina's dog, isn't it?"

"Brilliant detective skills, my friend."

"If that's your attempt at deflection, it's failing miserably. You know I'm not happy about you going to Gina's house at all, much less alone. Seriously. That's a crime scene. You could get into trouble for that shit."

"One, it wasn't a crime scene when I went. Gina hasn't even been officially identified. Two, I didn't touch any surfaces with my bare hands. I used gloves. And three, Frankie here would still be curled in a corner scared to death and hungry and thirsty if I hadn't gone over."

Zahra stopped next to the center island. It was only the second time she was in Katia's home, and it was the first time she'd seen her in any room on the first floor. Her eyes traveled up from Katia's bare feet to her camo-colored pants that hung loosely from her slender hips. "The dog would have been fine until detectives arrived." She tried to focus on the task at hand. It was a struggle between her brain and her heart, as her eyes rested on the soft, caramel-colored skin between the band of the pants and the hem of the fade- black tank top. "They identified her today. That's part of why I'm here."

Katia's voice pulled Zahra's eyes the rest of the way up to her face. "Figured. The detectives arrived a few hours ago. I watched them through the living room window." She gestured with her head in the direction of a large opening between the kitchen and living room. "I knew they were officially looking for clues."

Zahra temporarily forgot about the dog who took up residence on a patch of sunlight on the hardwood floor next to the back door. Katia pushed off from the countertop behind her and padded toward the opening.

Zahra followed her into the other room, and the two of them stood shoulder to shoulder and looked out of the large picture window.

Zahra spoke first. "They're bringing Paige and Bob back with another dog tomorrow. Just to be sure." She didn't know why she said it, she hadn't meant to. She rarely shared what she learned with anyone on the outside until it was public knowledge. In the middle of a serial murder investigation or not, that was the kind of hold Katia had on her.

After several minutes, Katia pointed to an alcove behind a large dune. "We used to kiss down there. We had no idea back then our parents could likely see us from up here if the moon was bright enough." She laughed. "Stupid young love."

Zahra nodded. "Probably. They're headed to her place today. May already be there."

Katia didn't respond. Zahra didn't push. Instead, she brought their discussion back to Andrew. "When did he come to this area? Do you know?"

"Who? Andrew?"

"Yeah."

"Year. Year and a half ago, I guess." Katia continued to stare toward the alcove.

Zahra watched Katia's tongue as she moistened her lips between sentences, thought about the way she used it on her nipples, her neck… She shuddered, told herself what a bad person she was for remembering sex at a time like this. It kind of came with the territory, though. If death stopped a criminal investigator's sex drive, she would never have sex. She reminded herself again that normal people couldn't reconcile the two.

Katia said, "Transferred from some little town over by Greensboro. Whit something, I think. I'm really not sure. I just try to avoid him. I told the guys he freaks me out. Always staring—asking questions about…" Katia's voice trailed off as if she suddenly realized where Zahra's line of questioning was going. "You don't think? Fuck. He did tell us he came here for years with his parents, sometimes alone to clear his head. Zahra…"

"I'll do some digging. Ask around the station. I'm sure they're looking into him. Into everyone, really. Buxton isn't big, and even if we consider surrounding towns, there aren't many possibilities for someone who could pull this off unnoticed, you know?"

Katia shrugged. "I just want to know Elizabeth is okay. For now, that's as far as I can fucking think. I'm numb. So numb."

Zahra pulled a buzzing phone from her pocket, looked at the screen. "I have to take this."

She walked slowly out of the kitchen and hit Talk. "Detective?"

"We found Elizabeth's apartment," the voice on the other end reported.

The words hung in the air. Zahra didn't like the way that sounded, but she didn't dare articulate her fear. She kept her voice low. "And?"

"Elizabeth isn't there. Neighbors say they haven't seen her in a few days. Say she keeps to herself, though, so they can't be sure when she was home last."

"Are they searching the apartment? They need to search the apartment." Zahra was pacing back and forth in the hallway, a nervous habit she inherited from her mother. She was suddenly glad she and Katia hadn't spent enough time together to learn one another's quirks.

"They will if it comes to that. There's no outward sign of foul play." The voice ticked off the grocery list of what she wanted to hear. "No one heard anything out of the ordinary. We have an officer stationed at her house. No one in or out without us knowing. A detective's going to talk to the curator at Stravitz Gallery."

"Is that the gallery where she's booked to showcase her work?" Zahra leaned against the staircase and nervously picked at her clothes in an attempt to stand still.

"Indeed it is. And where she hangs out most of the time when she's not home. I asked for an update as soon as they finish interviewing."

"Thanks. Let me know," she said.

Chapter Nine

After his epic fail with Katia, Andrew came home, booted up his computer, and started searching. If there was one thing he learned from all of his years as an Internet recluse, it was how to find information no one else could. He had many connections to the Internet underworld, connections that surface dwellers didn't know existed.

Andrew moved his cursor to the seemingly harmless green-and-black icon and clicked. Never enter a site through anywhere but the true Tor door. It's what sets the real players apart from the wannabes, the hidden from the found. Andrew Hunter was a real player.

He thought again about what the women said regarding the disappearance of the teacher. Are you one of those buried beneath the sand, Ms. Grey? Let's see who you're associated with in the deep dark corners of life.

A few keystrokes revealed Nadia Grey was at the high school that Katia, Elliot, Brent, Zahra, all of them, attended. Ms. Grey started the year Brent and Elliot were in eleventh grade. She died the year they were seniors. Andrew found that interesting enough to take a deeper look into the backgrounds of the two men.

Since coming to the island, he forced himself to get closer to Brent than Elliot. Elliot appeared too vanilla for his tastes. Trainer. Mentor. Faithful husband. Father to twin girls. He thought about the picture that Elliot kept on his desk at the station. Cute little things. Red-haired like their mamma. He didn't see the draw to redheads.

He touched the keypad and slowly typed out Elliot Palmer 1999 Buxton.

He found exactly what he expected. Elliot was from a family of six. Voted most likely to succeed and most liked. Met current wife, Josephine Baldacci-Palmer in his senior year. Every new click produced more of the same. Elliot Palmer was an all-American guy from a perfect home with professional parents. He tried various other ways to find hints of him on the dark web, but there was nothing, not even the slightest indication of his ever having loaded Tor. A real family man. Nothing else to see there. He was just as he appeared. Vanilla.

Andrew took a sip of sweet tea and thought about his mom. He missed her sun tea, missed the way it tasted exactly the same every time. He set the glass down next to his computer and rubbed his thumb back and forth across his fingertips to absorb the condensation before putting them back against the keys.

This time he typed faster. B-R-E-N-T. He was an only child of parents who still ran a local tourist shop. Brent wasn't as squeaky clean, but there wasn't a lot that looked dangerous, either. Unless you consider stealing a pack of cigarettes in the local market at thirteen dangerous. Other than a divorce and shared custody of a kid, Andrew didn't see much at this level. He was connected to the dead teacher, but so were other children. Andrew maneuvered his mouse, clicked into Brent's grades. Huh. Pretty fucking stellar grades in math for an average kid. He knew Brent was a deviant from the traces of him Andrew uncovered on the deep web. It was why he was nice to him at work. What he needed to know was how deviant.

Andrew scoured two years worth of yearbooks for clues. The math club was evidently a pretty important part of the lives of several football players. Nadia Grey was quite young and quite striking. Thirty years old, but she looked younger with her shoulder-length bronze hair pulled loosely back from her long, slender face. The speckling of freckles across her nose and high cheekbones complemented her light-blue eyes and light-peach skin in a way that screamed sensual youthfulness.

Can't blame a guy for wanting to fuck that. And she definitely resembled the current ex-Mrs. Grainger.

Andrew had seen the photo of the woman and a young girl on Brent's desk when he started working for Hatteras Island Rescue. He'd met the slight, ginger-headed woman at a fundraising event. The two, Brent offered when he saw Andrew looking, were divorced, but they remained co-parenting friends to their daughter.

"Look at you, Ms. Grey." Andrew scrolled down to get the whole picture on the screen. "You obviously had no problem pulling the guys close." In one yearbook, the teacher draped her arms loosely over two of the male students in a geometry club photo. "Hi, high school Brent," he said to the photo and wiggled his fingers in a wave. His eyes moved from the smooth-faced boy's eyes and mouth to his slim waist and hips that touched his teacher's in a way that said, "I'm accustomed to our closeness." In another photo, Brent glanced her way as she cheered her team to victory at a local math competition.

"Look at that look. You were getting that, weren't you?"

Could she have been molesting students? Only Brent, or others, as well? He looked deeper into the pages of eleventh grade and then twelfth. In every shot of the two of them, they were looking, touching, standing close to each other.

A thought formed in Andrew's mind as he studied the young boy and his teacher. The Internet became all the craze in the mid-nineties. By two-thousand, web crawlers were everywhere. New porn opportunities were everywhere, too.

Once you enter a search on the clear web, it never goes away. I wonder what ole Brent liked to search back then? Maybe I've searched your background with the wrong ideas in mind. Maybe you're not just a deviant fuck who likes to look at darkness. Maybe you like to create it, as well.

Andrew headed into the dark web to call in a favor. By this time tomorrow, he would know all about Brent's IP addresses, old and new, and he would have more information about him and his love of teachers, porn, children, death, killing, etc., much more than any cop on the current investigation would yet know about any one individual. Andrew's connections to the Internet underworld were years in the making, and they were deeper, darker, bloodier, and sicker than he ever said out loud. It was a job he wouldn't wish on anyone, and he couldn't think of a place he'd rather be.

****

According to the cable box in the space underneath the television, it was three in the morning. A solid five hours. Sandman stretched and reached for his phone. Holding his thumb down on the sensor brought it to life. He blinked, waited for his eyes to adjust, and tapped on the Calculator app on the second page.

Good morning, beautiful Elizabeth. He wished her blonde hair hadn't become matted so quickly. He'd have to make her wash it today, brush it. He wanted her to feel pretty before he killed her. So young. A pity she had to die. She could have made a name for herself. She could have done a lot of things, but her mother ruined that for her when she refused to stay buried.

Sandman stretched, muscular arms high above his head, the blanket falling down around his midsection. "Let's see," he said out loud and brought the phone screen back to eye level. "It used the bucket," he said, amusing himself by playing off of a line from his favorite movie, *Silence of the Lambs*. "Buffalo Bill, you have nothing on me."

He looked back at the dirty, tear-streaked face on his phone screen.

She stirred. Did she know she was being watched? People like her, like him, knew when they were being watched. It was something you learned. Sandman wanted to talk to her, to swap stories about their past. Did she hurt you, Elizabeth? Make you like the touches at night? Make you feel like you had to?

He hoped she wouldn't be like the others, but it was no use to hope. Hope helped no one. Agitation rose from his gut. He ran his finger across the picture on the screen.

He turned on his side, holding the phone with one hand, elbow pushing an indent into the mattress. With the other hand he reached for the glass of water from the bedside and took several long drinks. Elizabeth continued to be restless but still not fully awake. He supposed she would have quite a headache from the heavy doses of sleeping medication he administered over the last few days to keep her comfortable. It would be a couple of hours before she was able to talk to him.

"Your mom planned on bringing Katia to your opening," Sandman said to the screen. "Did you know that, Elizabeth? Did you? She told me she did. She actually thought it would be a good idea."

Thinking about Buxton's lifetime resident being pulled back into that web of disgusting homosexual filth made him cringe. He reached down and pulled the covers under his armpits. He wondered again what vile things Elizabeth's mom did to her daughter to make her think the only way she could be happy was to be with another girl.

"She should never have told me. She didn't have to. She could have left Katia alone. I wouldn't have had to kill again so soon." His voice was a deep whisper, full of pain and longing, like a little boy reporting to his mother he had to hit another child for trying to take his toy. "Will you tell me if you knew, Elizabeth? Will you tell me to save your own life?"

He could hear the seconds ticking by on the bedside clock. He laid the phone on the bed beside him and rotated both wrists until they cracked. He moved his head from side to side, rotated his ankles, and moved his toes up and down, prompting cracks from all his joints.

He touched the screen again and sent Elizabeth back into the dark corners of his phone. The Calculator icon appeared, innocent, uninviting. He swung the covers away and moved to the edge of his bed in one motion. Shit. Shower. Shave. Words of his father. Words from another life, a life where he was an innocent little boy, and his parents could still protect him.

Easing his feet onto the hardwood floor sent a shiver throughout his body. The air outside of the covers was a perfect sixty-eight degrees, exactly where he wanted it for sleeping, but cool enough to make goose bumps appear on his naked skin as soon as the covers were cast aside. Not innocent anymore, he thought. Never again. Auntie took care of that.

He stood, took the first steps toward the bathroom, and stopped. He looked at his own reflection in the dresser mirror. “Mirror, mirror on the wall, who’s the greatest of them all?”

He thought of all of the women who hurt children, about all of the women who thought they were getting away with their crimes, who would have gotten away with their crimes had he not crossed their path. Laughter exploded from his lips.

When he stepped into the shower, he was still thinking about all of the child-abusing mothers and aunts and teachers he stopped over the years. Women can convince you you need them, that you like it, and that you’re being a baby if you complain about it. They were all the same, these women who prey on children and make them do things, terrible things, until they’re no longer normal, can no longer be normal.

It wasn’t his fault Elizabeth was here. It was hers. If Gina hadn’t told him she was going to Virginia next month to see Elizabeth’s paintings in a real gallery; if she hadn’t told him she was going to invite Katia. If only. He couldn’t let her warp Katia any further. Katia could still be saved. He knew she could. He hadn’t seen Katia with another woman since Elizabeth left. Gina wanted to jeopardize her renewed strength. He would save her. He thought about another young person he tried to save. How long ago? 2000? 2001? He was the youngest of his kills. He was also the hardest. He almost hadn’t seen it through, almost let him live.

Missing: Seventeen-year-old Roger Townsend. He remembered the local headline. The article briefly attached him to his teacher. Model student. Geometry club. Parents indicate a love of school and no outward reason for him to leave. Geometry teacher, Nadia Grey, is also missing… The article went on to say the two were often seen together after school practicing for the competitions Roger competed in and the two may have been abducted together.

Abducted. They went right to abducted. Back then, he thought they would certainly assume the teacher convinced the boy to run off with her. But no. The idea he ran off with a teacher who convinced him she loved him and the disgusting things she made him do were normal wasn't even mentioned. No one entertained the idea the two were connected in that way, at least not for more than a gossiping moment.

A young girl and a male instructor would have changed things…

The thought returned to him over and over again through the years. Be a woman. Smile. Act innocent. Say the right things. It made him sick.

He tried to save Nadia Grey's newest victim. He wanted to let him live. When he walked in on the boy and Nadia in her classroom, his stomach lurched. The teacher had her hand flat against the chalkboard, her face inches from the face of the young man whose back lightly brushed the black slate.

He'd been told by another of the teacher's victims she would be alone. "Normally, I would be with her," he had sobbed. "I can't do it anymore. I don't want to do it anymore." The boy confessed to him sitting in the diner high atop the dune. The brand new diner built to appear old, nostalgic, with its silver and turquoise interior and old-fashioned jukebox. The diner of lies where the townspeople congregated during the long, winter months of inactivity, where so many abusers sat in all of their duality, putting dollars in the jukebox, lipping the words to old love songs, and intertwining their lives with the others waiting patiently for the return of summer.

He could still see the boy, now a man, legs dangling on either side of the silver leg of the turquoise-topped barstool, his lanky arms folded on the white-and-turquoise-swirled Formica countertop, the reflection of his wavy, light-brown hair against his red cheeks and those long, tear-stained eyelashes in the mirror behind the counter, his head hung in shame and heartbreak. He promised that boy he would handle it, and he had.

He told Roger to leave that day, to go home, but he wouldn't. Are you okay, Nadia? Do you want me to stay? He heard the boy in his head. Thought about the look on his teenage face. Like a little boy about to have his puppy taken away.

Roger called her Nadia, not Ms. Grey. He knew in that second Roger was another victim. Refusing to leave sealed his sentence of being with her in death as he was in life.

Several men, including himself, were questioned extensively when the pair disappeared. "You were seen chatting with Ms. Grey on multiple occasions," the police spat at him in that tiny interrogation room. "You seemed to have a relationship with her. Did the boy walk in on you harming her? Try to stop you? Did you hurt them both?"

He almost laughed out loud. They needed to blame a man, any man, and they needed it to be the woman who was the victim, always the woman. When no clues were found as to Roger's whereabouts, or hers, people went on with their lives. Fewer and fewer remembered.

But he remembered. For two weeks, he kept the two of them in the cell. For two weeks, they clung to one another. For two weeks, that bitch stroked and purred as she held Roger close. Roger wanted to let Ms. Grey have her way with him. That became obvious to him while he watched them wait for death. Every day, Roger begged him to let his Geometry teacher go, begged him to take him instead. Every day, that perverted bitch whined and cried and stroked and kissed her student. Every day, she begged for him to release them. But never once did the teacher beg to trade her own life for that of the child. Not once.

In the end, he was forced to take them both. Killing Roger was the only way to save him. It was his hardest kill and his sweetest. He remembered inhaling deeply as Roger exhaled for the last time. His whole body tingled, and a warmth spread from his gut outward until every finger, every toe, every hair on his head felt alive and warm with Roger's essence. It was like killing himself. Like taking all of the pain his aunt left behind, living in his own skin, and excising it. It was beautiful, and he thanked Roger profusely for allowing him to breathe, if only for a moment, pain free. He hadn't climaxed with him as he had with all of the others. He was thankful for that, a reaffirmation in his mind that he was doing the work of a greater power, but he had held him for a very long time as tears streamed down his face, as Roger convulsed and bled out in his arms.

Chapter Ten

Thursday, November 22, 2018

Elizabeth lay motionless, silent. She stared into the darkness through a small sliver between her eyelids and tried to separate the shadow that must be in front of her from the surrounding onyx of the room. It was a darkness profounder than she had ever experienced, a dark that stabbed into her chest, the pain as sure and real as if it were a knife plunged deep in search of vital organs. She heard breathing. She strained harder, but she couldn't make out a shadow.

"I'm going to turn the light on now, Elizabeth."

She struggled to keep her eyes open as light emerged from the womb of darkness. Even in its dimness, it burned. The grungy light splashed off a puddle where she urinated under the cover of darkness hours before. How many times has he been here? Twice? Three times? Four? She couldn't remember. Her mind reeled. Her neck ached. The air tasted gray, like the walls and floor in the empty room, sans the mattress she lay on, and her throat felt filled with lint. She remembered a shot in her neck and darkness. More came to her in bits. They found my mom. He blames her.

She expanded the squint, tried to enlarge her area of sight. The light was faint and hazy, but still it stung against the pure darkness she was in for what felt like days. He wasn't where she assumed he would be. Where are you? I know you're here. She moved slightly, eyes more open with each small movement. She tried to maintain the look of sleep in the windowless monochrome room. She hoped he would think she was only restless, still far away from the reality of this room, of him. No human form to her right, only an open doorway. She rolled to the left, chain clinking against chain. The sound startled her. Her eyes came fully open. There was nothing to the left. What the fuck?

And then another click by an invisible hand. And darkness.

Chapter Eleven

Katia turned onto Johnston Road a few minutes after one. The blacktop ended abruptly at the entrance to a large, dirt, parking area. She turned her car into a spot next to a trailer with the acronym CAMET on the side and the full, "Companion Animal Mobile Equipment Trailer" spelled out underneath. It was the trailer the brother and sister team parked on Buxton Beach for two full days while one body after another was uncovered.

She felt tears threatening. She reprimanded herself in the rearview mirror and wiped the corners of her eyes. "There's too much to do."

Images of the bright purple shoe and leg and partial torso blended together in her head. She needed to walk through what happened, and Paige seemed a good person to help her. The two were obviously in synch. Paige's text message inviting her to the facility came concurrently to the thought of texting the woman to ask if she was available.

Come on up to the facility. Training until one. Bring spoons.

Katia responded to Paige's text immediately. *Perfect. Be there at one—spoons in hand.*

CU then. Paige's reply quickly lit up her screen. And then again. *Invite Zahra?*

K, she typed back. *Texting her now.*

Katia looked over at Frankie. "I'll be back for you shortly, puppy face." She cracked all four windows and cut the engine.

The part of the training facility into which she entered looked to be part training hub, part office. She stood in the open doorway and observed the class and her surroundings. Two desks faced a string of whiteboards that listed the names of dogs and their proficiency in crucial basic skills. A dog-sized obstacle course of brightly colored ladders and balance beams crisscrossed the room. There were ramps and walkways of varying material and texture: metal, wood, and what looked to be sandpaper. Tin cans dangled from strings, and plastic-tube tunnels snaked around the room.

At the front of the facility, Paige stood with a group of eager students being dusted with a powder by her brother. "The powder simulates contamination," Bob said. "It will show up in black light." He finished the last trainee and returned to Paige's side.

"How many of you believe you put on your protective gear properly today?" Paige asked. She pointed to Bob, who in turn held up a black-light stick.

Katia found Paige's question ominous, as was her look around the room. You're fucked. The students looked at one another and down at their own gear. Most nodded as Paige made eye contact. A particularly cocky one said, "Yes," and, "Nothing's getting through this gear."

"Okay, peel off that protective equipment." Paige walked up and down the row of students. "Who wants to go first?"

One by one, the students untied, unwrapped, and stepped out of their gear. One by one, they walked over to the black light. Patches of white appeared on hands and arms, chests and legs, faces and hair.

"If this was a real site and there was real contamination, you could be dead," Paige said. She pointed to one of the students and then at another. "And you. And you." The students nodded and thanked Paige for another great class.

Katia leaned on the doorjamb and observed. She liked Paige's seemingly fearless and straightforward attitude.

A few minutes after dismissing the class, Paige made her way to Katia and the two women left Bob in the main facility and headed back the way Katia had come.

"What's in there?" Katia pointed to a building to the left of the one they just exited. She thought Bob said when she was here last year, but she no longer remembered what was where. And she needed a way to start conversation.

"That's the cadaver scent training lab." Paige looked over at Katia. "Want a tour?"

"No. Not today, anyway. Fascinating concept, but my new-experience meter has expired, and I'm out of quarters."

"Indeed." Paige smiled at her. "Fascinating. Once you get used to the smell. All dogs start in the big room where we were. Then they move into the cadaver room."

"Sounds charming," Katia said. "Speaking of dogs." Katia nodded toward her car a few feet away.

The two continued an easy banter as they reached the car and Katia retrieved the wiggling dog. She felt at ease with Paige in a way she hadn't expected.

"Join us anytime," Paige said. "Bring your new attack pup." She winked and tickled the top of Frankie's head. He twisted in

Katia's arms. He obviously enjoyed the scratch and wanted to get closer to the fingers that supplied it.

"Funny," Katia said. "And he isn't mine. At least not yet. Probably not at all. My dad is going to spaz out. He doesn't like animals in the house."

"Ever?" Paige scrunched her face.

"Nope." Katia shrugged. "Can't miss what you never had, I guess."

"I can't imagine not having a dog." Paige scratched Frankie's head again. "Zahra texted. She'll be here soon. She's dropping something at the lab."

"What?" She and Zahra had texted back and forth, and Zahra had said nothing.

"No idea. That's all she said."

"Why only one road through all of this land?" Katia asked.

Her attempt to steer the conversation away from pets and the warm fuzziness they produced in households worked. Paige launched into a mini, family-history lesson. Katia was grateful and genuinely curious.

"My great-grandpa was a barnstormer after World War I," Paige said. "Offered airplane rides, aerobatic flight demos, impromptu airshows. A lucrative undertaking, so the story goes."

Katia nodded.

"He bought this land piece by piece." Paige made a sweeping motion with her arm.

Obviously, the woman was proud of her great-grandfather. Katia turned her head slightly and smiled at Paige.

Paige smiled in return. Her gestures continued. "Left all of it to his only son, my gramps, who put in the road. Guess blacktopping was expensive, especially for a road that's a half-a-mile long."

"My dad would have a field day with all of the open space here," Katia said. "It's a builder's dream. And he would have roads in every direction." She used her free hand to point in several directions.

"And you? Would you have roads in every direction?"

"Me? Not so much. I like space."

"Me, too. Boys and their toys, I guess." Paige shrugged. "Gramps loved a nail and hammer, too. Did a lot of the work through here. He used to tell me stories of the land when he got it, his dream of expanding until he owned all of Manteo." Paige chuckled.

"What happened?"

"He and granny had four boys and a girl. Costs a pretty penny, he used to say. Guess work and time evaporated the dream. Who knows?"

"His kids all own one?" Katia indicated the houses to their left as she turned her body all the way around before falling back into step with Paige.

"One didn't make it to adulthood, a boy, Robert. Bob's named after him. The others all built along the road. My daddy had me and Bob. My uncles and aunts had two or three apiece. Gramps would have liked them to have more. He used to say, 'Plenty of room for more. Pick a piece of sand, and we'll buy some wood.'"

Katia smiled. Her father would have liked Paige's grandpa.

"I chose to have my house built closer to Great-grandpa Johnston's original house." Paige pointed back off of the road to a small plank house, obviously old, but not forgotten. "I keep it up, use it for storage mostly. It makes me smile. You can see where planes landed over and over again if you get closer. Everyone else was building farther away. I kind of felt like someone should want to be closer."

The women slowed as they came to the last house on the narrow road. "This one's mine. That one down there is the one Great-grandpa Johnston helped build for Gramps and Granny."

"Does anyone live there now?" Katia thought the house looked lived in when she passed. You couldn't grow much in the sandy soil, but someone had tried, had taken the time to put old half-barrels out front with geraniums.

"Gramps and Granny are gone now. Granny last year. I took care of her here until the end."

"Sorry." Katia glanced over at Paige. "I know the pain of losing someone you love that much." Her mom's face popped into her head. She missed her every day.

"Me. too, but she had a good life. She was ready. I miss her, though. Like, a lot. Anyway, we rented it to one of the trainers at the facility. Actually, a lot of the houses along here are rented out now. People move. Even family, you know? Gramps built mine. I chose where. It was his gift to me." She smiled and shrugged, leaning forward slightly. "It's a two-bedroom. He wanted to make it bigger. For a family, he said. I told him big houses make me nervous. They do. But so do kids." She laughed, shrugged again.

Katia wondered if it was a nervous habit. Guess there's a real person behind that tough, crime-scene, business-only, persona.

"I don't want any kidlets, myself. Just my pups." Paige looked at Katia. "That's it for me. Pups. How about you, Katia? You want kids?"

"Me? Hadn't really thought about it. Not particularly. I've got my brother, Marco. He's autistic. Smart. Cute as hell. And probably mine forever."

The two women stood in front of the door for a moment and stared at the row of houses.

"Ready to go in?" Paige motioned for Katia to go first.

Katia noticed Paige avoided further comment on children, or siblings. She tucked that away for another time. For now, the women had more-pressing matters.

They chatted easily as Paige washed up from her training session and filled a bowl of water for Frankie.

When the doorbell rang, Katia felt a tinge of sadness. She was enjoying the normalcy of the moment. "Maybe we can ignore it?"

Paige lowered the water bowl to the tiled floor. She stood and shook her head. "Nope."

"Fine." Katia stuck her tongue out at her. She stood close to the table in the small kitchen and listened to the front door open and shut.

Paige and Zahra rounded the corner and joined Katia near the small kitchen nook.

"I know I'm the bearer of shitty news," Zahra said. "I did bring coffee, though." She held up a carrier with three of its four cardboard slots filled with cups of steaming coffee. "Straight from the local coffee shop." A Cup of Inspiration was one of the few businesses that stayed open year round in the tourist-centered area.

Paige glanced from the coffee to Zahra and back again. "Coffee buys you a pass," she said. "Sit. Let's see what you've got."

The three women sat in Paige's cozy kitchen. Katia liked the way the nook sat tucked away inside the warm soft yellows that surrounded them on all but one side. It felt safe, secure. Her own kitchen with its beach-blue walls and large picture window was built to bring the outside in, and right now, that was the last thing she wanted.

"So?" Katia looked at Zahra. "What has the world of sterile, white rooms and little, silver knives brought us today?"

Zahra ignored Katia's nervous attempt at morbid humor. She opened the brown flap on her leather briefcase, pulled out a small stack of papers, and set them on the table between them. "You guys know we have fourteen confirmed."

"Fourteen." Katia stirred a spoonful of sugar into her coffee and repeated the word. It was surreal.

Paige nodded. "At least we didn't find any more yesterday. What we have is what we have."

"Not a lot of reportable information, yet," Zahra said. "Five days isn't a lot of time to review, you know? There isn't anything else I can do in Greenville. The specialists are doing their thing. It's all crazy." She paused, bit at her lower lip. "They're nowhere near finished in the bone room, yet. Additional specialists got there this morning." She reached over and took the sugar bowl before she continued. "Her team will be able to give us more information soon."

Paige nodded. "Might as well dig in." She raised the top sheet of the papers on the table and began to read out loud from left to right. "Name: Unknown. Decomp: Completely skeletonized. Age: Thirty-five plus."

There were several notes. The most jarring concerned the only male identified. "He was buried in the side of the same dune, above and behind the unnamed woman. The exact coordinates were also noted, as were identifying markers."

"A lot of unknowns," Zahra said. She looked from Paige to Katia. "Like I said, they haven't even started on the most decayed."

Paige didn't look up. She continued to read aloud. "Name: Helen Whitaker."

Katia knew the name. Her body reacted, sending a chill from her shoulders to her fingertips. She set her cup down, but not before a trail of coffee slid over the side and onto the table. She pushed her chair back and rose. "I've heard people talk about her. She disappeared from around here in like 1980."

"Eighty-three," Zahra said. "We got a hit on her dentals. Story is she was a recluse. Weirded people out, especially kids."

Katia returned to the table, paper towels in hand. "My mom said she used to have something sticking out of her yard with a cloth wrapped around it. Kids thought it was something to do with witchcraft. Turns out it was an old pipe contraption of some kind."

"Witchcraft. Idiots." Paige looked right at Katia. "Another reason I don't want kids." She scrunched her nose and gnarled up her fingers for effect.

"I thought humor wasn't allowed," Katia said. She balled up one square of the paper towel and threw it toward Paige.

"Humor without knives is acceptable." Paige lobbed the remark and the paper towel back in return.

"Humor with spoons." Katia said. Paige would understand the reference to their beach discussion.

"Spoons?" Zahra reached for the ball of paper that bounced from Katia's glasses onto the table. "Is that a secret code or something?"

Katia dodged Zahra's throw. She balled up another paper towel.

"Spoons are what we don't have enough of to battle this monster." Paige was on her feet. She retrieved the ball of paper from the floor.

Soon the three women were on their feet.

Zahra pulled an invisible sword from her hip and aimed at one and then the other woman. "Touché, and touché." Despite the solemn air around them, the three women danced around the small room in an imaginary sword fight.

It felt good to be in this moment with these women.

When finished, they settled back into their seats.

"Will the world ever be normal again?" Katia asked. The contradiction of feel good neurotransmitters and the pain of loss made her insides contract and expand rapidly.

The question sucked the momentary happiness out of the air. No one spoke.

Frankie, who bounced around the women a moment before, moved to Katia's side.

"You want up here again, boy?" Frankie's tail wagged. "Well, come on." She pushed her chair slightly back from the table and patted her legs.

Katia looked at her present company. "I didn't mean to ruin the mood."

"It's all good." Paige gave a half-smile. "This sucks."

Zahra pointed to Katia's lap. "What are you going to do with him?"

"Paige told me he could stay here until I get him cleared at home." Katia scratched the pup under his chin.

Zahra reached across the table, scratched Frankie's head, and returned to the notes. "Back to the little old recluse who lived in the dune."

"You're a sick fuck," Katia said. She pretended to cover Frankie's ears. "Don't listen, Frankie."

Zahra shrugged. "Some people like it. Just saying."

Katia looked at Paige and shrugged. "Some people."

Zahra indicated the paper. "You're deflecting."

"Fuck you. Fine." Katia sighed. She struggled with her anger. She enjoyed being with Paige and Zahra. They felt more like friends in the last few days than anyone since Elizabeth. On the other hand, next to the death of her mom, this was the worst thing to happen in her life. How could she feel anything but sad? Yet she did.

"Back to Helen." Zahra was fully in investigator mode.

"Teenagers mowed her grass and shopped for her," Katia said. "Story goes, no one realized she was gone until one of the kids said Whitaker hadn't answered her door for several weeks in a row and he wanted his money. Officers broke her door down. Found almost nothing personal. Not many clothes in the closet. Furniture went with the house. No signs of foul play." Katia's hand moved from ear to ear of the dog in her lap.

Paige jumped back into the conversation. She wasn't technically from Buxton, so she offered some distance. "It's hard to comprehend that this woman just disappeared and no one had a clue."

"Tools weren't as advanced then," Zahra said. "She didn't own the property. She rented it. It's easy to guess they didn't spend much time looking once the trail went cold."

"They did interview the boys, right?" Katia tried to remember the story.

Zahra reached into her bag and pulled out her computer. She talked while she booted it up. "I believe they did. Yes. There was one kid in particular. I remember my dad saying how weird he was."

Zahra typed. "Hm. This might take a minute. You two continue."

Paige nodded. Her finger skimmed over the coordinates and field notes and moved to the third line. "Octavia Quinn. Decomp: Completely skeletonized. Age: Mid to late twenties. Notes: Missing since 1984. Worked the Hatteras Ocracoke Ferry. Reported missing by father when she didn't come home after a shift. Cold case."

"Lived in Ocracoke," Zahra said over the top of her laptop. "With two sisters and her parents. Her father said all she wanted was to finish college and work with dolphins and kids."

Paige and Katia scanned the rows and rows of names and information. Much was still unknown.

"How'd you identify her?" Katia met Zahra's gaze.

"Dental records on her. Some of the remains will likely not be identifiable for some time, if ever. Got lucky on a few. Like Octavia. Her father also reported she was wearing dolphin earrings and a matching necklace made from nickel. She wore them every time she worked. We found the earrings with her remains. Jogged Detective Levine's memory."

"No necklace?"

"No." Zahra sucked in the corner of her bottom lip, made a tiny air sound through her teeth. She shook her head. "Not yet identified, anyway."

Katia liked the way she did that. It was one of the things she recognized immediately in the bar. Katia liked unconscious gestures, little telltale signs people used that they didn't realize they used.

"This unknown one…" Paige pointed back at the top of the first page, toward the first remains listed. "She was the only one found alone in a dune?"

Katia looked to where Paige pointed.

"Yeah," Zahra said. "Not sure yet what to make of it. She was completely skeletonized. Found with a knife. Likely the murder weapon. No other weapons were found in any other burial site. Working theory is she's the first. Helen and Octavia likely numbers two and three. Hard to tell for certain just yet."

Katia took off her glasses and set them on the table. She rubbed her eyes with her fingertips. "How many locals identified?"

"Four. Four so far," Zahra answered.

"Let's hope four total. In a population of barely over twelve hundred, how the fuck do even four people disappear without a trace and end up in a fucking dune?" Katia's frustration rose.

Paige ran her finger farther down the list. "That's what we're trying to figure out. That, and how bodies from anywhere could disappear and end up in a one-mile strip of dune on a beach that swarms with life for nine of twelve months per year. It's why I'm here. To put my head together with two other Buxton natives."

"Well," Katia chided her, "technically you're a Manteo native who went to school in Buxton because your father was the school principal. Special treatment and all that."

"Truth," Zahra said. "We joked about you back then."

"Speak for yourself." Katia puckered her lips to one side as she did. "I didn't joke about you. Hell, I didn't even know then your father was important or that you didn't belong there."

Zahra and Paige looked at each other.

"Is your name Elizabeth?" Zahra asked.

Paige moved her head from side to side. "Nope."

"Then I don't know you." Zahra finished the friendly jab.

"Fuck you both," Katia said.

"Oh, pick me." Zahra grinned.

Paige said nothing but continued to smile.

"Sorry," Zahra added. "I know this is hard."

"Fuck yeah. But, you know, laughing helps." Katia pointed back to the notes. "What else?"

"In addition to Helen and Octavia, there's Gina." Zahra's voice was even and low.

The girls all knew why she was easy to identify. You can't manage rentals along the Outer Banks and have your face on more than one Seaside Real Estate billboard and not be readily known.

"She was the least decomposed of the fourteen uncovered," Zahra said. "Still had fingerprints and other identifying marks." She paused and looked at Katia.

"It's okay." Katia gave Zahra a nod. "I need this. And I know this place. Know these people as well as anyone. Maybe I can help, pick up on a thread that pulls this fucked-up shit together."

"Two others," Zahra said. "Lacey O'Donnell and Nadia Grey were also listed as missing and easily identified from the database. Lacey was reported missing in Manteo in 2014 by her husband when she failed to return from a work conference. The husband was the prime suspect."

Katia latched on to the last words. Her back straightened, and her voice grew stronger. "So, are you all going to pick him up? Could he be the one who did all of this?"

"No." Zahra cut her off before she could get her hopes up. "He was cleared at the time. And he's thirty-nine now. The oldest decedents have been in the dunes for thirty or more years. Whoever this is, he or she has to be late forties at least. Probably fifties."

Katia nodded. "Who else has been identified? There doesn't seem to be any pattern at all. Different places. Different ages."

The women went through other names. They ultimately came back to Nadia Grey.

"There's a plaque in the hallway outside the classroom where she taught," Katia said. "It's probably still there." She turned back to Paige. "This world sucks." She didn't wait for an answer. None was needed.

Paige looked to Zahra who was now intently reading through something on her screen. "Wasn't she abducted with someone?"

"Who? Nadia? Yeah," Zahra said. "I was doing research on her this morning. There was evidence the teacher and a boy from the geometry club were together the day they disappeared. Caused a little stir, but none of that was proven." Zahra took a sip of her cold coffee.

"Want me to heat it?" Katia reached across the table.

Zahra shook her head. "Every student who was in the club or who was in her classes at the time was questioned. They all said she was an amazing instructor, that she was always there for her students. All of her students."

"Says in the notes her purse with all contents was found in—"

"Shit." Zahra's voice, low in her throat, drew out the word.

The other women stopped what they were doing and focused their attention on Zahra and her computer.

"Guess who the kid was who was a party of interest in Whitaker's death?"

The others waited.

"Shelton Fucking Easton."

Chapter Twelve

Marco heard his sister come in the front door, heard Papi yell. He didn't like when Dad drank bourbon. It made him act like someone who didn't belong in their house. When Katia smelled like that, she didn't yell. Why did Dad have to yell? It made Marco's head spin faster. It made the sounds in his belly louder, until he had to open his mouth and let the sounds out.

"He's been like this since I picked him up from school. Sounds like a wounded animal. You need to get him to shut up. Where've you been?" His dad swished the ice in his glass. Too loud. The ice was too loud. Like the sounds in his own belly. His sister's voice was lower, not soft like his mami's used to be, but nice. The sounds in his belly that always tried to get out when he was spinning in his head liked her voice.

"I texted you, Papi. Paige's training facility. I met Zahra and Paige to talk about the beach."

"The beach isn't our concern. Your brother—"

Marco listened to the pause in his papi's yelling noise.

"Your brother is our concern. I told you. You want him home; you be here to help when you're not working. And… Tonight. You. Are. Not. Working."

"I know, Papi. I'm sorry. It's just we may have found something. Someone Gina dated one summer."

"Katia Pilar Mercedes Billings-Castillo."

"Yes, Papi. I'm sorry. I'll calm him and get him to his appointment."

The sounds in Marco's tummy were alternating between something that resembled a howl and a chant. "One-six-six-M-P-H. One-six-six-M-P-H." Marco rocked back and forth on the edge of the periwinkle-colored chair in the tiny room his sister decorated for him with periwinkle-blue walls and trim. It felt good to rock. Good in his spinning head. Good in his mad tummy. No white paint. He didn't like it. "Just periwinkle, Katia. Marco likes periwinkle." He handed his sister the square in the paint store eight years ago, when he was just a little boy. After mami died in the fiery car, there were so many people around. In and out of his house. Periwinkle helped. His sister's nice voice helped.

"Autistic. Not stupid. Katia tell the people. The people in my head, too. Tell them, too." Spinning. Drowning. The taste of dirty ocean water. My lungs. My eyes. My nose. My ears. Piercing shards of pain. He didn't know why Papi wanted him to go away. Katia said it was the bourbon. Only the bourbon. Did Katia want him gone when she smelled that way?

Marco looked around his space. It was perfectly square. He liked that, too. He liked squares. And he liked the soft pillows thrown on the floor. They were all the same size squares. Marco liked to pile them into walls around him. They felt like clouds. His mom lived in the clouds. The pillows made him feel close to her. When he needed to be soundless, alone in his environment, he brought his books into the center and sat on the big, square pillow Katia bought just for him. This is where he sat now. Right in the center. Legs crossed. Sometimes Dr. Abney gave him a camera. He liked cameras. Take pictures of what is loud, Marco. Take pictures of what makes you happy, Marco. Dr. Abney had a nice voice. Not as nice as Katia or his mom, but a different kind of nice.

Marco turned his head left, then right, then left again. Books and magazines about weather were piled everywhere. He kept them precisely stacked by type and date.

His rocking, which had slowed as he thought about his mom and Katia and the white clouds, increased again. His dad's voice was loud in his head, not calming like Katia's.

He blinked rapidly. The sound hurt inside his head. Too loud. He raised his arm to his mouth, bit down on his forearm. Hard. Harder. Blood. My blood. Good. Rock. Bite. My blood. Fill the black noise with pain. My blood. Not hers. I can smell it. Go away, Marco. So noisy. Marco doesn't like noise. Make her stop screaming. Bite harder. Blood. My blood. He rocked and rocked, faster and faster.

He knew Katia was right outside, back against the wall, sitting, waiting. She always waited for him to center, to regulate against the overwhelming sensory input. "One-six-six-M-P-H. One-six-six-M-P-H. Katia. One-six-six-M-P-H."

Tell her. She might want Marco gone. Tell her. No. Tell her. Can't leave the square periwinkle. Tell her, his mind repeated.

His body rocked.

****

Katia sat still, waiting. The fact her little brother was able to add her name into his stream of repetitiveness told her he was almost calm. She was proud of him. Marco was mildly verbal on a good day, but when overwhelmed, all he wanted to do was be alone in his safe place, lights off, and rock to the rhythm of whatever weather stat he most recently read. Weather was one of his special interests, just as it was an interest of most everyone on the island. You couldn't live on a sliver of sand in the Atlantic Ocean and not be aware of weather. As a child, you learned to listen to weather reports. In the spring and summer, you listened to anticipate tourist season. In the winter and fall, you listened to anticipate storms. Marco internalized the importance of weather and turned it into a compulsion that few understood.

Taking pictures was another compulsion. No one was sure where that one came from. Perhaps from all of the discussions around the island of tourists and their cameras. Whatever the draw, when he combined the two intense interests, he was content for hours. There were hundreds of pictures of raindrops on flower petals and on sidewalks, hundreds of pictures of paper blowing in the wind and hair blowing in Katia's face or Marco's face, hundreds of pictures of the sunlight on the floor, on the fence that surrounded their ocean-facing home, on a tiny sand crab on the beach.

She thought about the last seventeen years. She was ten when her brother was born, fifteen when their mother died. Since their mom's death, Katia was the one who fed his passion for more and more specialized knowledge about weather. She was the one who bought him a digital camera. And she was the one who watched him struggle with interaction, the one who stayed alert to his desire to run away, even from his own home. "Elopement," Marco's psychologist called it when Marco was diagnosed at age four. "Very common in autistic children."

For Katia, it felt personal back then, like Marco was trying to run from her. It took years of therapy sessions for both of them to learn it wasn't about her or him.

"He has misophonia," Dr. Abney told her and her parents. "A hatred of particular sounds that can lead to a flight-or-fight-type response. You will need to watch for triggers. Once you learn them, you can avoid them, or at least be aware of them."

Before their mom died, Katia tuned the doctor out as he rambled on about what was happening in Marco's head. She remembered words: "meltdowns," and "stimming," and "developmentally delayed." All words she later would not only look up but study incessantly. "My own special interest," she thought, remembering another phrase Dr. Abney used that day.

She did remember that she felt good after the meeting because it meant Marco didn't hate her and their parents. She hated that her little brother had to deal with this for life. She vowed that day to pay more attention, to learn all she could about autism, and to always be there in whatever way Marco needed her to be. She watched and listened and took notes. Wrappers were the worst offenders for her brother—and plastic bags that crinkled and rubbed. They sent Marco into flight mode in seconds.

Over the years, the problems with elopement and meltdowns lessened. When he was four, they all worried about him constantly. Locks were placed high on doors and windows, where little fingers couldn't reach. Everyone walked through the house as if on eggshells. When he was eight, all plastic bags were removed from the house. For a period of time, dinners were eaten only with a plastic fork so metal didn't scrape plates. Nothing was done without thinking about how it would affect the boy with autism, the boy who couldn't or wouldn't talk, the boy who rocked and rocked and rocked.

Now Marco was a teen and, mostly, he learned to self-regulate, to monitor his own world, to communicate his needs through short semi-sentences and sounds. Now he went to his space and into his head until he was able to return.

So what the fuck happened in the school today? Why was today different? Of all fucking days.

Katia thought about the laughter of the afternoon. She almost felt normal. Maybe she shouldn't have. Maybe the universe was reminding her how fucked up it was that her ex was missing and Gina was dead. Fourteen people were dead.

She took a deep breath to keep herself from banging her head back and forth against the wall. It might actually feel good, she thought. Might feel better than the pain inside, better than the pain in her heart she felt for the young man on the other side of the wall. Today it was like he was five again. He was alone in a world that he didn't know how to share, and Katia was outside, shut out and afraid.

****

Marco slowed his rocking and looked at the door. His mind was full of sound bites and smells. A deep voice: Pretty little thing. Almost a whisper. Why? Whispers are for secrets. Grumbled whining in a throat, deep, a sound like when his friend's dog got hit by a car. Not a man sound. A girl. Blood and sweat: mixed-up. Different. Fear, yes. Smell fear, and taste it. Whose fear? Whose sweat? The person making the hurt-dog sound?

Run, Marco. Run. No. That is called elopement, Marco. Go to your safe place. Go to your safe place. Safe place. Katia. Safe. Home.

When he was three years and 100 days, Marco eloped. He remembered. It was raining. Marco loved rain. Dad loved rain. Katia loved rain. Rain tickled your face when you looked up at it. He only wanted the rain to tickle his face. He didn't understand why, but Katia smelled like fear when they found him. His mom smelled like fear. She smelled like fear when she took him to Dr. Callum Abney, too. He didn't understand that, either. Dr. Abney was good. He liked him. He looked forward to his mom and dad taking him there every Monday. He fitted Marco with a special tracking device, one he said would keep him safe. Then his mom didn't smell like fear so much.

He reached down toward his foot. He felt the thin strip securely fastened around his left ankle. He rubbed it between his index finger and thumb. Safe here. Katia. Safe with the periwinkle. Safe with the monitor. Safe and sound. Still here. The sounds. The smells. Get out! Get out, you fucking retard. Get out. Why did he say that? He rocked and felt and tried to make the words work together to tell Katia what he had seen. He wished he could remember the words for the blood, for the sweat and fear, for the other pictures in his head.

He didn't like blood. He rocked. And rocked. Trying to control the sensory input, to re-center his own body.

"6:30 is time for Dr. Callum Abney." Marco almost hummed as he said the words "6:30 is time for Dr. Callum Abney." The sounds followed him today. "6:12 PM." The smells now in his safe place. "6:14 PM." Have to tell Katia, tell Dr. Callum Abney. "One-six-six-M-P-H. One-six-six-M-P-H. Katia. One-six-six-M-P-H."

****

Katia waited. Marco rocked.

"Which will win? The need to self-regulate or the time showing on the clock in your safe room?" Katia waited in the hallway for Marco. She glanced at the door. The waiting was always the hardest part. No matter how many times she sat against the wall outside Marco's safe room, it never got easier to feel the helplessness that came with an episode. Her head hurt and her eyes burned. "Come on, little brother." The numbers on her phone moved to 6:15 PM. And then 6:16. Marco's rocking slowed. His chant softened. Katia waited.

At exactly 6:20, Marco's lanky, teenage frame emerged. The clock won.

"It is 6:20 PM, Katia. We see Dr. Callum Abney at 6:30 PM. Katia and Marco leave the house at 6:20 PM."

"Yes, Marco. We do." Her voice was quiet. She took her baby brother's hand, and together they headed toward the door.

Katia took her brother's hand again when they exited her car and walked past several reporters outside Dr. Abney's office. They hurled questions at Katia:

"Have they identified everyone in the dunes?"

"Are you still in contact with the dead woman's daughter?"

"Can you give us background on Gina Dahl?"

"Why did you run from the scene?"

She gripped Marco's hand more tightly as she felt him tense. She swallowed and took several deep breaths. Her brother would feed off of her reaction. Another meltdown might just take her down with him. "I'm sorry." She made eye contact with the one reporter she recognized. "I'm taking my brother to a doctor's appointment. You know what I know. Please ask an officer or the coroner about the beach."

Marco's palm was sweaty. She felt it slipping out of hers. She held even tighter. She guided him through the front door and down the hallway.

Dr. Abney told her years ago to let Marco's hand go when he relaxed his grip. Don't overprotect, Katia. Let him grow and learn, Katia. She tried. She really did. But Marco was all she had, the only person who needed her. She wanted to hold his hand, wanted him to stay a child. Tonight she needed to hold his hand, possibly more than he needed to hold hers. She suspected the reporters would be their new normal, at least for a while.

She looked over at Marco after they were greeted by the receptionist and led into Dr. Abney's office. She let go of his hand. While Katia and Dr. Abney spoke, Marco sat silently on his end of the black-leather couch. At some point in the conversation, she realized there was stubble on his face. She made a mental note to buy shaving cream and a razor.

When the conversation turned to Marco's well-being after school that day, Marco picked up the melon-colored pillow from his end of the couch and hugged it tightly against his chest. Katia reached for his hand, stopped herself, looked at Dr. Abney and then at the gray-and-black cat-shaped clock on the wall. The inside of the cat's ears was the same melon color as the pillows. 7:30 PM. Katia and the doctor talked for thirty minutes while Marco gently rocked and hugged the melon-colored pillow.

"Marco, do you want another one of my special cameras?" Dr. Abney asked.

Marco bobbed his head, but he didn't speak.

The idea for the disposable cameras came up a few years ago. "We'll always look for ways to play to his passion, Katia," Dr. Abney told her then.

"He has a camera, though, and a drawer full of memory sticks, and a computer for larger display," she said.

"Let's think about that," the doctor said and smiled.

Katia hated when he said things like that, hated that it made her feel like she was being analyzed as much as her brother, hated that it made her feel dumb for not already knowing what it was they should be thinking about. She expressed as much to her father once. What is dumb, he chastised, is that you let someone make you feel dumb. We're paying for the doctor to help Marco. You're Marco's sister. You know him. Ask whatever question you want to ask, and ask until you have the answer you need. End of story.

Her father wasn't much on what he called psychoanalyzing B.S. In fact, when he brought Marco on the rare weeks Katia couldn't, both he and Marco typically left agitated and it took Katia the entire next day to get her brother calm.

The doctor didn't have to say, "Let's think about that," anymore. Now Katia knew. A disposable camera allows for those with sensory issues to photograph what his or her mind's eye is perceiving as a threat. It will do so without the photographer having to look at it again on the camera or on the large screen. Processing the difficult information happens as the picture is taken. Anxiety of repeated visuals is lessened, and the person analyzing the pictures gets a clue about the cause of the meltdowns.

Dr. Abney pushed back from his black, lacquered desk, stood, and looked again at Marco. "One or two, Marco?"

Marco raised two fingers. "Please." Marco spoke for the first time since leaving the house.

"Two it is." Dr. Abney smiled.

Marco smiled in return.

Katia's heart felt lighter. Since the day of her mother's death, others accused her of being dark and uncaring. Dark she was. But not uncaring. For Marco, she would lie down and die. She looked at her brother. His eyes were following the doctor who made his way to the far end of a stark-white bookshelf that ran the entire long wall behind his desk. Katia liked how everything in the room popped from the black-and-white background, the way his purple tie and lavender shirt popped from his white coat, the way the melon pillows popped from the black couch, the way the colorful bookbindings popped from the white shelves. It felt like they were in one of Marco's old, pop-up, nursery rhyme books now stored in the closet under the stairs.

Dr. Abney rummaged around in the drawer for a moment and came up with a yellow-and-black disposable camera in hand.

Chapter Thirteen

The day was emotionally exhausting. All Katia wanted to do was strip off the day in a hot shower and crawl between her cool sheets. She picked up a burger for Marco in Avon before they headed home. It was one of Marco's weekly rituals. Whoever drove to the therapy session stopped at the same place and ordered the same thing. The owner never wrapped it in a crunchy wrapper. Instead, it was handed out the drive-through window wrapped in a napkin. No fries. Only a burger. Marco ate it on the way home.

"Teeth and bed," she said as the two walked in the front door.

Marco headed straight for the stairs. Nights like this, she was thankful for routine and for a brother who didn't argue. Scratches. Rocks. Spits. Spins. But doesn't argue. She laughed at herself. It's the little things.

Katia went into the kitchen and took her own burger out of its napkin wrapper. She didn't even sit down while she watched the second hand move around on the clock. Tick. Tick. Tick. 8:05. Her father was already in his room. Just as well; she was too tired to fight with him tonight. She planned to catch him early in the morning to tell him about Frankie. She wasn't sure yet what they were going to do with him. She hoped their father would let him stay. He would be good company for Marco.

Katia thought about her plans for the next day. She wanted to see Elliot and Brent. They would be at the station. She pulled her phone from her back pocket and texted Elliot.

Meet tomorrow? Fill me in?

Pretty uneventful 24, he texted. And then, *You aren't missing anything.*

Nothing?

Everyone is gawking at the beach. Absolute madhouse there. FBI now swarming.

They agreed on a time, and she slid the phone back into her pocket.

Tick. Tick. 8:11. She started for the stairs. At the top, she glanced out the large picture window. A light-blue Volkswagen van was parked on the edge of the side road.

Andrew.

She kept her cool while she gently laid the covers up close to Marco's chin. Not touching. Never touching. Just ever so close. "Sweet dreams, Monkey Head." She looked at the clock on her brother's nightstand. 8:15. Marco smiled. Crossed his arms under the covers in the symbol for hugs.

Katia reached down and pulled the tiny chain on the lamp with the cloud-covered shade of periwinkle blue next to Marco's bed. The same lamp that had always been and would always be.

In the darkness of the room, Katia walked over to the window direct center of the periwinkle wall. She reached for the string and pulled it inward and over.

Before she eased the blinds closed, she looked to where the van was still parked. Old school. She shook her head slightly. Weird and old school. The movement briefly brought something else into her line of sight. Then it was gone. What the fuck? A gun? Is that motherfucker going to try to kill me? She tried to remember their conversation earlier, the words he said before he left. "I thought you might want to know what I heard today." Was that it? Why are you here, you weird shit? I'll slice you to bits before I allow you to hurt us.

She let the blinds fall softly into place. She considered waking Papi. After their spat earlier, she wasn't ready to do that unless it was absolutely necessary. She loved him, and he loved her, but Katia suspected the older she got the more she reminded him of their mom, and those memories were still too painful to overcome, even for the sake of his children.

Katia paused outside Papi's closed door. No light shown in the small crack between the solid wood door and the hardwood floor. A moment later, she took her cell phone out of her pocket and moved quietly down the stairs. She briefly considered another text to Elliot but decided she didn't want to involve him and potentially bring harm to his family. Brent still kept the early morning hours he established in high school when he worked with her father. That meant 4:00 A.M. She certainly didn't want to send him a whiny "Andrew is creepy and he is sitting outside my house and I want him to leave" text.

Zahra or Paige would come. She didn't know Paige well enough yet to assume how she would react. Zahra wanted to hang out. She wanted to hang out with Zahra. Elizabeth was heavy in her head, though, and it felt like cheating to admit it.

Her mind whirled with the events of the last few days. She felt bruised and vulnerable and pissed and perplexed. What do I have to do with Gina's death and Elizabeth's empty apartment? The other bodies? Why in the fuck is this happening? Haven't we been dealt enough? She wished her mom was alive. She would know what to do.

If she got to the front door and Andrew was still there, she would text Zahra. She leaned sideways against the door and tried to get an angle on the van. She tapped her screen and immediately swiped down from the top and moved the sliding bar to the left to dim the brightness.

Andrew is outside. Parked. Watching the house.

Zahra's response was immediate: *I'm coming over.*

Katia checked Andrew's position before she answered: *He is just sitting there. My dad's here. Just sleeping.*

Katia's phone buzzed in her hand, and Zahra's face lit up the screen. She put the phone to her ear.

"You text me that, and then you want me to just sit here texting back and forth like you're telling me about a kite gliding contest or some shit?" There was obvious concern in Zahra's voice.

Katia adjusted her body against the inside of the front door, trying to get a better look at the van from the adjoining window. "I have no idea how long he's been there or why he's there. He said something today about what he heard at the beach."

"Before he took the kids to the school?"

"I don't know. He freaked me out. I made him leave. I feel like a fucking idiot. I should have kept him talking. Maybe he knows something. Or maybe he was going to confess something."

"I don't get that vibe," Zahra said.

Katia felt her face flush. She swallowed hard. She wanted to go out to the van and yank Andrew out by his shoulders. If Marco wasn't asleep upstairs, she might. She knew herself well enough to know that.

Zahra interrupted her thoughts. "I told the state detectives about his visit to your house today. They may have already questioned him."

"Fuck." Katia peeked out the window again.

"Yeah. I'm almost there."

"I told you—"

"I know what you told me. I'll be there in a few."

Katia stood guard. It was comforting to know she would have someone to hang out with in a few minutes. And Zahra had a gun.

****

Marco kept his eyes squeezed shut. One. Two. Three… He counted his sister's footsteps as she headed down the stairs. Thirteen. Fourteen. Fifteen. He knew she was at the bottom. He counted every night. It's what he did. I am Marco. I have autism. Go to sleep, Marco. Mom isn't coming home, Marco. Clouds. She is in them. He started to hum. In his head, he heard her sound. He missed her. Sweet dreams, Marco. Hummmmmm…

He wanted to get up. No, Marco. Bedtime means bedtime.

He listened. He heard her talking. I hear scared. He put his feet over the edge of the bed and went to his door. He stopped just inside the doorframe and looked down at his bare feet against the hardwood. He heard Katia's voice better from here.

"Fuck."

Katia stop saying that. My head remembers it and says it inside. Fuck. He didn't like when Katia said that word. Papi says it's bad. Katia isn't bad. He didn't want to hear any more of that. He left the doorway and padded over to the window.

Two fingers to peek. Why are there cars outside? A white Aveo. A blue VW van. Nighttime is for sleeping. Not for driving. He stood and watched a man in the van. He looked at the front door of their house. The man's eyes shifted toward the window, toward Marco. Marco waved behind the tiny crack in the blinds. The man waved back. He slowly opened the car door. The man is coming to the door. Don't tell Katia. Nighttime is for sleeping.

Marco went back to his bed and slid under the covers.

****

Zahra was unsure as to how she wanted to handle the newest situation. As soon as she hung up from Katia, she checked in with Xavier. He was on duty tonight at the Hatteras Island Sheriff's Office. Zahra was an officer out of Southern Shores. The two worked together multiple times over the last few years.

"No," Xavier said. "Andrew hasn't been questioned. We didn't have anything to make us think he's connected. No prior convictions. He's a fellow town employee, at the beach to do his job."

Zahra suspected Andrew was more than he claimed. She could feel it. She just didn't know how or why. She was hoping Xavier's soft spot for her would get him to speculate with her based on what they did know. It didn't take long for him to begin.

"Profilers are working hard to put together a statement for the press, so I heard."

She waited for him to volunteer more information.

"Probable psychological orientation," Xavier said. "Includes chronic sexual deviance and peculiar sexual experiences throughout his life. He is likely an avid reader and watcher of pornography and may have been involved in experiments including forced sexual acts on children as either the perpetrator or perpetrated."

"Seriously?" she said, her tone dripping with sarcasm. "That couldn't have been too hard to figure out." She pictured Xavier's signature shrug and the straight line of his lips.

"He's most probably a white male, late forties," Xavier said. "The burial site is visible from the row of rentals above. This specific location means something to him. He has likely navigated it many times, telling us he's not a stranger or a transient."

Zahra thought about Andrew. Thirty-five at best, probably less. He visited the OBX many times, but it wasn't his home until last year. "If his family stayed in a rental, would that be enough to learn how the town moves through tourist season and into hibernation?" She didn't think so. She was interested in what he thought.

"Maybe. This is a predominately white area, so men of other nationalities would have likely been noticed spending excessive amounts of time on the beach."

"So, probably white."

"The crime indicates some level of intelligence and preplanning, too. He would have a place to complete the killings and a way to get the victim and tools to the burial site."

"Right. He's strong and has a vehicle and a license to drive on the sand."

"Definitely. Brief mentions serial killers are typically creatures of habit. They have a reason for what they do. We may or may not understand it, but it's a valid reason in their mind."

Zahra mentally ticked off recent events. Andrew lives in the upper half of a converted beach house—an unlikely place to kill. It didn't fit. And yet, he was outside Katia's home three nights after she found the most recent victim of a lengthy killing spree.

"One more thing," Xavier said.

She swore she heard his male ego inflating his chest.

"The killer may have been absent from his employment for several days before and after each kill. The time around a kill is usually significant to a serial killer. So significant, they often remove themselves from their usual routine both before and after."

"Thanks, Xavier. I owe you." Zahra disconnected the call just as she rounded the corner onto Katia's street. She passed the light-blue VW parked several hundred feet from the pale-green Victorian beach house. The blond hair of the tanned driver was situated just shy of center in the driver's seat. She wouldn't have noticed him at all if she didn't already know he was there. He blended in with the sand against the turquoise of the sea. Zahra hoped her nonchalant speed and body movements would convince Andrew she wasn't here because they knew he was outside. It was imperative she not hand him any power or control over the situation.

Zahra pulled as far up in the driveway as she dared do without causing suspicion. Her hand went to the bulge under her jacket. The gun gave her a sense of freedom she never took lightly.

She reached for the door handle. Being in proximity of harm never came easy to her. She wasn't afraid, but she wasn't comfortable, either.

****

Andrew sat alone in his van. He thought Katia saw him from an upstairs window earlier in the evening, but there was no sudden burst through the door, no screaming into his cell phone by the irate teammate. Did she have his cell number? He doubted it. She could have gotten it easily enough from the directory, or her buddy Elliot, but she wouldn't. She didn't like him. After this afternoon, she probably hated him. Andrew wished he could let them know he wasn't a bad guy, that he was on their side. He knew nothing he could say would matter. He was the odd man out, and it was going to stay that way. And it was best that way.

He rolled his neck, sat up straight, and thought about streaming some music on his phone. Probably not a great idea. A bright screen might bring attention, even if only for a few minutes.

Instead, he contemplated his first days in Buxton. When he started with the Hatteras Island crew, he was in awe of Katia. He thought about her all of the time. He wanted to talk to her; he wanted to get to know her. He was mesmerized by her strange beauty, by her soft golden-brown skin hued like a page in one of those adult coloring books. The woman was a walking tattoo. He loved the way the reds and blues swirled with the greens and yellows to form pictures. When Katia caught him staring the first time, she didn't ignore it like other women he met. She pushed her perfectly chopped, black hair away from the edge of her glasses, stepped into his space, and smiled. It wasn't a smile that said, "Aw, thanks for noticing." It was a smile that said, "Not in a million years, asshole."

In that moment, Andrew knew he had zero chance with her. He wasn't stupid. He was a man nearing thirty-five with an Ichabod Crane nose and a bit of a belly. He was also a man. Elliot warned him about that long before Katia caught him staring.

What Andrew could do was make sure Katia and those around her stayed safe. It was his goal to make sure she stayed alive while they sorted out these murders on the island.

He looked back at the house. There was movement at the upstairs window. Was Katia watching him again? He thought she was downstairs with Zahra. He looked closer. It wasn't Katia. It was Marco, Katia's autistic little brother.

Not autistic, he corrected himself. Little brother with autism spectrum disorder. Marco was waving. Andrew waved back.

****

He sat silently, staring at her, willing her to break through the fog of her drug-induced sleep. *Open your eyes, Elizabeth. Realize what fate your mother has sealed for you.* When he learned the storm uncovered Gina Dahl, he knew he must retrieve her daughter and kill her, not only because she was a deviant soul, but because she knew too much about him and her mom.

Sandman looked down at the blade in his hand. Even in the dim, windowless room, the edge created starbursts of light as he moved it from side to side. He watched it, tilted it to catch the light from above in a way that made the starbursts play along Elizabeth's cheek and down her throat.

Elizabeth's eyes flew open. Her head jerked away from the starburst.

There we are. "Hi, Elizabeth." Wide eyes, so wild and afraid. He could see her chest heave, feel her fear as it climbed up her throat. She surveyed her surroundings, probably making mental notes, feeling her chains, testing her limbs. She moved her arms, yanked hard. He watched her eyes travel over her legs.

"I've been waiting," he said. "I cleaned you up as best I could and changed your clothes. I attempted to comb your hair. You wouldn't think it would be so tangled. It's short enough. It's thick, though, isn't it?"

Elizabeth remained silent, but her eyes spoke to him loud and clear.

"I know it still smells like piss in here. I'm sorry about that." He could see her repulsion, her attempt to breathe through her mouth. "Can you taste the smell?" He leaned his head back against the concrete wall and closed his eyes. "I can." He took a deep breath. He enjoyed the realness of being a human that repulsed others. "I like it, the way it sits in your mouth and clings to the inside of your cheeks. Would you like to shower, Elizabeth? Would you like to feel clean?"

"Why am I here?" Her voice sounded raspy from four days of drugs and a lack of water.

He opened his eyes and looked across the small space between them. "You'll feel better if you shower and put on clean clothes. I brought you some. And when you're ready, I'll tell you a story."

"I'm not a three-year-old. Just tell me why." Her tone indicated anger and impatience, but the rising intonation at the end of her sentence told him she was failing at being strong.

"Suit yourself." Sandman was tired of her voice. He didn't have time between Gina and Elizabeth to rejuvenate and prepare. He told her about the bathroom like a steward would announce exits on a plane. "If you change your mind, your restraints will allow you access to the toilet and shower area. I won't bother you in the room—unless you don't respond, or come when told. I'm not a pervert."

Her words were gruff. "Fuck. You."

"That's not why we're here," he said. He heard more force in her voice that time. It gave him strength. He stretched his legs out in front of him and moved his head from side to side until a loud pop filled the gray air. "Although fucking you can be arranged. I've fucked others, Elizabeth. Fucked them while I waited for the perfect moment. Would you like to cum while you die, Elizabeth?"

"Why?" she asked again. She yanked at the chains, held them forward. "I've done nothing to you, to any…"

And back to whiny. Her voice droned on in his head. He hated their voices, the way they pretended they were innocent and he was somehow to blame for their fate. "Your mother, Elizabeth. That's why you're here. She did this to you. Her laissez faire attitude about women and sex. Your attempt to do to Katia what your vile mother did to you. I would have let you live if your mother hadn't come back. I would have. But she did, and here we are."

Sandman thought about Gina. He wanted to take the time to relive the beautiful moment when her breath left her body and she gave in completely to his touch. Elizabeth was like a younger version of her mother, like a living trophy. He felt himself harden under the constraints of his jeans. Not now, he scolded himself. You promised Elizabeth a story, didn't you? He closed his eyes, breathed in the smell of fear and sweat and piss and darkness. He would save that memory for later.

"Did you know," he said, looking directly into Elizabeth's eyes for the first time, "from birth to age six or seven is when a child learns what love is? They…" He paused, letting the thought sink into his own psyche as much as that of his guest. "Who are the infamous *they*, anyway? Stupid, whoever they are."

Elizabeth's breathing was rapid, shallow. He liked that. He also liked that she was now quiet. He pulled his legs back up from the floor and rested his arms across his knees. "They say children deprived of love end up paying for the deprivation for the rest of their lives, that serial killers tend to fall into this group. But you know what, Elizabeth? I wasn't deprived." He tilted the knife in his hand, watched the dim light dance off of the sharp silver. "I wasn't left alone in my crib or banished to my room. I wasn't an unwanted boarder in my home. No. I was quite loved. Like you were loved. You were loved, weren't you, Elizabeth?"

He knew she was loved. Her mom and dad doted on her as a baby, as a young child. People in a small town talked. Everyone knew everyone. Stories were told and retold. "Yes. You were loved. And then everything changed. Didn't it, Elizabeth?" He felt for her, knew she was used as a pawn in her parent's divorce.

Elizabeth pulled at the restraints again. "Undo these," she said. "Let me go. I won't tell anyone I was here."

Sandman nodded. He pointed the knife in her direction. "From eight to twelve, negative predispositions are exacerbated and reinforced."

"Listen to me."

He didn't. "Wrong again, they." He smiled at her. "My parents didn't divorce. My father didn't drink or disappear. Hell, he didn't even drift away emotionally. He did love his sister, though." Saying the words out loud made him so angry. Your auntie loves you. She loves being near you. "My dad trusted my aunt. Believed her. While she was pulling me close late at night, running her sweaty palms across my stomach and around my young-boy-sized dick, making me grow hard against her fingers and against my will, my dad trusted her. He trusted her, and she used that trust to manipulate him into leaving me with her. A lot."

"Your aunt and my mom are not alike." She spit the words at him from her place on the filthy mattress.

"I killed her, you know," Sandman said. His voice was steady and calm. "My aunt. Just like I killed your mother. I made her trust me, and I yanked her head back and killed her."

He looked at Elizabeth, sitting there, just looking forward, as if she was looking through him. Bitch. He could feel the anger growing from a dark place inside. "I was right to bring you here. You would never have left her alone. Now you will die for your disgusting ways." He knew she would die. He didn't know where he would have her buried. He needed a new graveyard. It came to him then. Ocracoke. Plenty of quiet, deserted real estate in Ocracoke.

Having decided that piece of the plan, he felt a renewed sense of purpose. He returned to his story. "Proper socialization," he said. His head nodded slowly up and down. "That's key. I know what your mom did to you, Elizabeth. I know she made you sleep with her for comfort."

"What are you talking about? She is—" Her jaws clenched.

"Was, Elizabeth. Was."

"You sick fuck." Elizabeth's hands formed into fists. She lunged against her restraints until they pulled tight against her wrists and ankles. The red moving up her neck and taking over her face was obvious even in the dim light. "My mom never touched me in any way that was inappropriate."

He was impressed she still had so much spunk. Her mom was far less fun. All she did was cry. Criers were the worst. "That's what I told myself about my aunt, too. Until I couldn't pretend anymore. You don't have to pretend, Elizabeth. I can help you. Sexually stressful events. That's what shrinks call them. Sexually stressful events. My sweet, lovely, auntie liked for me to masturbate into her clean panties while she touched herself. What did your mom like, Elizabeth? What things did she ask you to do to help her make it through the night? Tell me. And perhaps I'll let you live."

"You won't let me live, asshole," Elizabeth said. "I already know that." Her rise in pitch at the end of each sentence hinted at sarcasm. Otherwise her voice remained flat, resigned. Her body shook. "Fuck you."

"Suit yourself." He shrugged and shifted his position against the wall. "You're right, you know. I can't let you live."

Neither spoke for several minutes. Elizabeth, chained, in a T-shirt and soiled underwear, sat on the mattress he laid on the concrete floor, while Sandman, clad in an ironed, button-down shirt, a few shades lighter than his dark-blue jeans, sat with his back against the wall, feet flat, knees bent by his chest. The five feet between them was dim. A light fixture shone overhead, but it never burned more than a twenty-five-watt bulb while they were alive. He liked it dim. Until cleanup. They were nowhere near that yet. He wanted her alive, wanted to enjoy her fear and sweat, wanted her to know what happened to women who tried to force their sick fantasies onto children. Katia isn't a child, the voice in his head reminded him. But she can still be saved. She isn't one of us. She's unharmed from within.

"That painting you were working on," he said. "That was Katia, wasn't it?"

Elizabeth didn't respond. She stared at the wall behind him. She held her hands together, one in a fist and the other wrapped tightly around it. He assumed she was trying to stop the shaking.

"No need to answer. I know it was. I can't risk you trying to expose her to our kind of sickness. You can understand that, can't you, Elizabeth? Your mom was going to bring her to you. Did you know that? She was going to bring her to your little art exhibit." He leaned forward against his legs. His face contorted. His mouth felt dry. "It wasn't enough she turned you into a lesbian with her coddling. She was trying to do the same to Katia."

A single tear made its way down Elizabeth's cheek. "You killed my mom because I'm a lesbian? You think my mom was a child molester?"

He leaned back. He hit a nerve.

Elizabeth managed to get herself into a kneeling position on the mattress. "You sit there with your back against the wall, contemplating your next words. You're not taking a lunch break on a job, sitting with friends, chatting about life." She moved forward until she reached the end of her chain. Her head was slightly above his level. She lowered her gaze. Meeting his eyes with her own. "You know nothing." This time the pitch was on the first word in the sentence. "My mother was a kind and gentle soul."

Sandman heard Elizabeth, but she sounded far away. Her voice became background noise to his own thoughts. He started to talk over the sounds of her. "I knew long before I started killing that I would kill, that it was going to end up that way. The more she touched me. The more I responded. The fantasies of her death just became too strong. It felt good. Really good." He ran his finger over the blade of the knife he still held in his hand. His breathing slowed.

Elizabeth stopped talking and sank back onto the mattress.

"After the first time, you want to get better. Your fantasies become more elaborate. You play the moment over in your head as you drift off to sleep at night." His voice was soft, as if his words were a bedtime story he had read a thousand times. "What needs to be changed next time? Done more slowly? What went well? Could I hold my hand differently for a cleaner slice, a faster death, less mess? What if I toyed with her longer, let her climax? And the next time, what if I take something to hold before I bury her, something to help me relive the moment?" He paused. In his silence, he licked his lips, remembered tucking Gina into her sandy grave. "It's all about choices, Elizabeth. Choices and control. Did you ever fantasize about killing her, Elizabeth? When she pulled your young, nightgown-clad body into hers? Did you want to hurt her?"

"Sick bastard. Who are you to presume because Katia and I were in a relationship my mother molested me?"

He felt betrayed by her words. He wasn't sick. The world was sick. The men and women who assumed women were kind and good were sick. He only wanted to save them. "Don't. Ever."

"Don't ever what?" Her body shook so hard her words came out in a vibrating tone. "Why don't you just kill me?"

For a full ten seconds, he was silent. Breathe in. Breathe out. It's all about control. My control. In. Out. "I was fifteen when I killed her, Elizabeth. My aunt. They found her bones in a dune on the beach. They don't know it yet. Maybe they never will. Can't be much of them left to go on."

She shook her head from side to side, her eyes closed. Tears streamed across dirt-crusted cheeks. "You killed her when you were fifteen?"

"I was frightened. And thrilled. And aroused. I expected to get caught. Arrested." He moved his index finger across the blade of the knife, stopping at the tip. "Open your eyes, Elizabeth."

She did.

Her chest heaved with silent sobs. "People like you deserve to die." He pushed the blade against his fingertip until one drop of blood formed on his skin. He met Elizabeth's eyes and smiled. "The arrest never came. Perhaps it was God's plan. I don't know. What I do know, Elizabeth, is the universe accepted my gifts of sinful flesh for more than thirty years. The beach kept my secrets."

He looked again at the blade in his hand and then toward Elizabeth. He moved forward and placed the tip of the blade against Elizabeth's neck. He swiveled the blade ever so slightly until it produced a blood-red starburst in the exact spot he chose as he watched her sleep in the wee hours of that morning. The exact spot he planned to return to when the time was right.

****

Elizabeth loved walking into the white of her art room. It was like living in the middle of a clean canvas full of opportunity. Her palette of colors called to her, beautiful in their rainbow of possibilities. Only recently did she choose the bright primary colors again, after a long time of being drawn to grays and blacks. Katia's colors. Elizabeth didn't want to live in the dark anymore. She needed to feel colors again. Moving to Virginia and using disposable phones and keeping a low profile had given her back her life.

There were colors, and she was happy. Her eyes opened and then there was gray, Buxton gray, like the fog swirls of early morning in the winter. She willed herself to wake up. Light was breaking through the thin veil of gray.

Someone was breathing near her. Elizabeth felt it under her skin where fear lives. Steady, calculated, methodical breathing, in and out, like the room was exhaling, feeding the monster at the edges of her thought, the monster who was, in turn, inhaling the dank darkness of the space, consuming it as he would any food. She was in the belly of the room waiting to be exhaled to feed the monster. Would he swallow her whole or chew until her bones crunched between his teeth? She tried to acclimate, to withdraw into herself. Another starburst. It was no use. She willed her eyes to stay open and follow the light and sound.

"Hi, Elizabeth."

Her insides tried to get out, through her throat, her nose, her intestines. He had a knife. In the dim light of the dank room, she could see the sharp blade rotating slowly, catching the light. Her arms felt heavy as she lifted them. Elizabeth then remembered why—she was chained. It slowly came back to her. She was painting, using all the colors of the rainbow, feeling free from the heaviness of her past, and then he was there. And there was darkness and this room and him.

"I've been waiting."

Elizabeth heard his words, but they were melting together. She felt as if she was losing control. She tried to focus. She sat on a urine-stained mattress. Not just mine, she thought. Others, too. Did they die here? No blood stains, at least none that could be seen in the dimness of the little room. How many? My mom. Was she here? She swallowed, steadied her breathing, and looked at her captor. Her body shook; her skin rippled with little bumps of fear.

Get hold of yourself. She forced her mind to focus on the walls. Gray. So much gray. There were holes in the wall where chunks of concrete were missing. Had someone tried to chip away at the prison when their captor wasn't around?

She licked her lips with a swollen tongue. She was being offered water. She didn't take it. Elizabeth wished she could put the bottle to her chapped lips without worry, but she remembered the rim of a bottle against her bottom lip, fingers on each side of her nose, pinching, the water running down her chin, into her shirt, until she opened her mouth.

More disgusting filth oozed from his mouth.

"Why?" she asked. The confusion and drug-induced stupor caused a slight slur and drawl in her voice.

"Your mother, Elizabeth. Remember? That's why you're here." His words didn't make any sense. Elizabeth's ears were ringing. She was only getting about every third sentence.

His smile made her want to puke. She needed to pee, and she wanted a drink. Her eyes burned from lack of sleep, tears, and the stench of the room. She tried to focus on his words and not the way his lips turned up as he spoke.

He kept talking. His words picked and crawled their way across her skin causing the tiny blonde hairs on her arms to stand on end. Bits of light bounced off of the knife he twirled between his fingers while he rambled on. Her eyes shifted between the glints of light and the spot she chose on the concrete wall. Do not let him get to you. Do not let him get to you.

Elizabeth looked from the twirling knife to the space next to the man who killed her mother in cold blood, killed his aunt in cold blood, and who continued to kill in cold blood. A picnic basket. What the fuck? A picnic basket?

****

Katia and Zahra sat in Katia's living room and talked about every man of the right age they could think of who lived in Buxton. Slightly before midnight, Katia noticed the weight of her eyelids. Shortly after that, she realized both she and Zahra were quiet. She blinked several times and stood. She touched Zahra's arm softly. "Hey. Wake up. It's after midnight. You better go."

Zahra took a minute to respond. "I'm not leaving. I can sleep on the couch. You got a blanket?"

"Andrew's gone. My father and brother are upstairs. Whoever did this horrible thing is probably in another state by now, at least if he knows what's good for him. You don't have to stay. I'm good."

"Look. I'm tired. You're tired. Andrew may come back. We don't know where—"

"Fine." Katia gave in. Zahra was right. They were both tired, and neither wanted to be alone. "Let's go upstairs."

Katia had no energy to argue. Besides, it felt good to have Zahra there. It also felt wrong to ask Zahra to sleep in bed with her when Elizabeth was so heavy on her mind. "You mind taking the spare room?"

"Not even slightly. I'm beat. Why in the world would I want to sleep with you?" Zahra bumped Katia's shoulder as they ascended the stairs.

Katia grinned. The response made her like Zahra even more.

****

Zahra's presence in the house calmed Katia enough for her to fall asleep and stay asleep through the night. It didn't keep away the demons.

She awoke to thoughts of death. It crawled from her belly to her throat like a snake. Gina's dead. Elizabeth's missing. She swallowed the bile that made its way into her mouth and reached for her phone. The numbers read 7:30. Seven hours. She laid the phone back on the nightstand and closed her eyes. Seven hours felt like seven minutes.

Her head relaxed against the headboard. She drifted in and out of a light sleep for several minutes before bits of the night's dreams returned. She forced her eyes open and pushed her body into a fully upright position against the pillows. The nightmare was important. She felt it, but she couldn't hold on to all of the pieces.

Marco was there, as was her dad. And then they were gone, and she was driving an ambulance, watching the speedometer. One hundred. One hundred and five. One hundred and ten. One hundred and twenty. She watched beachfront views whiz by. She was searching for Gina and Elizabeth. In the dream, she knew they were both dead.

Elizabeth is not dead.

At one point, Marco was there again. The ambulance was racing toward him. She felt like she needed to lure Marco from the Sandman. Something was at the edge of her memory. Something important. She strained to see out the window of the ambulance, but it simply wouldn't reveal itself.

Aggravated with her inability to reconstruct the night, Katia showered and dressed in a faded-gray T-shirt and black jeans and followed the smell of coffee toward the kitchen. What a strange week it was turning out to be. She was sore deep inside, the pain worse than any she experienced in the field. Katia thought about the reporters who waited outside of Marco's therapy session and the helicopter that hovered over the beach the first day. She was the woman who intimately knew the daughter of the deceased, the Buxton native who may have connections with more than one of the mysterious victims. She simultaneously wanted to protect her brother and her hometown and to run from all of it.

When she reached the kitchen, she found Zahra pouring a cup of coffee from a red warming carafe.

"Morning," Zahra said without looking away from the steaming brown liquid moving from carafe to cup.

"Never had coffee made for me at five thirty in the morning," Katia said. "In my kitchen, by a knight in shining armor." She tried to sound more okay than she felt.

"Good thing you added the, 'in my kitchen,' part." Zahra presented the coffee mug to Katia.

Katia held it in one hand, and with the other, opened the refrigerator to retrieve the vanilla creamer. The mug was printed with blue lettering. "Look beyond the autism to see the incredible." Katia turned toward the spot in front of the television where she knew her brother sat.

Zahra continued to talk.

The words weren't important. Katia was just happy that she was there saying them.

"Want some?" Katia set her mug on the counter and popped the top on the creamer.

"Indeed." Zahra held out a cup that read, "World's Best Carpenter & Dad."

"Great cup choice," Katia said. She smiled at the woman who stood before her in a gold-colored sundress and sandals. "I'm not sure how you would manage the tool belt."

"What? Are you dogging my carpentry skills?"

Katia shrugged. "Maybe. Can't say I would mind watching you climb a ladder or swing a hammer, though." She picked up her mug and headed to the table.

Zahra followed. "Can't say I would mind you watching, either. Hope I got the strength right. Figured between the shower and a strong cup of coffee, you might make it through the day."

Katia wrapped her hands around the steaming cup and brought it to her face. She closed her eyes and breathed deeply before taking the first sip. "Here's to making it through." She released one hand and let it fall into her lap, tapped mugs with Zahra, and took another sip.

The women sat quietly for a few minutes on either side of the wooden table next to the picture window in Katia's dining area. Both looked toward the beach. The view was as breathtaking as it was six days ago, but somehow Katia couldn't see it through the fog of death that settled around her.

Zahra broke the silence as Porky Pig proclaimed, "Th-th-th-that's all, folks," from the living room. "Haven't seen your dad. Marco came down, made a bowl of cereal, and turned on the TV. I assume that's ritual."

"You assume right." Katia's voice sounded as tired as she felt. She sipped her coffee and stared at the waves lapping the beach. The peaceful scene gave no indication of the horror of the last week. The two sat quietly for several minutes as the *Mighty Mouse* theme song played in the other room. Zahra, the beach, and the cartoon character who came "to save the day," mixed together to create a calm in Katia that until this moment she didn't know she needed.

"I won't ever be able to look at a dune again without wondering." Zahra appeared to be talking to the beach and not to Katia.

Katia absentmindedly ran her finger back and forth across the slightly raised ribbon of colored puzzle pieces on the side of her cup. "Me, either."

She pulled her gaze from the window and looked through to her little brother, empty cereal bowl by his side. "He has my workdays programmed in his head, like a little computer. And a clock. He has one of those built in, too. He'll bring his bowl to the sink at precisely 6:10. He will brush his teeth, get dressed, and be at the door at 6:25."

"Does he talk at all?" Zahra asked.

Katia forgot how little time they spent together before this started. "A bit. My name. Papi. Want." Katia smiled. "You know, the important things." She let her eyes wander from Marco's cross-legged posture up to his rounded shoulders. His arms hugged his sides, closed off. The little finger on his right hand tapped methodically against his right knee, the tap in perfect time to the slight rocking motion of his head, neck, and shoulders.

She looked back at Zahra. "He's still freaked about something. He isn't right."

"What can we do?"

"You know what? I appreciate you." Katia meant it. She liked Zahra. A lot.

"I'll take it." Zahra laid her hand over Katia's on the table. "And I mean it. I'm here to help. Not just through this shit, either."

Katia changed position in her chair, moved her bottom lip in and out between her teeth. She wasn't used to getting this close. She looked at their hands together. She didn't pull away. She did change the subject. "My dad leaves super early. He likes to make rounds to his sites to make sure all are making progress. He was probably gone before you even turned over this morning."

"How many sites?"

"Ten or more, I guess. His teams work their asses off in the off season. Try to get all of the repairs and shit done all up and down the island and build where there's still room to build."

"Not much left, is there? Room, I mean."

Katia took another drink of coffee. "Not like when we were kids, for sure. But people still move houses out on a regular basis and have new ones put up in their place. Probably always will."

Zahra looked where Marco sat rocking and tapping. "Is this about whatever brought you home yesterday?"

"I think so. He hasn't been right since whatever happened at the school." Katia gave Zahra the blogger's version of what she came home to, about her dad being agitated because she wasn't there when he got him home, about the doctor giving Marco a disposable camera in hopes it would calm him.

"Did he take photos?"

"Yeah. When we got home."

"How about we go have them developed? You can surprise him with them this afternoon."

"I need to talk to them at the school. See what spooked him. He loves it there. I don't get it. My dad didn't pry. Said he was leaving that to me."

"He's the parent."

Katia could tell from the abrupt way that Zahra ended the thought she wished she hadn't said it as soon as it came out of her mouth.

Katia raked her lower lip between her teeth again, using the nervous habit as a placeholder while she thought of what she wanted to say. Something told her it was okay. Zahra was safe. "I do wish he took more interest." She paused. She had never said the next sentence out loud. "He has no interest in Marco, because Marco will never be able to inherit Papi's business. He thinks that's what sons do. Instead, Marco flaps and taps and watches cartoons now just like he did when he was younger. He understands. I know he does. He just can't get it from in there to out here." Katia stopped short of telling Zahra about their arguments over special equipment for Marco and over how each of them felt Marco should be raised.

"You're a good sister."

Katia felt the heart palpitations that meant she was reaching anxiety-level high. She eased her hand out from under Zahra's. "Getting the pictures developed sounds like a great idea. Marco can finish snapping this morning at school."

Zahra stood and took their cups to the sink.

Katia stayed where she was. "I'm meeting Brent and Elliot for breakfast after I talk to the folks at the school."

Zahra obviously got the hint. "Sounds like you might need to handle a few things alone. I should check in with Dr. Webb to see when they want us back in Greenville, and I have a friend at the college I need to catch up with. How about we meet up after?"

Katia heard disappointment in Zahra's voice. She chose to ignore it. "Perfect. Say one?"

"Whenever is good. Just text. I'm off all day." Zahra's eyes moved to the clock above the sink. "Um. It's 6:15."

Katia tapped her phone to bring it to life. It also said 6:15. She looked at Zahra, her eyebrows moving in toward one another, her forehead creasing. She gazed at Marco sitting cross-legged, shoulders still rounded and little finger still tapping What the fuck? She looked again at her phone. 6:16.

"Marco?" She stood and moved toward him. When she was directly beside him, she knelt and touched his shoulder. The move would go one of two ways: Either he would turn to her and use his limited vocabulary to welcome her into his world, or he would start screeching, freaking out because she entered his world uninvited. The former would allow her to draw him out of whatever was happening. The latter would bring forth spitting, hitting, biting, or flapping. Maybe all of the above. She waited.

No change. Little finger, right hand, still tapping methodically against his right knee. The tap still in perfect time to the slight rocking motion of his head, neck, and shoulders.

"It's time for school, Marco. Marco? We have to go."

"No. no. no. Marco does not want it."

"You don't want to go to school?" She spoke in a low voice. "I'm going to talk to them. I want to know what happened."

"No. No. No. You. Kaaaaa. Tiiiii. Aa. Here. Bad. Here. One-six-six-M-P-H. One-six-six-M-P-H."

The wind speed of the hurricane, again. "What's bad at the school, Marco? Why do we need to stay here?" Katia felt so useless and frustrated. She wanted desperately to help him. She just didn't know how.

The camera. Maybe it will at least put his mind on something else before we enter into a full-blown meltdown.

She turned her attention to Zahra but stayed in a kneeling position by Marco. "Zahra. See if there are any pictures left on the camera. It's in the drawer of the computer desk. In here. In the corner."

Zahra made her way to the desk. "There are two." She picked one up. "Shit. None on this one." She reached for the other one and flipped it over in her hand. "Jackpot."

"Hey, Monkey Head. Want to tell me a story?"

Marco's tapping slowed and then stopped. He reached for the camera.

"Go ahead. Snap away."

Marco put his eye to the hole in the back of the camera, pointed the lens at Katia, and pushed the shutter release button. "Ka. Ti. A. Stay."

"Yes. I'll stay."

Katia phoned the school to let them know Marco wouldn't be in. She didn't mention his meltdown. She wanted to talk to them in person. Fewer things were miscommunicated that way. Then she texted Elliot to see if he and Brent could come by the house instead of meeting for breakfast. *Really want to hear latest station buzz*, she typed when Elliot responded they could do it another day.

No buzz to tell. Men in blue are all out taking reports of every strange or suspicious incident that residents can remember.

Some are contacting vacationers who stayed in the beach houses during times they are attaching to disappearances.

Anything stand out?

Nothing yet. Have you talked to Zahra? How goes the bone work?

She's here. I'll fill you in later. Nothing on bones.

"I'm so sorry. I know you have things to do," she said to Zahra as she punched letters on her phone's keyboard. "I can still meet you at one. I'll just have Marco in tow. Looks like the guys aren't coming here. Sounds like they both want to get home."

"I'll go in and check on the doc, meet with my friend. She teaches classes on profiling in the criminal justice program. Maybe I can find something to help." Zahra moved back into the kitchen and picked up the coffee cups.

"I'll get that after I calm the beast." Katia motioned toward Marco, who was mid-snap of a great picture of the doorknob leading to the garage. "And there you have it, ladies and gentlemen," she said in her best announcer voice. "Marco's doorknob masterpiece." She shook her head. "I'm not convinced the pictures can tell us a thing, but at least they're calming him down."

Chapter Fourteen

Friday, November 23, 2018

Zahra arrived at the large, brick building that housed the office of Dr. Harper Iacovelli. She used to love to visit here. Now it was a place to explore the psychological workings of a serial killer on the loose in Buxton—nothing more. Try as she might to avoid it, Zahra was falling for a certain tomboy Latina in a big way. When this was behind them, she planned to tell Katia that she couldn't think of being with anyone else, not even Harper.

In the five years since Harper kicked Zahra to the curb, the two women spent eight nights tangled in what Harper called "comfort sex." Zahra knew Harper had no idea how many nights they spent together. It meant no more to her than exactly what she called it: comfort. For Zahra it signified hope that the two of them would eventually find their way back to one another, at least it did until Zahra reunited with Katia at The Pink Clover.

As she stood in front of the red bricks, Zahra realized she hadn't spoken to Harper since the first night she spent with Katia. Now she needed to get up the courage to face Harper. She looked straight up the wall of the old building and back down to the glass doors. Butterflies be damned.

Harper's office was tastefully decorated with a deep-chocolate, wood desk and matching round table. In the table's exact center was a decorative, black, square bowl swirled with reds and tans. Zahra silently counted her steps until she was close enough to touch the fresh fruit that filled the bowl. "Thanks for agreeing to see me." She waited for the woman in the black pantsuit, white button-down shirt, and red skinny tie to ask her to sit.

"Hi, Zahra. Sit down." Harper motioned to one of the chairs that faced her desk.

"Thanks." Zahra glanced at the large piece of contemporary art that hung behind Harper's desk. The four women—almost caricature, almost real—danced in a whirl of reds and blues.

Harper would have been at home with the women in the picture.

"I have a class at 11:15," Harper said. "Until then, I'm yours. It's good to see you. Are you doing okay?"

Harper's red lips formed perfect words. Zahra willed herself to look at the fruit instead.

"I cannot even imagine what it must be like to have that many decedents at once. I bet Dr. Webb is exhausted. And of course, you, too."

"I'm okay," Zahra replied. "Doc and I worked some in Greenville. He made me take today off. Forensic anthropologists are all over. I think a crime scene investigator from a small town is just in the way."

"Does that make you angry?" Harper asked. "You sound irritated."

"Just aggravating to have so many people around. Can't keep up with what's happening. This is our fu…" Zahra caught herself. Harper didn't curse. She didn't tolerate it in her office. "Sorry. My bad. It's just frustrating to not be in control of the room. That's all."

"So. You indicated you wanted to bounce some ideas off of me."

Zahra nodded.

Harper opened a drawer of her desk and pulled out two waters. She put one in front of Zahra. "You cannot take what I say as gospel. Just because I teach classes on profiling does not mean anybody in your world wants to hear me tell it."

Harper also refused to use contractions, which made Zahra feel as if conversations took twice as long, and like Harper tormented her on purpose.

"I know," Zahra said. "I just want to get an idea about the organization of the killer. The reports we created from what we know so far show a thirty-year span of time with large intervals."

"He's organized. He isn't impulsive or haphazard. Thirty years is a long time for someone to kill in a small place like Buxton. It is an even longer time to do so without being apprehended. What are the intervals? Do you have a timeline?"

Zahra looked at Harper's hands as they rested, entwined, on her desk. Thumbs up and touching at the tips, glossy red to glossy red. Her long, honey-colored waves of perfectly groomed hair framed her slender face, and her emerald eyes had the darkest orbs at their center Zahra had ever seen. She was breathtakingly debonair. No one could deny that.

Zahra was a struggling student when they met, and she wasn't then or now what anyone would call debonair. She loved to let her bouncy, umber coils puff out naturally around her face, and though quite feminine in looks and actions, she preferred her nails short and her clothes comfy.

She pulled the timeline information from her bag and put it on the tidy desk.

Harper let out a low whistle as she ran her finger down the page. "Fourteen people over thirty years without being seen, without leaving telltale clues, without making mistakes. That is impressive."

"Truth." Zahra nodded. "Do you think it has to be a Buxton resident? I think it must. How else could he get away with it?"

"If not Buxton, I would say Hatteras Island. It is someone who blends in, leads a seemingly stable life. Someone methodical and intelligent." She studied the timeline for several minutes.

Zahra already knew it by heart. She was the one to painstakingly add the information to the computer as it was determined.

Harper started thinking aloud. "Let us go with thirty years for the first kill, subject to adjustment later. Based on how well we can determine time with today's technology, let us assume the gap time is correct. Something happened to pull his attention away from his surroundings and help him redirect. A marriage. Returning to school. Perhaps moving away for a while."

That was something Zahra hadn't really thought about. Shit. There could be other bodies in other places anywhere. "Do you think we should be looking in other places?"

"I am sure the FBI's profilers are coming to the same conclusion. They will likely do something to rule that out."

"Or not." Zahra let out a breath and shook her head.

"Yes. Or not." Harper continued. "All but one of the victims is female. All of them are Caucasian. He is likely seeing them as resembling someone who has harmed him in his youth, someone who has the same traits as that person."

"Someone with a mom complex? He's killing his mom over and over again?" Zahra leaned forward in her chair. Harper did know how to weave intrigue.

"It is hard to say, based on the decomp and incomplete data. I would lean more toward it being about a particular act rather than the actual person. According to this, each decedent already identified is different." Harper ran her bright red nail across the pages on her desk. She leaned back in her chair. "Here is the thing that stands out to me. There are varying ages, different hair color, length. And there is the boy, which adds an interesting element. He was buried with the teacher. Perhaps he was in the wrong place at the wrong time, but I doubt it. He will likely prove to be a huge clue to the solving of this."

"Like the boy could be a representative of someone or something?" Zahra's mind was racing. This was exactly what had drawn her to Harper.

"I would say quite possibly a representative of himself. He was likely an older teen the first time he killed."

Zahra didn't mention the knife found with the first victim. She debated with herself as to whether or not she should. Harper was trustworthy with any information shared and she wouldn't breathe a word of it outside of this room. Zahra decided it was worth the risk to see where it would lead them. "The first victim, the one from thirty years ago. We uncovered a knife with her body. No one else had that, not that we've found anyway, and Paige and Bob's pup was all over that strip of sand."

Harper didn't answer. She just let that information sit in the air between them.

Zahra looked at the swirls on the bowl and in the picture and back at Harper. She played with the hem of her shirt and thought about all of the forty-plus men she knew across the islands that made up Hatteras. The area was small, relatively speaking, but that was still a shit load of men. And then there was Katia, the woman she crushed on since high school. What part did she play? Why Gina? Why was Elizabeth missing now? How did they all connect to a death thirty or more years ago?

Harper leaned over the pages on her desk, still quiet. Zahra could almost hear the wheels turning in the older woman's head. Finally, Harper looked directly at Zahra. Her words were calculated. "The last body, Gina's body, was in the dune for approximately two weeks."

Zahra nodded.

"It is November. It is a time when the beaches are bare save the fishermen and women at particular times of the day and the occasional bonfire and volleyball game." Harper paused.

"What does that have to do with the knife?" Zahra's hands rested on her knees, now, and her full attention was on Harper.

"Maybe nothing. But I can tell you this. Your guy likely kills at the same time of year unless provoked in some way. The same time he killed the first time. Reliving the kill. He is likely a survivor of abuse. And your first victim is likely his abuser. As for the knife? My best guess is that, as a teenager, he felt he could not keep it."

****

Paige awoke to the wet tongue of Frankie on her hand. It had been over a year since she had a dog in the house. The German shepherds she trained and used in her work weren't allowed inside her home. They stayed in the training facility. "Are you hungry, little fella?" She moved her hand around to the small mutt's head and scratched behind his ears, which perked up at the sound of her voice.

She picked her smart watch from its charger, attached it around her wrist, and tapped the face. 5:17 flashed on the screen. "I wouldn't mind having you around all the time," Paige said. "But you would need to learn the days of the week." She pulled him in for a squeeze. "Adulting doesn't start as early on the weekend."

Frankie gave her a few seconds and then wiggled free, jumped to the ground, and headed toward the bedroom window. He looked back at Paige and barked.

"What is it, boy? Do you hear the shepherds in the facility? They can't tell time, either, can they?"

Frankie took a few steps toward the bed and then back toward the window, repeating the action several times. "Come on, Frankie. It's too early. There's nothing out there you need."

Frankie whined his response.

Oh well. Paige stretched and moved around to get her blood flowing. "Fine," she said. "I'm up. I'll take you out in two minutes." She stretched one last time and headed to the bathroom.

She sipped iced tea on her small, enclosed porch and browsed her notes from the work on Buxton Beach. Her copy of the recordings and the painstakingly accurate transcriptions helped her deconstruct each scene, each move she and the dog made, each command given, and how it was followed. In turn, this helped her create the best facility on the East Coast.

She drained the last of the tea from her cup and sat her pen on top of the notes on the small wicker table next to her rocker. She thought about Frankie's reaction to the noise in the training facility. In addition to the three dogs she and Bob were currently training for a police facility in Tennessee, they had three dogs they used for search and rescue missions.

Derrida was the oldest and semi-retired. She named him after the writer of *Cogito and the History of Madness.* Jacques Derrida was a philosopher whose work was cerebral and difficult, much like the work of a cadaver dog.

Voltaire came to her by way of a breeder in South Carolina who said he was too difficult to train as a cadaver dog. She took him anyway. She chose to name him after the great philosopher who spent much time in exile.

The youngest of the trio was Nietzsche. He was her favorite. The gorgeous, large, black-and-tan German shepherd who worked tirelessly for two days on the beach was named after a man known for his tenacity and intellectual prowess, traits also seen in the four-legged namesake.

Paige picked the pen and pages back up. She could spend thirty more minutes with the transcripts before she needed to head to the facility. The farther into the retracing of steps, of terrain, the more Paige found herself making the same notes: "Area of sand between dune and sand wall, area of sand between two dunes with a fence to the right, area of sand shows signs of depression behind long stretch of dunes." In every instance of a burial, there was an area where someone could have easily gone unnoticed by anyone passing by. In every single instance.

Paige had no idea whether or not this information was of any importance, and she suspected the police and FBI already noted it, but she would reach out to Zahra with the information, just in case.

She looked over at Frankie, who repeatedly picked a piece of food out of his bowl, carried it to the feet of his current master, chewed loudly, and repeated the ritual. "You're a strange sort, Frankie," she said. "Cheap amusement. I like that. Wonder what your new momma is up to? Shall we text her? Perhaps she's still sleeping since she doesn't have a small yippee alarm clock." She looked at her watch. 6:50. Before she could decide if it was too early to call, her arm vibrated and her phone lit up with her brother's smiling face.

"Hey. What's up?"

"Come down to the training facility," Bob said. "Someone's been here and our records and transcripts are all over the place."

Paige heard something else in his voice. A shiver moved through her skin. "What aren't you saying?"

"Voltaire's dead."

Paige felt her heart drop to her feet. Voltaire had a cold. She had put him in the main facility last night to keep him away from the other animals. "Dead? How? It was just a cold." The reality of what her brother was saying wasn't sinking into her morning brain.

"There's blood everywhere," Bob replied. His voice sounded frantic, filled with pain. "I didn't hear anything until the other dogs started barking. Thought it was a rabbit or something poking around their cages. Took my time. Fuck, Paige. I took my time."

"Don't touch anything." Paige was already standing. She debated on whether or not to leave the current transcripts spread across the table. Decided against it in case whoever did this was still close. She looked down at Frankie. "Is that what you heard, boy? Were they outside?"

In the time it took her to slide her feet into her boots and run the distance between her home and the facility, she had played a multitude of scenarios through her mind. None of them prepared her for what she found when she made her way through the animal obstacle course and to the office door. Pieces of paper were strewn from wall to wall, wall to door, across the small desk. One of three filing cabinets laid on its side next to the phone, which was ripped from the wall and shattered, its insides spilling across the cement floor. In the middle lay Voltaire, his coat now a crimson red. Paige knelt next to her beloved pet. Tears dripped from her chin and landed on his sweet face. She slid her hand under his head, lifted gently, kissed his nose. The smell of blood almost overpowered her senses. "I love you, old man." She kissed his snout and eased his head back to the ground, careful to keep her knee and foot out of the pool of red.

Bob stood off to the side. "Looks like his throat was slit wide open." He stood with his arms crossed over his chest. His fingers massaged his triceps.

"Who would do this? Why?" She couldn't think clearly.

"They wanted something. Voltaire obviously startled whoever it was. Best I can tell they didn't take anything."

Brother and sister remained still as the sound of sirens drew near.

****

"I'm going to kill you now, Elizabeth." His words were said with little enthusiasm. He was tired. Death took massive amounts of planning, sometimes years. Gina Dahl's death was seven years in the making: seven years of thought; seven years of watching. Hers was the longest. Of the more than twenty women and one boy he killed, she was the most time consuming. It wasn't because she deserved the extra years to live and pretend, but because she was the most visible in the community, the most vocal at events, the most easily missed. Thinking about it now was tiring. "I'm sorry it won't be a more appropriate death. I do like to enjoy them. Your mom has ruined that for us, though, showing up so soon." He moved the blade in his hand and watched the starburst play across her neck, trying to position it at the exact spot where he would slice.

Elizabeth stayed quiet.

They often said nothing when they knew it was time.

He stood a foot in front of her and waited. The room smelled like fear and urine and blood. It seeped out of the pores of the walls. He breathed deeply. "The paper said fourteen." He spoke in Elizabeth's direction but not really to her. "There are more, you know. Not all here. Fifteen here. You'll make sixteen. Well, seventeen, if you count the goddamn dog I killed this morning. Stupid creatures. Noses that won't stop. Bark at everything." His eyes met hers. Hers looked to be filled with so much anger. "Are you angry, Elizabeth? You should be. Angry at her." He paused. "I wonder who they missed?"

Sandman pondered his latest adventure. He had traveled into Manteo, to the edge of the property owned by ancestors of Paige and Bob Johnston. He walked from a half mile out in order to go unnoticed. Getting in was effortless. He easily jimmied the door, and the file cabinets were unlocked behind what the idiot brother and sister assumed was the safety of the office door.

"I went in search of a file this morning. And the damn file wasn't there. Not mine. Not the one detailing my hard work. All I found was an obnoxious dog."

Elizabeth visibly shivered. He smiled.

"The dog was a surprise. I didn't see that coming. Course, he didn't see this, either." He held the sharp blade up high so the light brought it more clearly into focus. "Thought the fur and thick skin might make it harder. It didn't." He pulled the knife through the air quickly, making a "fwoosh" sound through his teeth. "Like slicing through butter."

Elizabeth began to shake harder. Even in the dimness of the small concrete room, he could see the increase in movement.

"They took my bones, my work, and they left me with nothing but a goddamn dog to kill. That makes me angry, Elizabeth." He rubbed his temples in tiny circles. He didn't like to kill animals. He didn't like to kill without a plan. There was so much wrong with this week, so much cleanup. "I deserve to know who's still out there. Her transcripts would have told me. How dare she not file them appropriately? How dare she?" His agitation built. "I thought about going into her house. Paige, the dog whisperer. But those canine crusaders made such a racket that I left. We're going to have to finish up soon. I have so much to do. So much to do."

He took a few deep breaths. So important to plan. Think. He watched her chest heave as she apparently tried not to cry, tried not to give in to her need to scream. That calmed him. He was in control. Everything was okay. He was actually enjoying this part more than he anticipated, even in his exhausted state. But he couldn't linger much longer.

"Your ride will be here soon, Elizabeth," Sandman said. "You'll travel to Ocracoke, where people feel safe and secure, secluded from the world. I made the arrangements before I came today. A ride in a covered truck bed on the ferry. You'll be buried in a dune at the end of the island. I'm sorry for that, too, Elizabeth. I would like to have you here, with the others. But it's impossible." Sandman remembered the swarms of police and rescue workers, his aggravation as he watched them wade through the flooded beach. So many people on our island the last six days. So many dogs sniffing and people poking, disregarding the need for order and respect for the beach.

One tear escaped Elizabeth's left eye and ran down her dusty cheek.

Finally. Full recognition of her fate. "Elizabeth." He reached down to the basket at his side and opened the lid. "My auntie and I picnicked together on the day she died. There was a storm off the coast. The wind felt good on my bare skin. So good…" His voice trailed off into a dreamy pause. He reached in and pulled out two cans of beer. He stacked one on top of the other and popped the top of the first. He held it toward his captive. "Would you like a beer, Elizabeth?"

No words from the mattress in the dimly lit room, and now almost no movement. The shaking had completely stopped. If not for the tear and the slight rise of her chest as she breathed in and out, he might have thought she died sitting up, legs crossed, fists shoved into the creases of the back of her knees.

"Suit yourself." He put the unopened can back in the basket, moved the open can to his lips, and sucked the foam from the opening. His stomach held a restless energy. He knew it was time, yet he toyed with her, missing the formulation of a well-orchestrated plan. Six days wasn't enough. "You have to be thirsty, Elizabeth."

Sandman would miss saying her name. It was one of his favorites, second only to Judith. He remembered the woman from long ago. It was in New York, while vacationing with his parents. They wouldn't find her amongst the Buxton bones. That kill was spontaneous, like this one, too quick to plan. He closed his eyes and leaned his head back against the cement wall. He could hear her voice in his head. Georgie. Hold Aunt Judith's hand. No. Like this. The way she intertwined their fingers, the way the young boy looked at her. That's right, sweet Georgie. The two walked hand-in-hand to a hotel in a seedy part of New York. Sandman followed.

Hug me, Georgie. Her head leaning down to rest against his, her words almost too soft for him to hear.

Sandman waited and watched. She sent the boy up ahead, stayed down for a smoke. It was easy to offer a light and a walk.

He left her body at the bottom of a dumpster, and the next day, he traveled home with his family. He missed having her near.

He opened his eyes, opting to keep Judith tucked away inside himself. Instead, he talked about Helen. Her they would find in Buxton. "After my aunt, I didn't kill for a while. The psych-babblers have that part right. We can be satisfied with reliving the moment over in our heads for quite some time as long as something doesn't trigger us. Helen was my trigger, at least the one after my aunt. She lured boys into her home, boys like Sammy, who I babysat for when I was in high school. He was a sweet kid, unsuspecting. He never had a chance."

Elizabeth stared at him, unmoving.

"She was easy. You just have to know your prey. She knew the young boys. I knew her. No one even started questioning her whereabouts until she lay in her dune for almost two weeks. I was a kid with no record, good grades, a quiet disposition. She was a recluse with no known family in the area. Sammy told me about her letting him drink." He paused, remembering Sammy's innocence. He took a sip of his own beer and wiped his mouth with the back of his hand. When he did, the blade held loosely in his fist sent a prism across the shadowy room.

"She let me drink, you know, my aunt, that is. That's how they get you." He made a sound of disgust and changed his voice to something resembling an older southern woman. "Only beer, Little Man. Wouldn't want you getting addicted to hard liquor, now would we?" He tilted the can and drank, not stopping until he finished half of what the can contained.

"Did your mom let you drink, Elizabeth? Did she force you and Katia when you were teenagers? Did it make you feel better about what you were doing?"

"She. Didn't. Do. Anything." Elizabeth's voice was louder than he anticipated it would be when she finally gave in and spoke. Her words throbbed in his temples. It felt good.

Sandman reached back into the basket and pulled out rope and plastic and laid it to his other side. He watched her reaction, felt her fear increase, felt the walls breathe it in and add it to the fear that already lived there.

"Why won't you listen?" Elizabeth's voice cracked. "She is…"

He waited. Excitement built.

"She was. My mom was supportive. She never touched me in any way that was inappropriate. She didn't make me gay. I didn't make Katia gay. I am gay. Katia is gay. She was supportive because it's the twenty-first century and everyone has a right to be who they are. Straight. Gay. Bi. Trans. Gender fluid. She loved me. She. Loved. Me…" Her voice trailed off again, but not before he heard the catch in her words.

He could tell she was trying to save her own life, trying to get him to buy into her lies. Sandman looked at her, and this time it was he who didn't respond right away. Partly because he wanted to see if she would say anything else, and partly because he was reveling in the fact she gave in and gave him this gift. Their begging, pleading, rationalizing, fed him in a way nothing in any of the twenty-plus picnic baskets he prepared ever had. When he did speak, it was in a soft, satisfied voice.

"Gina loved you. You loved Katia. My auntie loved me. That much we have established." He put the can to his lips and pulled the last drizzle of brown liquid into his mouth. He made a soft slurping sound. He bent the empty can in his other fist and set it on the floor.

"I will be ready for you shortly, Elizabeth. I need to get our blanket ready." He stood and moved through the doorway to the second of two rooms in the small underground area. He planned the space carefully. He killed ten women in this room over the years. Each time, he improved, perfecting the ritual. He went through the steps: Lay down the plastic. Pull it just so to cover the tile. Leave bare the drain.

He heard Elizabeth behind him. Her chains scraped the lacquered, concrete floor as she tried to break free. Why do they all try? Spread the red-and-black-checkered picnic blanket. Smooth out the wrinkles. Wrinkles annoyed him, made him less satisfied with the moment of release. This situation was a wrinkle, one he was going to have to maneuver carefully.

He set the basket on the edge of the sink, making sure it was balanced evenly across the two sides it touched. He almost didn't add the sink when he laid out the plans for the room. It protruded from the wall. It required a faucet and pipes that couldn't easily be concealed. It was important the women had nothing they could use to harm themselves. In the end, he decided it was worth the minimal risk. He chose a heavy concrete base he could build right into the wall and a spout that did the same. To the right of the spout was a single button that, when pushed, produced a stream of water.

Nothing to adjust, nothing to dislodge. It served him well, as had the large, shower area with its varnish-covered sides and bottom, large drain, and large, removable showerhead. He smiled at his ingenuity as he thought about the time taken to figure out how high up the wall to place the head to ensure his guest couldn't reach to remove it from its place.

He opened the basket and pulled out the plastic and the blanket. It was just like the one he brought to lie on with his aunt. Time for a picnic. He hung the blanket over the edge of the basket and eyed the plastic, looking for the end with the small pinholes that were cut to fit perfectly over the drain. He could already feel the warm blood pooling around his legs and ass, feel it moving slowly toward the drain, the holes allowing for a slow release of the fluids.

When he was satisfied with the positioning, he moved back to the basket to retrieve the blanket. He closed his eyes, enjoying the feel of the fabric that initiated the ritual. So thoughtful, Little Man. Auntie loves you so. He took the blanket edges in his hands and flicked his wrists to fan out the fabric. The unrestricted parts of the blanket puffed out and floated down, coming to rest in the area that was slightly lower than the rest of the room, the area with a showerhead and a drain, the area where he washed the blood away after each guest.

He repeated the ritual between shower and basket until he secured each corner of the picnic area with silver duct tape and put the cheese, bread, and knife within reach of his place on the blanket. In death, others live. In death, others live. In death, others live. In death, others live. In death…

His whispered chant eased and stopped. Look, Auntie. Perfect.

He returned to the room where Elizabeth waited. Her eyes held the knowledge of her impending death. Wild. Afraid. “Do you want to confess your sins, Elizabeth?”

He stood, studied her face for a full ten seconds. “Very well. I’m going to unlock your feet and hands from the chains, but I’m not going to remove the chains from around them. If you don’t fight me, I’ll give you the dignity of walking to the picnic area. If you fight, I’ll take you by whatever means necessary. Do you understand?”

Her eyes widened, and her chest rose and fell quickly. He could tell she was debating his words, deciding. He looked down at her, the air in the room growing stuffy. Two more steps. Kneeling, hands moving toward the lock, key at the ready.

She spat, the bubbly white strand missing what he presumed was its mark and landing on her own leg. She looked from the wetness to his face and back again. Her hair hung in strands on either side of her chin. She didn’t look up again.

Chapter Fifteen

Andrew sat at a table overlooking the Pamlico Sound. Across from him was Gerald Wells, the assistant director for the FBI Cyber Crimes Division. To his right stood a young man, poised, pen and pad in hand, ready to take their order.

"Good afternoon," the young waiter said, looking from one to the other of the two men. "Welcome to Café Pamlico."

Andrew motioned for Gerald to go first.

"Water with lemon for me," Gerald said.

"Same. No lemon."

Gerald's eyes scanned the menu. "These vegetables really from your own garden?"

"Yes, sir."

"You wash the dirt off before you cook them?"

"Sir?"

"Kidding, kid. Kidding." Gerald pointed at the menu. "Give me the crab."

Andrew realized two things as he listened to the two men banter back and forth about the menu. One, his boss was a condescending ass, and, two, he himself felt a duty to the people in this town. He dare not say anything, but he was relieved when Gerald ordered and shut up.

The two men made small talk while they waited for their meal of fresh crab cakes and potatoes from the cafe's garden.

"What do people do here in November?" Gerald asked. "I drove in on that two-lane road and felt like I was driving into a ghost town." He tucked his tie between two buttons on his shirt as he spoke.

The tie was worth more than most of the folks on the island made in a week. The assistant director had no point of reference for the community building he witnessed on the island. "Some kiteboarding and windsurfing. And lots of fishing. Lots. November and December are prime months."

Andrew tried fishing several times on Cape Point at low tide. It was Brent's and Elliot's favorite spot. They went on and on about catching blue fish and sea trout. All he could think about at the time was trying to stay balanced in the ridiculous thigh-high fishing boots. Now he wished he paid more attention. He didn't particularly care for Brent, but he found Elliot to be a good all-around guy, even if he was one of the most boring he ever met. If there was bad-mouthing to be done, he would decide when it was appropriate.

The waiter sat a plate in front of each man. "Can I get you anything else, gentlemen?"

Gerald answered for both of them. "No."

The young man retreated. Andrew said, "You could be a bit more pleasant."

"Fucking lagoon life." Gerald pointed with his fork toward the window to his left before maneuvering the squashed potato and butter that rested on the tines to his mouth.

"It's not so bad," Andrew replied.

"Says the man who has lived in his computer for years. Since when do you think being in the land of people…" Gerald paused, looked around the empty dining area, shrugged. "The land of few people, isn't bad?"

"Not as horrible as I thought when you asked me to take it on last year." Andrew stopped to put a piece of crab cake in his mouth and continued while he chewed. "Some of the best seafood I've ever eaten. Nobody much messes with me. They think I'm a bit off." He gave a crooked smile and widened his eyes.

Gerald told Andrew once that he reminded him of Ichabod Crane with his pointy nose and long neck. Now Andrew pushed his shoulders down and stretched his neck as far as he could. He opened his hand wide, put it in front of his own face, palm in, and made a circular motion. "All this? All this and a few inappropriately placed comments? Well, let's just say I'm not a town favorite."

"You play your part well," Gerald said. "Just don't play it too well. We need an in. And soon."

"I'm in," Andrew said. "I just need to somehow make my obsession with the morbid a bit clearer. Damn bodies at the beach didn't help. Everyone's going to be on high alert."

"You think it's connected with our baby porn and death whacko?"

"Such a way with words, Gerald. Can't say, but the sick shit I have access to online is beach and dune centered. Whoever's taking them loves the sand." Andrew took a drink of his water.

He secured the position as an undercover agent for the FBI's narcotics and violent crimes division several years prior. His focus was dark web crime. This time, that focus forced him out of the safety of the Internet and into the Hatteras Island EMS, an assignment he argued against when first presented with it.

He had pointed out tons of reasons for not getting assigned to Buxton Beach as a paramedic, not least of which was the years he had spent away from the business of saving the lives of his fellow marines.

Yet, here he sat, across from the man who had insisted his background was exactly why he was the perfect person to take on the persona of a slightly creepy newcomer to the quiet little piece of the Outer Banks known as Buxton.

Gerald thought it was his power over him that ultimately made Andrew agree to the job, but it wasn't. It was actually Andrew's parents, who decided to sell their home and kick him out, that sealed the deal.

The assignment forced him to leave the obscurity of his room and the darkness of Tor, where you are a click away from guns, drugs, and far worse, and to enter the face-to-face world where he bounced between sleepy serenity and siren-screaming, tires-screeching, adrenaline-pumping ambulance driving and bad-guy chasing. He found it suited him.

When Andrew finished his bachelor's degree in 2013, he never dreamed he would be a small town emergency worker putting his paramedic skills to use to catch a criminal who plastered the dark web with anonymous exploits of rape and murder. But his exceptional hacking abilities and his blurring of dark and light in a way that kept him barely on the side of right, made him an integral part of the FBI narcotics-and-violent-crimes task force.

Andrew currently had two identities. Agent Hunter, a man focused on bringing criminals to justice, and "The Darker the Better" Andrew Hunter, who worked virtually with evil to monitor evil. Some days he thought he might be a little too comfortable in the second skin, but he never dwelled on that.

Before coming to Buxton, Andrew was recognized for preserving the integrity of a bust in one of the largest child pornography websites found on the dark web to date. In that instance, he went deeper than he had ever gone before and had seen things he would never be able to wipe from his mind. He also found evidence that someone here on this island might be connected to some of the images on that bulletin board website. With that site shut down, hints of new sites popped up throughout the dark web, but they were buried deep, deeper than even Andrew was currently able to navigate. The mastermind was still on the loose, and if clues proved true, he was close by.

Until they found the person or persons responsible for obtaining and maintaining the new sites, millions of people would continue to obtain the deviant material they desired at the expense of millions who may not even know they were being exploited.

"What's on your mind?" Wells said. "I know it isn't singing 'Kumbaya' around a campfire with the locals."

"Thinking about the Lullaby bust, actually. I've managed to find my way into the invitation-only site, but being invited in beyond the bullshit outer layer has proven to be more of a challenge."

"You do love a challenge. What's the wall?" Gerald asked around the final bite of sweet local crab.

"The person who goes by Ted who may be anyone except Ted." Andrew placed emphasis on the word "except." "That's who's keeping me out. At least out of anything worth a flying fuck." Andrew took a deep breath. He wanted to find this man and chop his nuts off. "He let me in, but only on the fringe." So far, Andrew knew the person behind the pictures was near a beach and had access to emergency equipment, including an ambulance.

"It's a sick fuck who gets off on death." Gerald folded his napkin and laid it on his plate. "And you need to find him. Connected to this other shit or not."

Andrew looked across the table at Wells and then turned his gaze out the window at the Pamlico Sound. His next words were pointed away from the two men, as if he wanted to save them the ugliness of the human condition he was coming to know in ways even he hadn't guessed. "He reached out to me recently," he said. "He got me deeper into the onion. Not all of the way, but deeper. I'm peeling layers."

Gerald put his elbows on the table and leaned forward. "Layers you think may reveal a connection to what's happening on the beach?"

"Maybe." Andrew pulled the cloth napkin from his lap, put it over his mouth, and cleared his throat. He debated on how much to share with his boss. Gerald was the only man who knew the depths of his involvement in any undercover operation. This included the one that put Andrew in the center of darkness that now swirled around Buxton, North Carolina. Now he was here to check up on him. That didn't sit well with Andrew.

Andrew took a breath and moved his gaze back to Gerald. "You know my past. You know that in my purgatory-life between military and undercover, I wrote code for people who could wipe me away without a trace." He shifted in his seat. He wasn't scared, but he damn sure understood the risk. "I made connections between people who traded guns for drugs, drugs for absurd sexual favors, absurd sexual favors for power. You have to trust that I know what I'm doing."

Gerald was silent, but he offered Andrew a slight nod.

The waiter returned and looked straight at Gerald. "Would you like dessert?"

Gerald shook his head. "Just the check. Together, please. Thanks."

When the waiter was out of earshot, Andrew said, "Last night I spent hours scouring pictures and videos of some of the most sickening graphics I've ever seen, trying to find clues to who's behind everything. I need more time."

"Time is something we may not have much of." Gerald motioned to the scene outside the window. "Some sick motherfucker provided your sick motherfucker a candy store of picture opportunities."

Gerald was good at his job. But running a team wasn't the same as working as part of the team. Andrew needed his boss to understand. "Gerald." Andrew's voice lowered, and he met his boss's gaze. "My involvement just became about a lot more than whether or not a local is the sick fuck supplying the juice for our dark web, death-porn sites."

Gerald waited.

"You know I've been watching Brent Grainger and his EMS pals for this."

Gerald placed his elbows on the white paper that lined the tabletop. His fingers formed a steeple that leaned against his chin. "And?"

Gerald wanted the "So what?" of the statement. "I plan to tell him I was quite aroused at the scene, that I never saw anything like it, that situations like that are why I became an emergency worker." Andrew leaned back in his chair and rubbed his hand on his chin. "There's more."

"Figured." Gerald tapped the tips of his fingers together.

Andrew heard the impatient tone loud and clear. "Some of the pictures I've been privy to in the last week show a woman with her throat slashed wide open. She's lying on a beach." He paused while the waiter moved back toward the table and presented the check.

"A man in dark-blue work pants is straddling her. Can't make out her face or his, but she's blonde."

"EMS life definitely gives him access." Wells took a deep breath in and exhaled loudly.

"He's smart. Blurs his close-ups just enough to prevent recognition."

"But…"

"Yeah. I know. We may be looking for more than one person on this little bitty island."

****

Katia stood behind Marco, watching Yogi Bear trying to steal a picnic basket. She allowed him to have a large glass of thick, sweet *horchata de chufa* while he watched, hoping the tiger nut cinnamon milk would call forth thoughts of their mother and help him to re-center. The beverage was their mother's favorite. It was also Marco's. The tiger nuts needed for the drink demanded a twenty-four-hour soak before the process of grinding and sweetening could even begin. Katia hated the chore but loved the memory of her mom's stories of grinding the nuts and cinnamon by hand back in her home country when she was a young girl. She looked down at her now still brother with his milky mustache. His camera sat next to his right knee. She whispered, "I wish she was here with us, Monkey Head."

In response, her not-so-little brother lifted his empty glass over his head and said, "More sweet?"

"Hmm. Taking advantage of your distraught sister, are you?" She took the glass.

Marco dropped his hand back into his lap without another word.

Katia was handing her brother a second glass of the feel-good beverage when her phone buzzed. The text was from Zahra.

How's Marco?

Katia typed, *Calmer. Took every pic on cam.*

Want 2 talk.

Katia looked at the time. 1:00. There was that punctuality thing again. She assumed it was part of being a cop. She didn't want to take her brother to the school, but she wanted time to talk to Zahra without fear of Marco's reaction. Perhaps Mrs. Ellington, their neighbor, would look after him. She was widowed a few years back and never turned away a chance to care for someone.

Katia's phone buzzed with another text. *No worries if you can't. I get it.*

The corners of Katia's mouth turned upward. She visualized a worrywart Zahra on the other end of the texts. She genuinely cared and never wanted to cause undue stress. It was one of the things Katia found herself drawn to these days. Also the hugs. Katia wasn't a hugger, but when Zahra hugged, she hugged with her whole body. Her hugs told a story. It was a perfect depiction of how she approached life. Katia liked that, too.

Katia put an end to Zahra's suffering and responded. *No. Thinking. Give me 5.*

Roger that. Zahra followed her words with lots of symbols—a smiley face, yellow heart, blue heart, red heart, and green heart.

Katia dismissed the text box and hit the little phone icon on her screen. "Mrs. Ellington," she said when the line was answered. "This is Katia."

"Oh, honey," Mrs. Ellington said before Katia could finish. "I heard about our Gina."

"Yes, ma'am." Katia made sure her words were even and slow. She knew Mrs. Ellington would have it no other way.

"Can't say it's too big a shock. You know, with all of those houses she takes people in and out of."

Katia ran her fingers through her hair and walked toward the kitchen. "That's what I'm calling about, Mrs. Ellington. I need to meet with the criminal investigator."

"That sweet Knots girl? What's her name? Saw her momma just last week in town."

"Yes, ma'am. Zahra. Can Marco hang out with you?" She hoped the woman wouldn't ask about the school.

"The world isn't like it used to be. Real pity about Gina. Such a nice woman."

"She was, Mrs. Ellington."

"You bring Marco right on over, honey. I was just about to whip up some lunch. I'll turn on his channel."

****

Katia sat sideways on one end of the big beige sofa. Her shoulder pushed into the softness of the back cushion, and her legs, tucked up under her body, pushed into the seat. All of the beige made Katia feel like she was in a cocoon. She faced Zahra, who sat cross-legged on the other end, an overstuffed beige-and-burgundy pillow hugged tightly in her lap. "So, our killer is someone we know."

Zahra corrected Katia. "Likely someone from the island. Harper didn't say someone we know. Xavier didn't say someone we know. Not directly."

"Zahra. Seriously." Katia adjusted her posture so she was sitting away from the back of the couch and opened her hands, palms facing each other. "We fucking know everyone on the island."

"Touché." Zahra played with the edges of the pillow.

"Okay. So someone who blends in, leads a seemingly stable life." Katia needed to do something, and building a profile from the information gathered seemed the only way to add to the investigation while they waited for the specialty teams to do their work. "Someone methodical and intelligent. Someone who can leave their home in the fucking middle of the night to go bury a body." Katia rubbed the back of her neck. She ached all over. Not the ache of someone with a fever or an overused joint, but a deep ache in the bones. This was personal.

She made eye contact with Zahra, looked away, and then back again. In the middle of everything, this woman made her warm inside. She didn't have many friends, at least not the kind who you want to be around all of the time. But in the last week, she found herself wanting to be around two people in particular, Zahra and Paige. Mostly Zahra.

She didn't want Zahra to think she was nonsensical in any way, so she kept those thoughts to herself. "Do you think the storms have anything to do with it?"

"Like, does he kill and bury them during a storm?" Zahra's fingers quit pulling at the pillow fringe.

Zahra looked like she was thinking about that, about how it might line up with what she, Dr. Webb, and the others were finding in the lab.

"Something like that, I guess. I mean, Harper told you there's a pattern we haven't seen yet, right?" Katia tried to think back on storm dates. She, her dad, and brother tracked them on the storm boards at home. Her mom had tracked them, too. Some town folk were addicted to storm-tracking like poker players were addicted to poker. There were storm boards all over town. Heck, Katia had one at her house. "It would create a good cover. No one would be out in a storm." She paused. "No one would be watching or hanging out that close to the beach. They would be across the bridge, or at least hanging out farther in. It would make perfect sense."

Zahra was quiet.

Katia wished she could read her mind. "It's stupid, isn't it?" Katia was supposed to be listening to the profile Harper constructed from Zahra's information, not play junior detective.

"It's possible, I guess." Zahra's brows were pulled in at the center, creating a crease in her forehead. "Let's think about this. Think about Anna. Here's what we know." Zahra held up one finger. "She was sitting well off the coast." She held up a second finger. "We almost drowned trying to work the beach."

Katia watched her fingers.

Zahra lowered her fingers and picked up Katia's hand. She brought it to her mouth and kissed it gently before lowering it to her own lap. She looked at Katia. "If it's that bad out, do you think someone could get the tools and a body out to the dunes, dig, bury, and clean up, without being hurt or noticed? Fourteen times? I don't know."

"What then?" Katia dropped the topic of the storm for now. She didn't want Zahra to move their hands. She'd look at the boards on her own when she got home.

"Maybe let's look from a different angle and see what connects. Harper said the killer may be killing a pseudo-someone. Someone who harmed him. There was the teacher, the one who was rumored to have fondled more than a few male students, and the woman who gave piano lessons to kids in town to make money in the winter. Who else do we know something specific about? Oh, yes. There's the recluse who was reported missing by the boy who mowed her grass."

Katia heard the words—boy, harmed, women, kill. She thought about her dream. More of the pieces were coming into view. She could remember Marco. The ambulance was racing toward him. It was Zahra who stepped in front of him. Marco's face turned into a face without a name, featureless, dark, blurred around the edges. Marco was trying to get away from the Sandman. And then it hit her. What if Marco saw something related to this case? The idea that her brother might have seen something brought the bile from her stomach into her esophagus. She swallowed hard.

Zahra continued to run through what they knew. She seemed oblivious to the fact that Katia was no longer listening.

Katia thought Marco's breakdown was over something minor. A teacher who wanted him to sit in a hard chair or turn off the television for therapy time, perhaps. But what if he knew something? She bit her lip. Marco used a camera at school after a previous episode. He calmed quickly, though, and the camera was stuck in the drawer until this morning.

Katia dropped the two cameras off for the pictures to be developed before she came to Zahra's house. Until this moment, she didn't believe they would find anything of value when she picked them up. What if Marco captured something on the first camera? What if there was a clue buried in the pictures of teachers and playthings?

Zahra's voice took on a surreal quality. She sounded far away. Sounds of Marco's distress the night before mixed in and then her father's words: "He was like this when I picked him up. I can't calm him. Get home." And Marco, rocking, tapping. His panic at the thought of her taking him back to the center that morning. Could one of Marco's caregivers do this?

She thought through details of each teacher and each administrator in the school for disabled children.

Zahra shook her leg. "You're zoning again. You okay?"

"Yeah. Just thinking about Marco's pictures."

"Did you put them in?"

"On my way here. What if someone at his school…" She couldn't finish the thought out loud. Marco was her responsibility. Her dad made that clear years ago. She accepted that responsibility. Now someone had hurt him or scared him. Her breath came harder. She couldn't stand the thought of her brother in a bad situation.

Zahra stretched her arms toward Katia. "I don't know about you, but I could use a minute of quiet. Please?"

Katia hesitated. It felt like a sign of weakness. She wanted to be strong for Zahra, for Marco, not the other way around.

"Please?" Zahra repeated. "I need you."

Katia gave in and let her body turn and fall forward until her head was on Zahra's shoulder and their bodies were side by side.

Zahra rubbed Katia's back in a circular motion.

The women were still, their breath coming in synch. In and out. Smell the flowers. Blow out the candles.

"Do you think I'm weak?" Katia asked into Zahra's shoulder. "I should have gone back to work. Everyone else went back to work."

"Weak?" Zahra's voice was soft in Katia's ear. "Are you fucking serious? No. You're strong. Actually amazing. I don't know how you're doing this. As for work, you've got to be kidding me."

Zahra's shoulder moved from beneath her cheek, and hands moved to either side of her face, holding her up and bringing their faces close. "We will find him, Katia. We will find Elizabeth. You have to believe that."

"You think Elizabeth is okay?" Katia leaned into Zahra's hands. She trusted her to hold her up. Her lip was shaking, but she didn't shed a tear. The officers who went to Elizabeth's apartment in Virginia reported no signs of foul play, but Elizabeth was nowhere to be found.

"Honestly," Zahra said softly, "I don't know."

Katia felt puffs of Zahra's breath on her own cheek. It was warm and soft. In this moment, she trusted this woman more than she trusted any other person in the world.

"The FBI seems to think it's unlikely he would take the risk of going to Virginia to try to find her." Zahra kissed Katia's nose. "Let's hope she's with a friend."

"I think Marco knows." She couldn't believe she was saying the words out loud, even in a whisper against Zahra's skin.

"Knows what, Katia? Whether or not Elizabeth is safe?"

Katia swallowed hard, licked her lips. "Knows something about who is doing all of this."

****

Brent looked at the pictures on his computer screen. He was alone in his small, white-brick home. His mom said it looked more suited to a little Podunk town than to the beach at Buxton. It was one of the reasons he bought it. No one paid attention to it. It sat on a tiny side street no one travelled. It was plain and uninviting, just like him.

Brent liked being alone. The only person whom he liked being with more than he liked being alone was Savannah, his twelve-year-old daughter. She used to spend every other weekend here. As she aged, it became less and less. Her friends were all in Corolla, where she and her momma now lived. Savanah's picture hung on every wall, sat on surfaces in elaborate frames that proclaimed, "World's Best Daughter," and "A Family Makes A Home."

Savannah lived on in every room except the one he now occupied. No one lived in that room except Brent and his clients, those men and women who, like him, lived two lives. In that room, the walls were bare except for a large, round clock, the kind you would find in a classroom. It hung over a file cabinet that blended into the tan paint. Brent sat in an old, wooden chair at a large, and equally old, wooden desk, both of which were handed down to him by his grandfather. In front of him, a laptop computer, folded into the closed position, sat atop a docking station. Two large monitors, both alive with color, consumed all but the smallest part of the top of the desk. In the area were an ashtray, a pack of Marlboro Menthol, and an old flint lighter, also a gift from his grandfather. Two leather chairs separated by a round table completed the room. It was his favorite place to be when he was home alone.

He glanced at the long, black, hand of the clock. It rested on the twelve. The thin, red, second hand ticked past the short hand that sliced through the five. What is taking so long? He picked up the flip phone from its place next to the keyboard and opened it. Nothing. His brow furrowed. He snapped the phone shut and put it on the desk. The phone was the last of a batch he purchased several years ago on the dark web. He made a mental note to find more soon.

He gazed at the computer monitors. Years ago, he made a deal with the devil.

"I didn't ask for this," he said to the colorful image on the left screen. "Like you, I was recruited." He looked from left to right and back again. There were five shots of the partially uncovered corpse of Gina Dahl. He sat back to study the angles. His eye rested on the way a raindrop lay on a single speck of sand to create a tiny magnifying glass atop a perfectly polished red nail.

Not bad, he thought. Not bad at all.

His face flushed, the quiver in his stomach built with every click of the keys. He moved part of one picture and laid it over another and then another. After an hour of work, he pulled his shoulders back as far as they would go and cracked his neck. The perfect shot. Beautiful.

He named the finished product, "Meticulous In Death." He could hear the collective intake of breath of his Pain and Pleasure fans, a site focused on pain, death, and sex. Children and eighteen- to twenty-year-old women brought the most bitcoins. His account would grow exponentially over the next few days as word got out there were new shots from an active crime scene.

You're welcome, ladies and gentleman. Enjoy.

Brent zoomed in on one shot, on the vivid purple of the shoe. He used his manipulation tool to make it an even stronger color, a purple so majestic it demanded the observer's attention.

Gina carried herself like a majestic goddess.

He intended to give her the perfection she deserved.

He clicked the blurring tool and hovered it over the leg, bloated and splotchy. A light brush created the illusion of muted purple pouring from the majestic purple shoe.

He rested his hand on the mouse, pulled the corner of his lip between his teeth, and rolled title ideas around in his mind. The title, he knew, was as important as the shading and color and angle of every shot.

"I shall call you… 'Her Majesty 'Tis of Thee.'" He smiled at his choice and typed it into the computer, attaching the words to the corner of the photo.

Such a big personality you were in life; such a big personality you will be in death. He relaxed into memory of the smell, of the faces of those who were witnessing intense death for the first time. The beat of his heart was as strong as the moment he captured the shot. There were so many people around. Brent was so forward, so daring with his craft. Butterflies, almost painful in their tingling of his insides, returned.

When he was pleased with "Her Majesty," he moved the picture to the bottom of the right screen and clicked another folder on the left. This one held the children. Gina wasn't the only subject of his attention on the beach that day. The small Clark child, whom he carried to the transport unit, also made him move through his fear of detection to capture the sweetness of death.

"Breathless Innocence," he titled the picture that was now front and center on the screen. He ran his finger across the display, down the arm hanging limply across his own. From the angle of the shot you could see the blue of his EMS sleeve, the emblem edge on the chest. Enough to tease but not enough to know. He never let them know. He was too smart to make rookie mistakes.

He remembered news reports about the most recent bust of a group of those soliciting the porn he provided. The reports said, "Didn't change their screen names," and "Used gateway sites." Idiots. They deserved to get caught if they used unprotected proxy services to browse.

His eyes rested on the side of the boy's face. He contemplated whether or not to darken it slightly or trim it a bit more but decided it captured perfectly the way he felt the moment he slipped his phone out of his pocket and took the photo. There were people all over the beach who were so desensitized to technology that they didn't even look his way.

In the moments he rested the phone against his chest and snapped the shots, every nerve in his body tingled. He wanted to open the boy's eyes as he carried him, but he couldn't risk the attention a broken stride might create. Pictures with open eyes would have to wait. Now, looking at the photos, he was glad he hadn't. The result of the pale skin and blond curls against his uniform was beautiful. Open green eyes would've created a much different effect.

He thought about his audience and looked again at the photo. It showed the connection between man and boy but not rape or snuff. This would be a problem for his followers on the Pleasure and Pain site.

"A different site for you, my 'Breathless Innocence,'" he murmured.

He closed the image, went back to the folder, and chose another shot of the same Clark child. In this one, his eyes were open. He looked like a scared boy who stared blindly at the camera. If you weren't aware of his death, you might allow yourself to believe he was very much alive. His followers were going to love this shot of the child with strong male fingers wrapped in the soft blond curls. The other hand rested under the sheet that served as a prop to give the illusion of nakedness. He had no desire to actually fondle the young boy. His job was to make it appear as if someone did, someone just beyond the reach of the camera's eye, someone who could be anyone his audience desired.

He titled the last edit, "Final Desire," and posted the shot to Pain and Pleasure.

"Final Desire" was a perfect shot.

He continued working as the minutes ticked slowly past. He checked his phone. Nothing. Waiting was the hardest part.

****

"He's asleep," Katia said, entering the living room. She plopped down across from Papi in the big, cushioned chair. It was obvious from his damp hair and clean skin he recently showered, though one would never tell from his dress. Richard Billings, carpenter extraordinaire, never wore pajamas or shorts. Always Levi's and T-shirts. Always. She liked the way he smelled after work, like wood and sunshine. As a small girl, she watched for his return and jumped into his arms to breathe in that smell. She wished she could do that now. She was mentally and physically drained from the last six days.

Telltale clues in the room told her that regardless of her exhaustion, of her wants or needs, a Marco conversation was forthcoming. She made eye contact with her father. His brow furrowed as he glanced down at the bourbon in his hand. She waited. It took less than thirty seconds to get to the conversation at hand.

"You left him with Mrs. Ellington," Richard said. His voice was stern, low. "Why?"

"I left you a—"

"A note?" His words cut into hers. "I read it. He's home now, isn't he?"

Sarcasm. Great. Katia started to remind her father she was told a million times not to text him or call unless it was an emergency. He was the one who initiated the notes in this age of technology. She decided to keep her mouth shut. This would be over more quickly that way. Maybe she would have a drink of her own.

Marco was in his safe space when she got home. He rocked and tapped no matter what she said. She finally left him to self-regulate and came downstairs. Her brother's setback this week was part of her father's choice for bourbon rather than a beer. Beers meant her father wanted to relax. Bourbon meant he was agitated. Katia saw it as the equivalent to Marco's tools. She didn't say that, either. Instead, she sat silently and let her words boil beneath her skin.

Her dad played with the condensation on his glass. "We need to talk." His voice went from agitated to kind, his brow less furrowed.

Fuck. Here we go. Katia leaned to her right and pulled her legs up behind her, her slightly muscular frame filling, but not overflowing, the big chair. She pictured Zahra's hands, recalled the feeling of her breath on her face, the slight hint of coffee, the sincere desire to be with her. She thought of her mother's arms before the accident, before Katia had to become an adult, when her mom was the one at the stove, stirring the boiling milk and lemon, whisking the egg whites into beautiful soft peaks. When she had filled her body with all of the positivity she could muster, she spoke.

"Papi, I'm tired."

Her father sat with his forearms resting on his upper legs, his right hand swirling the golden-brown liquid across the ice cubes.

She looked past her father and out the big picture window behind him. It was dark now, but she knew exactly what lay on the other side of the glass. From the time she could stand, she spent hours looking past the large, white, windowpane, hours enjoying the way the stark white framed the tans and greens of the beach and the greens and blues of the sea. She was glad the blues and tans of the room were the same as they were when she was small enough to do somersaults across the overstuffed cushions. She looked around the room and absorbed the memories.

They sat in silence a moment more. It was impossible, but she swore she could still smell her mother on the strands of soft fabric. She inhaled deeply, gathering strength from the past. "Papi?" She wasn't going to help him get to his point.

"I found a place for Marco."

There it was. The sentence she heard once before and never wanted to hear again. She pulled herself upright and hugged her knees to her chest. Her whole body tensed. Every inch of her being threatened to betray her. Breathe in. Breathe out. Breathe in. Breathe out. She swallowed hard and spoke evenly and with conviction. "He stays with me, Papi. I promised her."

"Promised who? Your mom? She's dead, Katia. She's dead, and we're here, and he's not happy here."

"Her. Yes. I kissed her good-bye and promised." Katia waited. She looked between the bourbon in his eyes and the one in his hand. Neither gave her a clue as to what was coming. The silence engulfed her, engulfed them both, until she felt dizzy. Her throat closed around words that tried to escape. Her lead-filled feet refused to carry her away from this moment.

He looked through her. The glass rested against his right knee. She waited. The seconds ticked past. Katia's insides filled with lava, hot and oozing across her organs.

"Do you think she wanted you to waste your life sitting around here with a brother who doesn't even know what you do for him?" He drained the last of the liquid from his glass and put it down on the table with more force than necessary. "For God's sake, Katia, he can't even stay home alone or tell us what in the hell is wrong. He's not going to get better."

"Papi. Please." Katia yearned for his understanding. "It wasn't that bad. He barely ever has them anymore."

"You weren't here, again."

"But, Papi—"

"Katia. He's a teenager now, with teenager thoughts and teenager strength. How much longer do you think you'll be able to guide him out of these episodes?"

Her hands shook in her lap. She looked at her father's glass. The drops of condensation ran down the sides and created a ring of water on the lighthouse coaster. Katia wanted to throw it at him. Right now, she hated him, real hate. She felt her hand move toward the glass. It would be simple. He was slightly inebriated. If she threw it hard enough…

"Katia? What are you thinking?" His words broke her from the horrible thoughts. "I know you love him. I love him, too. He's my son, for Christ's sake."

"Love him? Love him?" Katia's voice rose. She felt her cheeks grow red. "Love isn't putting him somewhere to make our lives easier. Don't you get that? I'll give up everything, anything, for him. That's love."

Her father's chest rose and fell methodically. His face appeared to be a mix of sorrow and pain.

"I get it, Papi." Katia adjusted her voice to a more respectful tone. "I really do. It's hard. He doesn't talk much. It's hard to figure out what's happening. He's loud. He flaps. But he needs me. Needs us." She looked directly in her father's eyes. "I need him."

Still he remained silent.

Katia debated on how much of the past few days to share with her father, especially tonight. She was twenty-six-years old, but she still felt like a child in his overbearing, overprotective presence. He wouldn't approve of her playing detective with the county's criminal investigator and search and rescue dog handler. She wasn't going to stop. She also wasn't going to let Marco go anywhere she couldn't protect him. She didn't know how they all fit into this sick fuck's game plan. But she didn't need one more thing to worry about, and she would worry if her brother was in a strange place without her. She tried again.

"I know it's bad right now, Papi. But it's only bad right now because of whatever happened at the school." She paused to think about her next words. "Maybe someone there has something to do with what's going on." She let the words hang in the air until he answered.

"What makes you think that?" His voice was steady, even.

Katia feared him turning the conversation back to the home for developmentally delayed youth, so his question pleased her. "You said he was like this when you picked him up. He freaks at the mention of me dropping him off there." She talked faster than she meant to. "He's suddenly afraid to be without me. Even Mrs. Ellington took a few minutes to convince him it was okay for me to leave, and he loves going there." She took a deep breath. Her lips moved back and forth between her teeth.

Her father picked his empty glass off of the table and sucked the bit of moisture that had pooled around the ice into his mouth.

Katia needed to get it all out before she lost her nerve. "It's just weird. He's gotten much better since the last time. He's learned to communicate better. The doctor gave him another camera. I dropped it off. I need to pick up the pictures tomorrow. They'll soothe him." She didn't mean to tell him about the pictures. He'd think she was stupid for the indulgence.

But he didn't tell her she was stupid. He didn't argue or bring the conversation back around. "For now," he said. "For now, I'll let him stay. But Katia?"

"Yes, Papi," she answered quickly, her voice more cheerful. "I know. I promise. I understand we may have to place him one day."

"Go on to bed. You need rest. I need rest."

Katia wanted to cry, she wanted to scream, she wanted to ask her father to hold her and say that everything would be okay. But she didn't. "Good night, Papi."

Chapter Sixteen

Sunday, November 25, 2018

"Death is dark. And then…"
Nothing.

****

When the text finally arrived late Sunday night, Brent was delighted.

Ready.

No more. No less.

He closed the phone, slid it into his pocket, and moved quickly toward the closet in his bedroom. Before he lost himself in preparing the photographs for his customers, he had carefully poked the edges around the entire back wall with the sharp tip of a pocketknife. The advance planning decreased his arrival time to Elizabeth when the call came, and it left the wall intact to the untrained eye.

He put his hands against the drywall and pushed, eased up, and pushed again. He lifted the drywall to the side and stepped into the small three-by-five-foot space that lay behind. He looked at the boxes of decals and pictures and newspapers and VHS tapes that sat alongside an old player he still occasionally brought out to relive the early years. He ran a finger through the light film of dust on one of the tapes. Nine of the people presented on these videos, in these papers, were from his pact with the devil the media recently named Sandman.

Sandman. He was Sandman. The man they were after was the Devil. He felt his pulse in his temples. He inhaled deeply. He needed complete focus for the job at hand.

He moved past the memories and to the shelf that held a stack of truck decals, also courtesy of the dark web. He already decided on the decal for tonight. He sifted through several until he found the one that read, "Gecko Sportfishing." A green-and-brown gecko in captain's gear, one hand on a large, wooden steering wheel, looked up at him from the center of the clear vinyl circle, the name of the company curved across its top. It was a legitimate business down the coast in South Carolina. He had done his research. It was perfect. The owner was a night fisherman. His boat ramp, dockside café, and store would be as dark as the night, and his dark-colored truck with the gecko decal would be stationary in the darkness.

Brent used his shirttail to wipe the surface of the decal and laid it to the side. He reached into another box and sifted quickly through a small stack of fake driver's licenses. He settled on a scraggly-haired blond. Jasper Rigby. He said the name silently, but with the best deep-south accent he could muster. Sounds nautical enough. The patrolman loading the ferry wouldn't even glance at it. They rarely did this time of year, as there were few visitors and few reasons to suspect anyone crossing was not as they should be. He ran his fingers through his own sandy-colored hair and thought about the other items on his list.

****

It didn't take long to get from his garage to his destination, approximately two miles away.

Nothing is far in Buxton. How many times had he said that to tourists stopping by the station? We're one of seven small villages along the fifty-mile stretch of Hatteras Island. Smile, nod at whatever witty comeback was presented, and point them on their way. The pointing and smiling was the mundane part of a job that allowed him access to the subjects of his art.

A block from the house, he pulled over and parked. It was late evening, and dusk had settled, but blackness hadn't yet blanketed his route or his midnight-blue, newly decaled truck. His fingers fumbled with the strings of the gray hoodie, his mind more on the sweet artist who lay waiting for him a block away than on getting the loops just right to secure the hood around his face.

He glanced into the rearview mirror and tucked his unruly curls back beyond the scrunched edges of gray. He lifted thin, gray gloves from the passenger seat and pulled them on. "Don't let the anticipation get the best of you," his internal creature from the deep said silently. He looked down to the phone in his hand. With one finger, he tapped out one word: "Here." When he crossed over to Ocracoke tonight, the phone would be discarded.

He waited a few seconds to make sure there would be no response, pushed the back of the flip phone with his index finger until the spring let loose and the top popped shut, opened the truck door, and slid down to the sidewalk. Head down. Hands out. He fought his natural urge to put his hands in his pockets as he walked. Move slightly slower. Jasper's a fisherman, not an EMS worker. He has nowhere to be and is in no hurry to get there.

He watched his feet all the way to the side door of the structure. The man is brilliant. I'll give him that. The two purposefully passed in the grocery store yesterday morning. The man dropped a piece of paper into a pile of Granny Smith apples, and Brent picked it up with his forefinger against the green apple skin. He slid the apple into a plastic bag and the note into his jeans pocket. It was all so simple, and the crisp pop of the apple busting against the power of his teeth as he unfolded the note and read the words felt good:

"Wait for completion notification. Suitcase ready. Coordinates inside. Ocracoke. Last run. Away from the trails that coil from the stacking lanes. Dune marked."

There were no plazas or businesses off the dock on the Ocracoke side. The deserted beaches ran for miles next to the road that led into town.

Brent reached the door in exactly one-hundred-and-one steps. He stood motionless for several seconds and let the sound of the ocean and the descending darkness move through his body. In front of him was the entrance to the now infamous Sandman's lair. He shook out his arms at his side, letting the movement track naturally from arms to hands to fingers.

Like a ghost writer for the famous, Brent wanted recognition for his part in the production, but he knew his emotional and monetary livelihood was tied directly to never being acknowledged for his own creativity.

The crack in the whitewashed, wooden door wasn't noticeable until you stood right in front of it. He reached forward. The door moved silently at his touch. For a moment, he let his eyes adjust to the new level of dark. Then he moved into the belly of the beast.

He stood in the dim light of the room. Eyes closed softly, he breathed through his nose, meditating to the scent of death. For a moment, he could take as much or as little time as he liked. The room was soundproof, the walls and floor concrete, thick, layered with varnish that made them easy to clean. The Roto-Rooter man. That's me. In his mind, the old jingle started playing.

In the beginning, he was appalled that he allowed himself to be sucked into such circumstances. He even refused to help the third time he was summoned, but Sandman made it clear that refusal was not an option. "Watch what you say, boy. You're part of my mess, and we both know how I clean up my messes." His voice presented as even, soft, but Brent heard the message loud and clear. He never refused again. The rules of their relationship were simple ones: fewer words are always better; use a phone only until a job is finished; dispose of the phone the moment the word "complete" is typed; leave no trace in this room, in the yard, truck, or trail to indicate she was anywhere near; leave no trace he was here, no trace his boss was here; get in and out without raising suspicion; crop and Photoshop all photos so as to show faces in unnamable fashion; wait one month before posting any picture taken.

The last two rules were added in the years since the Internet had grown useful. Prior, he took photos only for himself. "A hobby," he told the man. "Payment for keeping quiet."

Each time Sandman needed his services, Brent would receive a note passed discreetly from hand to hand. Until 2004, the notes were their only communication. Then, for a while, a new phone was placed in a plastic bag in a dune as soon as another one was discarded. When there was a job to do, a one-word text came through: Apple, for the grocery store; Hole-in-one for the putt-putt windmill; Read, for the bookstore, third shelf, third book, mystery section. Now he found the phones through the underground web. They were untraceable that way. The key words remained the same.

When Brent wasn't at work, he was content to spend his summers like any other twenty-something male raised on the water: windsurfing, kite-gliding, and looking for love. But as the years passed, he grew more agitated between kills. His job and his hobbies paled in comparison. His love life was nonexistent. He constantly craved the thrill and the artistry that could be achieved only when he was able to use a professional grade camera, like tonight.

He remembered the first time: Nadia Grey.

Nadia. He loved her so, as well as a sixteen-year-old could love. He remembered the curve of her breast under his shaking hand and her soft moan as he followed the instructions she whispered in his ear. He thought she was the one. He would have done anything for her. But she didn't love him. She loved attention. Brent's. Roger's. Casper's. Greg's. How many others? He wanted to ask her after he found her with Roger that day. But his voice didn't work when he opened his mouth. She didn't see him in the doorway of her classroom, but Roger did. She was seated, head forward, gorgeous auburn hair flowing toward the desk, almost brushing the papers sprawled in front of her. Roger's hands rubbed her neck, her shoulders; his fingers moved farther down her chest with each squeeze. As his eyes met Brent's, he touched his fingertips to the edge of her breast and smiled as if to say, "I win. You lose."

Brent wanted to hit him, to push him away. And then she moaned, a moan like he heard when his own fingertips moved across her skin. He felt a sob build that threatened to give him away. He ran down the hallway, past the blue lockers, past the trophy case where his science trophy sat alongside all the others, past the cafeteria, and out the heavy double doors. He ran and cried until his legs ached and his breath came in ragged gasps, until he was alone on the beach, away from all of them.

But he wasn't alone that day. A man sat by himself on a checkered blanket, eating a sandwich. "Hungry?" the man asked him.

His stomach churned. He wanted to say no, but his body disobeyed his mind. He walked over and sat. For years afterward, he played the scenario over in his mind. Each time he chose to run. His fantasy didn't change reality. He was a hero. He saved other boys from her spell when he sat with the man and told him why he ran and why he cried over his teacher.

As the horror of what happened faded, and as the man praised him over and over, the fantasy changed. He felt good about his part in Nadia Grey's story.

By the time the man told Brent about another bad woman the next year, Brent was fully invested in their crusade against evil. With the second woman, he found himself turned on by the smells and drawn to the pale skin. She was like a blank canvas, and he was an artist.

He wanted the man to kill more, to give him more, but the man refused.

"No, Brent," he said. "Taking a life is revenge for a crime so horrible that prison isn't an option. These are crimes society ignores. Only a woman who viciously wrongs a child will pay this price."

Brent really didn't want people to die, but he did want the smell of blood. A body drained of life was quite beautiful. At nineteen, he became a volunteer for the Buxton Rescue Department, and two years later, he was a full-time paramedic for Hatteras Island Rescue. The job fed his basic need.

On those occasions, when a woman committed the ultimate sin, he was gifted not only with death but with death delivered to a quiet cell where he could spend hours posing and photographing his subject in exchange for his services. He learned quickly that the most horrific women in life were often the sweetest in death. Their photographs fetched a handsome penny on the dark web where men and women searched for fodder for their darkest fantasies.

The room was dimly lit with one bulb that hung above a concrete floor. He moved farther into the room. To his left, the dark was darker. Elizabeth was in there. He moved through the entryway and flicked the switch. The room flooded with light. The sharp contrast to the light in the outer room assaulted his sight. He blinked rapidly as his eyes adjusted and he could cross the few feet from the entrance to the shower.

"Hello, Elizabeth. I've looked forward to meeting you."

His eyes took in the pale beauty of her exposed skin, her pale blue eyes, and her pale pink lips. For a moment, he avoided the wide slash in her throat. Red. One of his favorite colors. It popped in the camera's eye. He would capture it in the photos soon enough, but first a close-up of the soft blues and pinks. He knelt on one knee, steadied the camera by placing his elbow on the other knee, and leaned in. With his free hand, he brought blonde strands across one cheek. The camera's eye captured one-and-one-half eyes, her nose, and three-quarters of her pale pink lips. He would blur the edges later.

His eyes traveled out to one shoulder and then the other. The man left her dressed. He didn't understand this. Elizabeth was young, blonde. She was a beautiful artist. Maybe that's the difference. He wouldn't connect to her in the same way: artist to artist. He admired Elizabeth's work that hung in the local beach gallery. It lined the walls every summer when tourist season began. People admired her use of vibrant color and bold brushstrokes, and by October each year, her work was gone. It didn't sell quite as quickly as his work sold on the dark web. Perhaps it would, now that she was dead. He made a mental note to see if he could get his hands on some of her pictures.

He slowly removed one piece of clothing and then another. Each time, he took a few seconds to fold the cloth neatly and set it out of the scope of his canvas. Several times, he pulled his camera from his chest to his eye, adjusted the focus, added more of the picnic blanket and then less, shot from the corner of the basket with the wine bottle peeking from the corner, and then from the band of her paint-spattered blue jeans.

This time was better than many times in the past. It wasn't unusual for the man to spoil the canvas before he arrived. He especially hated it when he had it packed and ready for transport. *Transport and bury. I didn't ask you here to have a party. She's dirty. Get. Her. Out.* The man's words echoed in his head. Those times the process was quick, and his pictures were few and imperfect. Tonight was one of the good times. As the clock ticked away the late evening hours, he took time to revel in his craft, time to create a true masterpiece.

After all of Elizabeth's clothes were removed, Brent let his eyes move to the slash. He remembered the first time, when he saw the same smooth cut through Nadia's throat. He loved her as only a sixteen-year-old can love. He reached down and touched the raw flesh. It was almost hard to the touch, but not quite. He touched the flesh around Elizabeth's wound. His finger sunk in the same way as it had that day. In both instances, too, the blood was congealed on the outside but released a sweet red stream when he pushed. He pulled his camera up to eye level and focused on the drop as it oozed downward. He turned the camera slightly to capture the trail of red from another angle.

His work focused on color. The right color pulled the personality from each person, like the purple that popped from his computer screen earlier in the day, the color of majesty, the color of a queen, a real estate queen.

He stood up and stretched. In the field, most of the photos were taken with his cell phone. Occasionally a medical investigator who fell for his flirting and kindness sent him high-resolution photos from her lab. But not for a while.

He looked at the screen on his camera and clicked back through a few shots. When he used a phone, he worked tirelessly at his computer to make sure he captured the true color and beauty of his subject. His continued success depended on it. When he used his high-resolution camera, the tool did the hard work for him and he could more easily relax into the shoot.

When he was satisfied with the current photos, he let his eyes roam over Elizabeth's naked form as he thought about additional staging. "Dear, beautiful, Elizabeth," Brent said, "I know just what we should do."

He felt as giddy as a child on Christmas morning whose ears are filled with the sounds of a puppy's yelp before they hit the bottom stair. The chains. He never used the chains. It would take planning to get Elizabeth from here to there without creating a mess, but he had several hours for that.

Silver and red. Merry Christmas to me.

****

Loud voices are not good. Marco cannot sleep when the voices are loud. Past eight fifteen. Lights out. Look out the window. No. Lights out. The lights are out. Where is the camera? Katia took it. Pictures coming out tomorrow. That's what Katia said at eight ten. Katia did not lie to Marco. Pictures tomorrow.

Marco squished his eyes tight and tried to count like Katia taught him. One. Two. Three. Four. Five. Six.

Loud. Papi is loud at Katia.

Katia is loud at Papi.

Go to the window. Marco likes the night. The ocean. The sand.

What if the bad man is on the beach?

Marco did not like the bad man on the beach, the man in the black clothes. All black clothes. No face. Just a black night face. He didn't like when he saw the bad man.

Pictures tomorrow. Marco liked pictures.

Good night, Katia.

Good night, Papi.

Good night, Marco.

Chapter Seventeen

Monday, November 26, 2018

Katia worked her first twenty-four-hour shift in over a week. It felt good to be back in the station instead of on the sidelines. She called home only three times from 7:00 Sunday morning until 7:00 this morning. In all fairness, she slept close to six of those hours. She was sidetracked by the continued harassment of reporters for another hour. And Papi told her not to call again after she called for the final time at 5:00 this morning.

"I told you I wouldn't take him to the school, Katia Pilar. He'll be in front of the TV when you get home."

"Thanks, Papi. I'll hurry." Katia didn't mention that she needed to pick up Marco's pictures before she came home. She intended to do it Saturday, but Papi was at a job site, and she didn't dare leave Marco with Mrs. Ellington again.

Katia looked at the two women who sat at the table with her. It still seemed surreal that one week and one day ago they came together with such force that their lives would forever be intertwined. Neither blinked an eye when she asked them to come over to look at the developed pictures, even though each was in the midst of her own crisis: Paige with the break-in and Zahra with her continued help on the case.

Now the three of them sat in Katia's kitchen discussing the break-in at the training facility.

Paige and Zahra were debating the how. Katia was half-listening, her chair leaned back on two legs. Her mind was reeling. Why in the world was someone interested in getting their hands on transcripts from the facility? Why would they kill a rescue dog? Would Frankie have protected Paige? Would he have been cut open, too? It was unlikely the small pup would have offered much in the way of keeping someone out and would probably have suffered the same fate as Voltaire.

Katia eased her chair back on all fours and tuned into the conversation. "Bob said the pups in the facility were going crazy,"

Paige told Zahra. "Woke him up. I'm far enough up the road I didn't hear much."

The ding of the oven timer interrupted their conversation, and all three women flinched.

Katia stood up and made her way to the kitchen. "My mom's cinnamon rolls are the answer to everything." She attempted a smile.

"Holy crap, those smell amazing," Paige said.

The women sniffed the air. Something about the sweet smell of fresh dough and cinnamon made the horrible easier to bear.

"Are those things ready?" Zahra asked.

"Yep. Ready." Katia placed the plate of steaming rolls in the middle of the table and returned to the kitchen for three glasses of milk.

Paige and Zahra chewed mouthfuls of cinnamon goodness as they welcomed Katia back to the table.

"Oh. My. God. These are the bomb." Paige swallowed and shoved another large bite into her mouth. "I need this recipe."

"No can do, my friend. My mom would roll over in her grave if I gave it to anyone."

The weight of the words turned the banter into silence.

Katia sighed. "Sorry. Bad choice of words."

Paige shook her head. "Don't be. We have to get used to it being a part of our life now."

The thought of a murderer being close to Paige made Katia's skin crawl. She cared about this woman. She wanted to kill the person responsible more in this moment than when she stood on the beach looking down at the bright-purple shoe of Gina Dahl.

Kindred spirits. Those were the words that came to her mind when she thought about her growing friendship with Paige. It was different from what she felt for Zahra. That relationship needed much more exploration when she wasn't so mentally exhausted. After Elizabeth left her, she saw other lesbians only rarely and mostly at The Pink Clover. Now she was here with two, and that felt good in the midst of this horrible new reality.

Paige broke into her thoughts. "Want to give the boy-child a roll?" Paige motioned toward the living space where Marco sat cross-legged in the middle of the floor, Frankie's head on one of his knees.

Katia looked through the archway at her little brother. Her father was right, he was now taller than her by a piece of an inch, and his voice, when he did talk, was growing deeper. "He had cereal. Maybe in a bit."

Zahra looked also. "They seem completely content to me," she said. "If the tail wagging is any indication."

"I think Frankie calms him," Katia said. "He's not tapping at all this morning. Now if I can just figure out how to tell Papi that Frankie is not Paige's and is here to stay."

"Oh, shit." Zahra tapped the screen on her phone. "That's my alarm to remind me I told Doc I would meet him at the sheriff's office to get a rundown of what he needs me to do here. He's heading back to Greenville this afternoon. We need to focus. I've got an hour before duty calls." She pointed to the transcripts and pictures on the table. "I also managed to get a little background on the three male caregivers who spent time at the center."

"What kind of background information?" Paige refocused on their task.

Zahra reached into her sling bag and pulled out a sheet of paper. "Maybe nothing of any substantial value." She put the newest paperwork on the table. "Two of the three males are young, about our age, twenty-five and twenty-seven. Neither has any history of violence or problems at home or school or in a relationship. Both have valid and up-to-date credentials and strong referrals."

Katia lifted one shoulder and made a face. "So at least we can rule them out as being Sandman."

"Looks like." Zahra indicated the last name on the list. "This one is old enough, forty-nine, but he's the owner. Rarely there. Never alone with the kids. He's a businessman, not a caregiver, best I can tell. And he isn't from here. Started the chain of caregiving centers in Louisiana. I have friends digging deeper, but I don't think he's a killer." Zahra looked directly at Katia. "I don't know what happened to your brother at that place, but it probably isn't related."

"Fuck." Katia pushed out a loud breath through her nose. "Fuck. Fuck. Fuck."

Zahra touched Katia's shoulder. "Let's focus on the pictures." Her gaze moved down to the end of the table where Paige sat. "That all of them?"

"Yeah. I haven't looked at them yet."

Zahra and Paige sat without moving. Katia knew they were waiting for her to open the package. Neither of them wanted to take the lead.

She reached for the envelopes. She didn't know what to expect from the second batch of photos, the ones from the camera Marco took to school, and was only minimally aware of what she would find on the first.

Katia opted to open the second envelope first and began laying out the four-by-six-inch glossy prints in a long row across the wooden table. Twenty-four pictures. Three of which were too blurry or bright to tell what was in the eye of the camera. That left twenty-one. Katia started naming them one by one, though they didn't need naming. "A Dixie cup half-full of Kool-Aid. A selfie of Marco's left eye."

"And part of his forehead," Paige added.

Katia looked closer. He had the same crease his dad wore when he was worried or angry, and his eye pupil was dilated. She moved to the next photo. "Crayons. Three in a row. Nothing extraordinary."

Zahra pointed to three separate photos. "These three all look like the same sky. Must have been before a storm. The clouds look angry as fuck."

"This looks like another one from school." Katia held up a picture of curls. "A classmate, no doubt. Looks like he has the same taste as his sister."

She looked over at Paige. "What do you have, there?"

"I think it's a box. It's blurry, though. Looks like just a bunch of crap thrown in."

Katia took the photo from Paige's hand and gave it a once-over. She was disappointed they hadn't found more. She wasn't sure why. What in the hell was an autistic teen's camera going to tell them? "Probably a box of toys that holds something he likes." She looked in where her brother still sat quietly stroking Frankie's fur and rocking to the beeps of the Road Runner on the television screen. She laid the picture on the table and reached for the next.

They spent the best part of an hour looking through the other fourteen photos, all taken at the home where Katia and Marco grew up. What they found made no sense, and Katia doubted it would make any sense to Marco today.

"Let's take a break from pictures and talk about the transcripts," Katia said. "You think these are what the person was after when he or she broke in?"

"I do, actually. Whoever it was took nothing. These are the only things that weren't in the office."

The three talked through possibilities for a few minutes but landed on nothing of value in determining cause or motive beyond the obvious: Someone wanted to know exactly what was uncovered on the beach. That could be a crooked reporter as easily as it could be the media's Sandman.

Katia noticed Zahra checking her watch. "Time for a few more pictures?"

Zahra stood as Katia pulled the other package of photos and put them in a stack on the table. "I would love to stay and go through more of these enthralling photos, guys, but I have a good doctor's brain to pick and much to investigate."

Paige nodded at Zahra. "I know you're disappointed." She turned her head slightly to meet Katia's eyes. "Do you think your neighbor would watch your brother for an hour? I kind of feel like a run."

Katia's hand rubbed the back of her own neck. She moved her head from side to side and in a circular motion. "I could use it, for sure." She considered the offer. Her dad was upstairs tending to paperwork for his business. The chore consumed him for hours when he did it, so he would be here for a while. She could ask him. He wouldn't be happy if she left Marco again, but he wouldn't likely put up a fuss in front of her friends.

She wanted to go for a run. She wanted to run until the fucking sand ended and no one knew her. She wanted to run until she forgot about Gina's death and Elizabeth's disappearance.

She debated a call to Mrs. Ellington. It would avoid a later argument with Papi. She weighed that against a satisfied brother in front of the television set, a brother who would likely flap and twirl and screech if she tried to coax him away from Yogi and Boo Boo. It just started, and it was his favorite. She wondered how many other families lived their lives by which cartoon was on the screen.

After several seconds in her own head, she smiled a weary smile and said, "He'll be fine for thirty minutes. I'll text my father. We'll be back or he'll be down."

Katia stood and shook out her arms and legs. "Pity you have to go, Zahra," she said. "We could have a threesome."

"Bitch," Zahra said and winked. "I'm not into sharing anyway."

Paige interjected a sigh and a shake of her head. "You," she said, pointing to Zahra, "go to work. And you," she said, turning to Katia, "are you good in that?"

Katia glanced down at her slightly wrinkled T-shirt and sweatpants, swallowed her grin, and met the eyes of Paige. "Yep. Ready, willing, and able."

Zahra pushed her chair under the table and walked into the living area. "Later, Marco Man. Later, Frankie." The pup's ears raised at the sound of his name, and his head cocked to one side as if awaiting further instructions. Katia and Paige came in and stood next to Zahra. The three watched for a moment as Yogi Bear tried to avoid being wooed by Cindy and to get to the cake in the picnic basket. "Shit still makes me laugh," Zahra said.

Katia agreed and let her hand lightly brush Zahra's. "Poor Cindy. Always trying to win out over food."

Zahra took Katia's hand in her own and squeezed.

Katia thought Zahra would always win out over food if she was Yogi.

"We better take Frankie." Paige motioned toward the pup when a commercial came on and broke the spell for all of them.

Katia nodded. "No way I want my father to find him here when I'm not. Come on, Frankie." Katia slapped her side. "Let's do this." To Marco, she said, "We're going for a run, Marco. Marco? Look at me." Her brother looked her way. He held Frankie down against his leg. "He has to come with me," Katia said. "We'll be back when The Flintstones come on."

Marco lifted his arm, and the dog stood, shook out his fur, and trotted over to Katia's side. The three women and their mascot headed for the door.

Chapter Eighteen

Zahra pulled into a parking spot at the back of the building that housed the Dare County Sheriff's Office. She glanced into the mirror and rubbed her index fingers under and around her eyes, trying to coax herself back into the day. Satisfied there was nothing she could do to get through this madness, she decided to get on with it. She reached into the cup-holder and unhooked her phone from the charger. The blue light blinked an alert that a text message was waiting. She swiped the screen and read the message from the doc that indicated another body was found on the beach.

"Shit."

Zahra slid the phone back into the cup-holder and put her car into reverse.

****

"Same M.O.?" Zahra asked. She stood with Dr. Webb on the portion of Buxton Beach that ran parallel to the ferry docks.

"Female," Dr. Webb replied. "Dumped, not buried. Throat slashed."

Zahra put her hand on her camera and pulled it away from her chest. "I'll get started."

"Zahra?" Dr. Webb touched her arm. His face looked somber, even more than normal.

"Sir?" Zahra caught his gaze. Something was different. A chill moved through her body.

"It's Elizabeth." His words were low, and Zahra could tell he was doing his best to stay calm.

She felt her equilibrium shift. The camera fell back against her chest. "Does anyone know?" Zahra really wanted to ask if Katia knew, but the words hurt too much in her mouth. The woman she was falling in love with was going to be destroyed by this, and there was nothing she could do about it. Zahra swallowed slowly, buying time, trying to think.

"No. Not yet." Dr. Webb's voice was soft, knowing. "Do you need someone else to do the pictures?"

"No. I'm okay. Really." She let her eyes fully absorb the scene. She stood alone with Dr. Webb and Elizabeth inside the yellow tape that wrapped around stakes pushed into the sandy ground.

Elizabeth was a small woman, likely no more than five feet two inches, petite in every way. In high school, Zahra envied her tiny pale body, small, pert breasts, her blonde hair and blue eyes that sat perfectly centered on either side of her perfectly shaped nose. She wanted to be her instead of who she was: a well-endowed black teenager with boring brown skin and boring brown eyes and hair to match. She wanted to be where she was, too: with Katia Billings, the class of 2010's most likely to be queer.

Zahra focused her camera to capture Elizabeth's full body. The top of Elizabeth's head was inches from touching her collarbone. Her small frame was folded in half at the waist, her breasts to her thighs. Zahra twisted the lens on her camera to zoom in on the woman's outstretched arm. Rainbow bands of vibrant color encircled the small forearm. Zahra moved the lens farther down to the woman's hand. Her fingers were lost inside a picnic basket. The faded brown of the in-and-out-woven pattern and the big, gold, turn-button latch on the front reminded her of the large basket her family used to pack when all of them went to the water for the day.

Zahra eased the camera back against her bosom. A picnic basket? What. The. Fuck. She turned back to Dr. Webb. "Doc?"

Dr. Webb hit Pause on his recording device.

Zahra motioned toward the out-of-place item. "Was she here with someone?"

He shook his head. "I suspect she was in it."

Zahra looked away. When she felt in control of her insides, she turned back. She studied the way the basket lay flipped on its side. The middle piece of wood that she remembered from her family's basket was gone from this one. She examined the position of the body. It was partially in and partially out of the large, cavernous space. Blood caked the inside of the thin wood slats, and flakes of the deep, reddish-black color had scattered on the sand where the body spilled out sometime during the night.

She raised her camera and concentrated on her hand placement. It was imperative she keep the camera steady until she heard the click of the shutter.

She took photos from all angles as she walked around the murdered woman. When she finished, she knelt beside Elizabeth and focused on the smoothly sliced skin. The cut started and ended in the same section of skin as Gina's had started and ended. The depth appeared to mimic the prior woman's as well. She moved her body and the camera to get pictures of Elizabeth's hand where it lay inside the basket. Through the lens, her eye caught sight of something.

"Doc," Zahra said, "there's something in the basket. Something shiny."

Dr. Webb knelt beside her in the sand and pointed his Maglite in the direction Zahra indicated. "A knife."

Zahra could feel the exhaustion in his words. Sadness seemed to seep through his pores and mix with her own.

"Get every angle, Zahra," he said. "Don't miss anything." He rose and made his way to the yellow line.

****

The shrill sound of the alarm startled Andrew. It always did. No matter how many times it sounded, he was always back in the field and surrounded by gunfire.

Elliot's voice brought him back to Buxton. "Chest pains. The beach. Let's go."

Andrew set his coffee cup on the counter and fell in step with Elliot.

When Andrew and Elliot arrived, FBI agents and police officers swarmed the area.

"What the fuck?" Elliot said. He slowly pulled the ambulance into a space of sand close to the new, yellow, crime scene border.

Andrew grabbed their gear. "Beats me. Let's find our heart victim."

Within seconds, they were at the side of a police officer who sat in front of a dune inside a new parameter of crime scene tape.

"I'm fine. Passed out for a sec. Boss says I can't go back unless you clear me."

"Tell us what happened." Elliot talked to the man while they checked his vitals.

The man pointed toward a body and a basket tossed against a dune. "We're all exhausted. I didn't have lunch. That's it, really."

"Vitals are good. I suggest food before you go back to work so it doesn't happen again." Elliot put the equipment away and stood.

Neither Andrew nor Elliot returned to the ambulance. They watched as Dr. Webb and Zahra moved around the woman.

Elliot was the first to speak. "Doesn't look like she was buried. Do you think it's our serial killer?"

Andrew's brain worked through the scene and processed it against what he knew about Brent Grainger. Brent wasn't the Sandman. Andrew was one hundred percent sure of that, now. Sandman was a zero-day exploit, a man who takes advantage of a vulnerability. He thought Brent was Sandman's partner. But this was sloppy. So what changed? If Sandman saw Brent as the clean-up crew only, Brent would now be a weakness in the network's defenses, a vulnerability. Brent screwed up this time. Sandman would soon know.

Andrew and Elliot weren't normally partners. Elliot worked with Katia, and he worked with Brent. But Brent called out today. It all started to make sense. Brent couldn't work anymore. He called off shift because he planned to escape, not from the police, but from Sandman.

Andrew nudged Elliot. "This has my gut on edge. I won't make it back without some relief. Give me five."

"Sure, man. Take your time." Elliot continued to watch the new horror unfold.

Distanced from the others, Andrew dialed Gerald Wells's number. When the man answered, Andrew filled him in on what he had learned so far.

Gerald asked, "So. One hundred percent not Brent. I agree. Who?"

Andrew stood in the background and watched Zahra snap pictures of the scene. Brent told him she and Katia were an item. It was hard for him to imagine Zahra's soft curves in bed with a woman, but he definitely understood the draw to Katia. He hoped Brent was right. After all of this, Katia deserved something good to happen in her life. "I don't know who kills them, but my guess is Brent has a contract with whoever does."

"Assuming Brent is our dark web porn-master, how does that connect?"

Andrew swiveled his head from side to side. "Watching the forensic investigator snap pictures just now got me to thinking about Brent's pictures on the dark net. Before Zahra took over as the forensic investigator for Hatteras Island, his pictures included a lot of different crime scene photos."

Gerald didn't respond right away. When he did, Andrew could tell he wasn't connecting the dots. "Right." It sounded almost like a question. "We questioned how many people were taking them."

Dr. Webb's team was wrapping up. Andrew talked faster. "I found enough proof to assume they came from all over the United States. Like whoever was responsible was able to get people to send them to him somehow. Now they're more concentrated. The backdrops similar. Like multiple angles of the same few scenes rather than spread out."

Gerald followed his line of thinking. "Something changed. What?"

Andrew continued bouncing ideas off of his boss. "What about the forensic investigator? Not Zahra Knox. The previous one. According to Zahra, she traveled with Dr. Webb to disaster sites a dozen or more times over the years she was in the position. Zahra told us she wishes the good doctor was younger. He doesn't travel much now."

"I'll see what I can find out about the last investigator. You figure out how a kid from a quiet strip of sand ends up as a porn lord and possible link to a serial killer."

"That's why I'm here, boss."

"It is now."

Chapter Nineteen

Brent shouldn't have dumped her body so close to the first crime scene. He knew it was dangerous with the constant flow of agents and reporters and curious onlookers.

But he had no choice.

"You understand. Don't you?" He touched the screen gently. Elizabeth's face came into view, then her body, then the backdrop, as picture after picture pinged into view on the computer screen. For a moment, Brent sat back and enjoyed the experience of the blurred whites, yellows, reds, and silvers coming together to create minuscule moments of memory.

He considered purchasing one of those new cameras, the ones with Wi-Fi built in to move pictures seamlessly to the cloud, but there was something about the cable lying on his desk, something about the connection, the pulse of the camera beating picture-by-picture onto his screen that made the experience of what he did even sweeter.

He had done so many clean-up jobs over the years. Each one went off without a hitch. Brent followed the rules, never veered from the plan. This should have been no different. And it would have been, except Elizabeth was an artist. Brent was an artist. He owed it to her to take his time, to make everything perfect, every shot perfect. Perfection takes time. For the first time since Nadia died, Brent ignored specific instructions. He didn't take Elizabeth across to Ocracoke Island. Instead, he worked long past the hour of the last ferry, which left him no choice but to dump Elizabeth sloppily onto the beach.

The thumbnails stopped pinging in. Brent clicked onto the final shot. It was the last picture he took of her on the red-and-black-checkered blanket in the washroom. The shot caught the edge of the brown picnic basket sitting open just above and to the left of her pale blonde hair. He loved her cut. Short. The front edging her celestial face like a gentle frame. A flawless shot.

Brent admired the contrast between the deep pinks and tans of gristle and the pale white of skin. His finger traced the bold line of red along the slash's edge. Exquisite.

You would be proud of this work, Elizabeth. You would love the ghastly pallor, the love story of a woman's last heartbeat. The representation of the last push of color up the long, slender, white neck. How could I not sacrifice myself for you? For us? For such a perfect masterpiece?

He would have to die to escape the man to whom he owed last night's experience. Brent was prepared to do so. But first, he would give to his followers his final artistic portfolio.

He opened each picture in turn. Hundreds of them. Each one took him back to the tiny room under the dune. It was a room so well hidden that even if they found Sandman's house, the room could easily go unnoticed.

He was the only one who knew what Sandman was capable of. Not even the police officers, rescue workers, and FBI agents that tirelessly worked his grisly graveyard knew his true potential. Last night, when he realized the time, fear swirled in the pit of his stomach. He thought about leaving, getting a message to his contractor, negotiating the move of the body the next night. Ultimately, his draw to being with Elizabeth was too great, and the awareness that breaking the rules meant his demise was too clear. Brent was a walking dead man the moment he missed the ferry.

When he should have been stuffing Elizabeth's lifeless body into the picnic basket and into the covered bed of his truck, he was rolling the edges of the red-and-black picnic blanket, instead. First one side and then the other, until the rolls of fabric tucked her in tight. He contemplated this last pose in the death room. It needed to be just right.

Should it be her hand or his? His face, perhaps. That would make a final statement. *If I pull this off, I will need anonymity. Not my face.* Brent decided on her hand, placed carefully between her own legs, one leg bent slightly, almost demurely, her head turned toward the camera and slightly down. He moved her mouth until the lips parted slightly, corners raised enough to give her cheeks the look of pleasure he was after.

When he should have been driving his truck onto the Ocracoke-bound ferry, he was moving the beautiful Elizabeth into the room where Sandman had watched her for the last week. He scanned the walls and ceiling to make sure the man hadn't placed any new cameras. If he had, and if he pushed the Calculator button on his phone to observe the progress, Brent would be dead before he left the room. But still he continued. The single camera Brent knew existed was covered with a black cloth. Sandman didn't like this part. He never watched. He covered the camera on the last day of her captivity for every woman who was held here.

"I don't want to look," Sandman said. "But I will. I know I will."

Brent liked that the man knew his own weakness. It guaranteed alone time to snap the pictures he needed to supply the demand of his followers.

Tonight was about more than his followers. This woman was his kindred spirit, a fellow artist, the only person since Nadia he had to get just right.

Moving Elizabeth to the holding room, the room with the mattress and chains, wasn't difficult. As he gently pushed his hands between her body and the blanket, he contemplated what he would do when he left. The ferry was out, obviously. Weights on her ankles? Risk digging in a dune? Head the other way on Highway 12, out of town? No. He would leave her where she would be easily found. Brilliant. All eyes on you, beautiful Elizabeth. And none on me.

He'd have little time before the Sandman was out for his blood. A merciless prospect.

Brent laid Elizabeth on the mattress that smelled of her urine and sweat. "Where shall I go, Elizabeth? Somewhere warm, with an ocean. I have to have the ocean. Somewhere with my own dunes, not his."

He smiled at the thought, at how far he'd come from that scared teenager who cried as he recounted the way in which his adult teacher broke his heart. He would be gone before the emergency task force finished working the scene, before the Sandman knew he was forsaken, before his own identity was traced.

He went to the computer. Pictures flickered past on their way to the folder marked Artist to Artist: Elizabeth against the wall, cross-legged on the naked mattress; Elizabeth with her head bowed nearly against her unclothed chest; a close-up of one strand of her hair that formed a comma on her cheek, the end touching lightly against her upper lip.

Brent paused the upload with the touch of a button and reached down to push the band of his sweatpants and boxers down toward his hips. He hadn't been able to relieve himself last night or this morning. It was too dangerous to leave behind any trace that would connect him to the murders he would never commit. But in the home he'd soon be leaving, he'd allow himself the few seconds to release the buildup of excitement that came from knowing his work was some of the most sought after on the dark web.

"E.Liz.A.Beth," He said her name in syllables that matched his rapidly beating heart. "I won't disgrace you by hiding your face. You're my masterpiece. Our work will gain you the notoriety you sought in life and me the fame I had no idea I wanted until we met."

He spent his remaining hours in Buxton in his hideaway closet going through the small personal items he'd managed to collect over the past ten years. Ten years he did this. Ten years of rage and despair and hope and ecstasy. He began his relationship with others on the dark web even longer ago. The web wasn't always the colorful, fast-moving realm of today. Once it was just bulletin boards and pseudonyms as gamers learned from one another the art of Thexder. For him, that was where it all started.

Every weekend, his father let him use the monstrous computer that sat on his desk. He knew it was because they didn't want to entertain him for that many hours, or for any hours, truth be told. The only person in his life that did matter, his grandfather, died when Brent was ten. With no one left to pull him away from the screen, he quickly became a regular on electronic bulletin boards where gamers exchanged information and learned the art of breaking the law. Being able to exert his will on system after system was invigorating. As the Internet grew, and the dark web grew, so did his skills. Brent became something of a celebrity in a wilderness where the sickest of the sick go to play.

This celebrity status put him in contact with a man who called himself Dr. Blanche. Together with an unnamed third party, Brent and the doctor made a fortune finding the names of babies who died prior to their second birthdays and creating false identities for those who needed to disappear forever.

This celebrity status also put him in contact with the most deviant of all humans on the planet—those who derive pleasure from pictures of small children, teenagers, and adults in various stages of death and sex. Fulfilling their need ensured Brent made more money through the partnership than he could spend in all of his life on the small island of Buxton.

After leaving Elizabeth on the beach in the wee hours of the morning, Brent reached out to Dr. Blanche. He needed a new identity immediately, complete with an impenetrable background in case anyone came digging. The good doctor didn't disappoint. He delivered in less than seven hours.

A few clicks in a different direction netted Brent a private plane and a ride in a car with tinted windows that gave the appearance of clear glass. He coordinated times and places.

He would have the early part of the day, but no longer. Someone would stumble upon Elizabeth. He tried to turn the basket on its side without her body spilling forth, but he miscalculated the weight. Even in the dark, he couldn't take the time to make changes to the scene. He was too close to the original sandy graveyard, and someone would patrol the area regularly. By noon, she would be on everyone's television set.

"Breaking news. The body of a woman has been found…"

Perfect. Everyone would be swarming around Elizabeth. Everyone, that is, except the Sandman, who would likely still be in his room, alone. It was Monday. On Mondays, he stayed locked away in his room to balance his books. After a kill, it was also his time to get his head back in the game as an upstanding citizen of Buxton.

Nothing tied Brent to the Sandman except for the summer after Nadia's death when he worked in his shop. I'll teach you to be just like me, he told Brent. And he had, but not as a carpenter. Brent was horrible with tools, and after a few months, the man resigned himself to the idea that Brent wasn't woodworking-apprentice material. There was also nothing to tie him to Elizabeth except for the cookouts he and his ex-wife attended where Katia and Elizabeth were guests as well.

Brent pulled the decals off his truck before going inside last night. All of them. And they were now in the little room where he stood. By the time anyone said anything about the truck, he would be setting up shop on a Costa Rican island, safe and secure.

He would miss his daughter. He would even miss Elliot and his wife, his own ex-wife, and Katia. These were his friends, his meat-world family. But they weren't his passion. Even his daughter couldn't replace what he had in the virtual world. Even if she could, staying in Buxton would end in one of two ways. With him dead or with Sandman dead. There was no in between.

A final look around the room, and Brent was finished. The pictures were uploaded; the gas was poured everywhere. He stood in the middle of the living room. In one hand, he held a T-shirt pulled from the back of his dresser drawer. Nadia had given it to him the first time they made love at her home. He swore it still smelled like her. In the other hand, he held the lighter his grandfather used until the day he died. He rolled the thumbwheel slowly. The metal ridges felt good against his skin. It seemed appropriate the shirt and lighter be the tools used to send flames into the room behind the wall and into the room that housed the computer. The fire would spread rapidly through the small, fifteen-hundred-square-foot space while he traveled down Highway 12 and across the bridge. He rolled the thumbwheel faster. He liked the way the blue-and-yellow flame turned his grandfather's face a golden hue as he puffed his pipe to life. He missed the simplicity of his grandfather.

He raised the old T-shirt and dangled the hem just above the flame. When the shirt started to burn, he dropped it to the floor and stepped out of the tiny room and toward the door. He crossed the threshold at the exact moment a black, Lincoln Town Car slowed in front of his smoldering home.

His grandfather used to say, "Money doesn't buy happiness, boy. Try to remember that." He slid into the backseat and motioned for the driver to proceed.

"Maybe not, grandfather, but it can certainly buy punctuality and anonymity. And today, that's close enough to happiness for…" Brent looked down at the passport in his hand. "For Quintin Finn." A slight smile crossed his lips. Good-bye, Brent.

Chapter Twenty

Sandman planned the death of Gina Dahl for seven years. Today, he sat in his room and thought through every detail. Somewhere, he made a mistake. It was the only explanation for the week's events.

When Katia was eighteen, she told him she was in love with Elizabeth. "A couple," she said.

"Over my dead body," he answered.

He lost it in that moment. This was his little girl. Rosario's little girl. Nothing could shake him more than someone who sought to harm his little girl. He shouldn't have threatened to run over his daughter and Elizabeth with the car. He shouldn't have chased them to the beach. He shouldn't have acted like he was out of control. Those choices cost him years. So much lost time while he regrouped and showed Katia he was okay with her choice. Time when she could have been saved.

She can still be saved, he thought. I can still fix this.

Gina laughed at him when he went to her to ask for her help. They sat in Gina's brightly colored kitchen, adrift in primary reds and yellows and blues.

"They're in love, Richard. Why in the world would you want to interfere with that?"

He kept his hands under the table, fists balled into tight circles. "Love? Are you serious right now? One, they're eighteen. Two, they're both girls. Three, they have no idea what harm they'll bring to themselves and their families with this bullshit."

Gina's lips puffed out with air as she blew an exasperated breath into a sunbeam. She let silence hang between them for a moment, obviously trying to decide the best way to approach such a sensitive topic. "I won't apologize or pretend I think this is wrong. I just don't. I told them they have my blessing. You need to get on board. It's 2010. Civil unions are becoming the norm. Hell, you can even be gay and adopt children in the Netherlands and Quebec. Let them be."

It was her fault this happened. He thought Gina and Elizabeth would be good for Katia. She appeared so sad since her mami died. She was a brave girl, strong and adaptable, but she needed a mother. I'm so sorry, Rosario. I've let the devil into our daughter's world.

"Richard?"

It was Gina's voice, but as his anger grew, Gina morphed into the demons he held inside. His vision blurred. His head hurt. He tried to focus on Gina's face. It twisted and became his aunt's face, and then it became the faces of the others. One after another, it blurred into the next. How many were there? Fourteen in the dunes counting his auntie. But there were many others. Ones he left exposed. Ones where he took unnecessary risks in response to his youthful needs.

Richard thought back to those early years. He could see them clearly in his head. He spent so many years naming, remembering, and associating—a game he played even today, a game that kept the fantasies, the feeling of completion and accomplishment, alive.

Helen. The Corkscrew. She gave the neighbor boy wine after he mowed her lawn each week, made him weak, made him giggle. That kill was for the pocket knife, blade out and ready; it met her throat at the same moment his fingers wound into her hair. Yank. Slash. Perfect landing. Beautiful. He let her head fall forward so her mouth was next to his face and breathed in her last breath.

Aunt Judith. Not his aunt. The boy's. Georgie, she called him. He could smell the city, feel the rush of his nineteen-year-old self surrounded by the traffic and lights of New York. Inside, his body thumped with adrenaline as he remembered following Judith and the boy, her hand on his back, her fingers in his messy, light-brown curls, her laugh, so much like his own auntie. In the moment, he forgot Georgie wasn't him and Aunt Judith wasn't his own aunt…

"Richard? Richard Billings. Listen to me." Gina's voice crushed the thought. "I don't know what your hang-up is with our girls and their love, but you need to get it together. We're all they have. They need us to be supportive, not to make them feel unworthy or disgusting or wrong."

Sandman pictured her blood dripping through the whitewashed boards of the kitchen table where the sunbeam played. He moved his eyes from his fantasy to her face. "You're right." He placed the words carefully into the air. "Absolutely. I just needed to talk it through with you."

For seven years, he pretended she was right, that he didn't hate her, that he didn't dream about the feel of the blade as it reached through layer after layer of her too-tan skin until the pink and white lay bare to the primary red she loved so much.

For seven years, when the draw was too strong or the need too great, he found other blondes, blondes who deserved the feel of his knife against their skin, blondes who preyed on the innocence of a child. He learned to swallow his food over the lump of hatred when Elizabeth stayed for dinner. He laughed at Gina's jokes when they were forced together at a neighborhood bonfire on the beach in front of their house. And he even agreed to attend numerous real estate events over the years as her plus one.

Along the way, Marco learned pieces of who his father was. Richard underestimated the boy who didn't speak. Each year, even as Richard refused to purchase speak aids for his son, Marco added words and sounds in new ways. Marco knew and now he was trying to tell Katia. Richard couldn't let this happen. He loved his children too much.

****

Paige ran alongside Katia at a laid-back pace. They ran the length of beach untouched by the catastrophes of the past week. An easy banter drifted back and forth between long stretches of comfortable silence. The last silence had stretched across a quarter mile of sand.

Paige thought about the pictures, about Marco, about the connections between the women who were brought together in this case.

Paige was good at puzzles, at clues. It was one of the things she loved about her line of work. It demanded she key in on minute details of each dog, to learn movements and desires and to use them to train and train until each animal reacted exactly the same way in a crisis situation. And yet she felt inept at piecing together the clues that could be hiding in the photos from one teenager's camera.

Paige went over them again. She tried to focus in on what they hadn't seen. The crayons. What colors were there? Deep blue?

No. Purple. Yes. Majestic Purple. And Gold. Purple and gold. How were they placed? She couldn't think of anything that made them stand out. What about the box? What was in it? She tried to picture the blurry items. Nothing stood out. A toy phone, maybe. A tiny statue of some kind. A box. Or was it a frame? A picture frame. What was a picture frame doing in a box of stuff set out for children and teens at the center for the disabled?

Her mind went back to Katia's table again. There was a picture of Yogi Bear and Boo Boo taken by a boy doing what he loved to do best, watch old cartoons. A door knob. To which door, none of them had any idea. The knobs were all the same. Marco's map. And his map again. And again. Obviously, Marco loves maps. What else? She thought about the mix-match of things, so much like Katia's brother's brain.

Paige looked over at Katia, who appeared deep in thought. She touched Katia's arm and signaled she needed to slow down. "You ready to head back?"

Katia nodded. "Probably should." She touched her watch with her finger without breaking stride. "Shit. We've been gone close to an hour. My father will not be happy."

Paige motioned toward Frankie who was happily talking to the waves and weaving back and forth between the white foam and the two women. "What about him?"

A half smile came across Katia's face. She pulled her upper lip into her mouth with her bottom teeth. "Come on, boy." She patted the side of her leg. "We're going home." Katia looked to Paige. "Papi won't question it until you leave." She shrugged and sprinted forward. She glanced back over her shoulder. "After you leave, I'll handle it."

Back at Katia's house, the women took the front steps two at a time. Until last week, Paige was slightly covetous of what Katia possessed. From her outsider vantage point, she thought Katia led a life to be envied. She had a sexy, bad boi persona that guys and girls both found attractive. She had the most well-built house on the strip, with the beach outside her back door. Her father doted on her and her brother, and she had no real need to work.

Paige's own mother was a strict disciplinarian who believed the saying, "Spare the rod, spoil the child." Her father was an equally hard-ass disciplinarian, a principal at work and at home. In high school, she watched the Katias and Elizabeths of the world float through life and she wished she was them. She hated that she was the girl who had to go to a school away from her friends, who had to come home and work with her mom in the training facility, who had to hide who she was from parents and brothers and aunts and uncles and cousins. She loved her adult life, but she was still not the openly gay Katia Billings. In that respect, her life still sucked, yet somehow today that was okay.

Katia was several steps in front of Paige. She held Frankie in her arms. Paige could hear her breathe, slow and deep, as she stood in front of the door. Katia was scared. That was a word Paige never associated with Katia. "You want me to hold him?" Paige asked.

"No," Katia said. "I got this. How can he say no to Gina's dog? It isn't like I just picked a stray up off of the street."

"True that."

The phone in Paige's pocket buzzed as she lifted her foot over the threshold. She was so into her run she hadn't noticed any of the phone notifications. She pulled it out of her pocket and pushed the door closed behind her. Seven messages. Paige read in order from the first one. It was from Zahra.

Another body. Take Katia home and call me.

Where are you guys?

Paige. Fucking answer me.

The fourth text was from her brother: *Did you hear? They found Elizabeth.*

Paige sucked in her breath. She hadn't expected those words, not from her brother. She looked at Katia's back as she rounded the corner into the living area. Paige touched the arrow to read another message from her brother.

Are you okay? Do I need to come get you?

The final text was from Zahra. *Can't leave beach. NEED to know you have Katia. That she is safe. PLEASE.*

The television was blaring Foghorn Leghorn and that pesky chicken hawk. Paige responded to Zahra while she walked to the corner of the living room.

With her. Will tell her in...

Katia's voice, high and full of palpable pain, pulled her eyes away from the screen.

Katia moved from object to object, calling for Marco. "Paige? Paige? Fuck! He isn't here!"

"What do you mean he isn't here? Where would he go?"

Katia appeared deaf to the question. She ran past her, headed for the stairs. Frankie nipped at her heels. Paige tried to keep up, sliding the phone back into her pocket and grabbing the banister for extra propulsion forward.

Katia opened her brother's door and called his name. And then the closet door. She spun in a circle, her black, fringed hair spinning out as if charged by an unseen current, Frankie still at her heels, spinning, too, barking. The two moved into the room adjoining his, a light-blue room with clouds on the ceiling.

Katia mumbled and Paige strained to hear. She couldn't get close enough to the spinning woman to make out the words, words that sounded like a chant. Everything was out of control. Paige's heart was pounding. "Katia. Stop. Just for a minute. Think."

"He doesn't go anywhere but these three rooms," Katia said. "Nowhere. Papi? Papi!"

"Talk to me," Paige begged. "What's wrong? Maybe they're together. Maybe they went to town. Maybe they—"

"Something's wrong. Very fucking wrong. My father doesn't, he doesn't take Marco out on Monday morning unless it's to school. He isn't happy I'm keeping him home. The TV's still on. It wouldn't be on. Maybe he made him go. Maybe you're right. Paige, what if he made him go?"

Paige thought about the message in her pocket. So many things seemed wrong. She desperately tried to hold it together for her friend. "Okay," Paige said. "You told me he has a tracker. Right?"

Katia looked at her. At first, it seemed as if the words didn't register, but Paige could see a calm slowly returning to her eyes.

"Yes." Katia sounded less frantic. "Yes. You're right. I keep it in here." She headed in the direction of what Paige assumed was her bedroom. She and Frankie entered a room Paige had never been in before. She followed closely behind. It was dark and dreary.

Katia opened a black drawer in a black dresser and pulled out a silver device. She turned it over in her hand, looked at the screen, shook it, looked again, and tapped it against her leg. "What is it," Paige asked, keeping her voice as even as the circumstances allowed.

"It's dead."

They quickly made their way down the long, upstairs hallway to a closed door Paige assumed belonged to Katia's father. Paige didn't know a lot about him. She and Katia weren't close in high school, and until this week, they saw one another only a handful of times. Katia seemed hesitant to open the door or to knock. Katia, who spun out of control two minutes ago, now stood unmoving, staring at the wooden barrier.

"Katia," Paige said in an undemanding voice. "Katia. Knock."

Katia looked at the tracker in her hand and again at Paige. "He's never been out of range. This tracks for up to five miles."

Paige understood. When Katia knocked on that door, whatever was happening would become very real. She thought about the phone in her pocket, wondered how Zahra was holding up with Dr. Webb on the beach. She needed to tell Katia about Elizabeth, but she couldn't. Not until they found Marco. "He's okay, Katia," Paige said. "Maybe your father took him for a ride. Maybe the tracker is broken."

Katia didn't answer. She made a fist with her right hand and slowly rapped her knuckles against the wooden door. No response. Katia knocked again, and again no response.

The two looked at one another. Paige reached for the handle and turned. Not breaking eye contact with Katia, she eased the door open, allowing Katia to take in the room. Silence greeted them. Total silence. "I don't think he's here," Paige said. "See. They're off some—"

The sound of the back door opening stopped Paige's words. The women turned in unison and bolted for the stairs. "Marco? Papi?"

"Marco?" Richard responded, his voice getting louder as he moved closer. "Isn't he with you? I got your text saying you were going for a run. I jumped in the shower and came down, but he wasn't here. Figured you decided to take him."

"No, Papi. No." Katia held up the tracker. "It isn't picking up his signal."

The women were standing mid-staircase, Katia's father at the bottom, looking up. Paige had her hand in her pocket, her fingers around the phone, trying to will away the text messages. This can't be happening. She wished she was anywhere but here; at the same time, she was thankful she was here.

Katia started down the rest of the stairs, taking her phone out of her pocket as she went. "I'm calling 9-1-1."

Chapter Twenty-One

Marco sat cross-legged on the mattress, the left side of his face on fire. He couldn't remember how he got from the front of the television screen to the room behind the workbench, but he remembered his father's words.

"This is all your sister's fault. Your sister and her new little band of bitches."

Why, Papi? Marco doesn't like that word. Katia loves us.

His eyes must have said what his mouth couldn't. He saw his dad's arm swing back. Something in it. What?

Marco brought his hand to his face. Blood. His blood. His father's hand on his shoulder. "Can you walk, son? I'm sorry. I didn't want to. Your sister made me. We have to hide, son. Another storm is coming."

Marco likes storms. Don't we like storms, Papi?

"Push the pin in right here, Marco. I put her right here." His father's finger on the map and his words don't match in his head. You didn't put the storm there, Papi. Why did you put that thing in my neck? Why do you hate Katia? Katia loves us.

He remembered his father's other hand, the one not on his shoulder, the one not spotted with blood, his blood. The burning from his head shot little electric waves down his arm and into his fingers. The pain made his vision blur. Everything turned black. He wanted to close his eyes, but he knew he shouldn't. If he held still, he could see a pinpoint of light in the black.

His brain tried to put the pieces together. He didn't like it here. He wanted the pictures. His pictures. From the toy cameras Dr. Abney gave him. The ones he took after the first time and the ones he took after the last time.

Why did Katia print them? He tried to stop remembering. Rock, Marco. Don't think about the pictures. About the times in the room. Marco rocked and chanted. But he couldn't forget.

Slash. Fast. Slash. Fast. Slash fast.

He hit the good side of his head with his palm. Over and over. Smells bad in here. Like the farm. Don't like the farm. Don't like the teachers who said learn about animals. No animals at home.

Except Frankie. Katia brought home Frankie. Don't tell. Papi will be mad. Don't make Papi mad, Katia. Papi doesn't like bad girls. Bad girls have to be punished. Marco doesn't like blood. Slash. Fast. No, Papi. Katia isn't bad. Why did Papi say she is bad? Katia brought Frankie home. Marco petted Frankie. Marco loves Frankie. Frankie loves Marco. Marco is bad. But not bad like Katia. Katia is a bad girl. Papi doesn't like bad girls.

The pain from the methodical hits of his palm felt good. His body reacted by slowing down. The rocking became less erratic, more soothing. He tried to focus on the outline of the door. "Duck your head, Marco. Do you know why the opening is so small?" His dad told him stories about the door, about the room, about the weather boards, while they sat on the blanket with the bleeding women.

"Before you were born. Before your sister was born. Your mom and I were so in love. She was good then, but I knew. I knew it was possible. So when I built this house, I chose a piece of ground right up against the largest dunes. I planned carefully, worked on this room foot by foot. I placed supports, poured concrete, brought in more sand. It's soundproof and weatherproof. I wanted it to be bigger, but that would have been a greater risk. Someone would notice the house stuck out here. Twenty-seven years, son. Twenty-seven years and not a single person has stumbled on my room, our room now."

Marco held still and thought about the cameras. He liked the sound the button made when he pushed, and the way his finger started to move and then stopped just as the click sounded in his ear. Slow and steady, Marco. Push slow and steady. Dr. Abney taught him how to put his eye against the little hole, to feel the button. Gently. Slow. Click.

Marco wanted to tell when he put the camera up to his eye and found the doorknob to the workshop. He wanted to tell when he put the purple and red and white crayons together. Gina's colors.

Gina loves purple. Marco loves Gina's purple shoes. Except when they jerk. Blood. Blood from the white skin on the purple shoe. Why were you bad? His breathing started to hurt again, and his eyes filled up with tears.

He wanted to tell when he snuck into Papi's room and bent way over to see into the box with the camera's little eye.

He learned about the box after the first bad woman, the one Papi hit in the head because she tried to run away in the garage. She was supposed to stay asleep. "You're ruining everything," Papi said to her.

Marco thought she sounded like the dog on the farm. It screamed because Suzi stepped on its foot. Was Suzi bad?

He only opened the door without knocking because he thought it was an animal in the workshop and it was hurt. He was supposed to be sitting still until Katia got home. Seven thirty at the end of the day. Katia comes home. Twenty-four on. Forty-eight off. Sit there, Marco. Nothing for you.

Papi didn't like him in the workshop during the storms. After the storm, they did the board together. "Don't go. Don't. Workshop," he said into the small, dark room. There are sharp things in the workshop, Marco. His dad's voice mixed with his own in his head.

He raised his arm to his mouth, bit down on his forearm. Hard. Harder. Blood. My blood. Good. Rock. Bite. My blood. Fast. Slash. Fast Slash. My blood. Not hers. I can smell it. The mattress. Like the farm. Screaming. Like the dog. Frankie. Where is Frankie? Go away, Marco. So noisy. Marco doesn't like noise. Make her stop screaming. Bite harder. Blood. My blood. He rocked, faster and faster, trying to get his mind away from the blood and the screaming.

Papi was nice after he showed him the room, after they took the woman there, after the blood. They went to his room. His dad spoke slow, quiet. Marco likes quiet.

"Papi keeps treasure in here, son. We can never tell anyone. This is your aunt. She was bad." She didn't look bad in the picture in the polished silver frame. She was pretty. Pretty like Gina. But she wasn't in color. No purple or red in the picture.

"Put the ring in the box, son." The ring was silver. Like the frame. Like the knife. The knife came back into his head. Papi loves knives. "Look at the glint in the light, son. Isn't it beautiful?"

The hard, silver edge. Shiny. Papi, why are you pushing so hard? Hard against the side of her white neck. Bad girl. Slash. Fast. Marco rocked.

"Someday you will make the slash, Marco."

Butterflies. Not good butterflies. Katia gave him good butterflies. Stories of Mami. Of tickling tummies. Good butterflies. He wished his words were better sometimes. But I might tell.

"Don't tell, Marco. Never tell."

Bad butterflies. Bad when the knife slid through the skin, when the blood came out in a line, fast. Slash. Fast. He rocked. Bad butterflies when the scream came out. Bad butterflies when she had good words and then had no words. Bad butterflies when his dad closed his eyes and moaned as he pulled the blonde woman's head back against his shoulder.

"Did you see that, Marco? Did you feel it?"

Only bad butterflies. And scared. Marco feels scared.

He had never been here without Papi. There was no woman. He thought there would be a woman when Papi took his hand and led him into the workshop, even though there was no storm. They only went to the room when there was a storm.

2-0-0-M-P-H.

Papi shook his head at him, pulled his arm. Asked him why he could say numbers and letters better than words. He didn't know why. He liked the weather board. Papi smiled when they put dots on the weather board. He hated the room, though. It was past the big weather board.

"Do you remember how to open it, son?"

Papi is proud when Marco opens. Reach way down. Stretch. Finger on the button. Move fast, Marco, or the workbench will scratch you. He liked the way the bench moved when he pushed the secret button. Good butterflies. He wanted to close it and do it again. And close it. Again. Again. Never go in the room. Never go where the bad butterflies live. Too dark. Smelly.

He rocked and chanted, wishing Katia knew his secret. Fast. Slash. Fast. Slash. His tummy was hungry. He wanted a cinnamon roll. He looked around the space lit up only by the yellow bulb. No basket. No woman.

"Sit here, son." Papi made him sit on the picnic blanket after the blood.

Too many smells. Marco's tummy didn't want food after the blood. Eat it, Marco. Papi's eyes are different. Bad different. Like the bad butterflies. Never tell, Marco. Never tell or we will put Katia here. Katia is a bad girl. Katia's neck is tan, not white. Papi likes white necks. Fast. Slash. Do you want to do it, Marco? Her eyes. The woman with the white neck has wide eyes. Blue. Like Gina. Like Elizabeth. Like Paige. Marco likes Paige. And Zahra. Marco likes Zahra. Zahra has brown eyes like Katia. Girls are bad. Fast. Rock. Tap. Slash.

****

It wasn't supposed to be like this. Why had Katia printed the pictures? Why had Paige befriended Katia? Why was Katia being targeted again by a lesbian? Look at them. He scanned the room with his eyes. Katia and Paige sat next to one another on the couch. Katia's face was buried in her hands, and her elbows rested on her knees. Paige touched her back. Paige's ridiculous mutt sat at attention with his back against the couch between the girls. One of the officers sat in the chair across from the girls. The other stood at his side.

"Take your time." The officer who remained standing spoke directly to Katia.

Richard watched his daughter. She's strong. I'll help her become stronger. I don't want to kill you. I don't. You're not like her. Like his aunt. He hated that Katia reminded him of the woman who hurt him so many years ago. Not in coloring—his aunt was pale, had blonde hair and blue eyes—but in build and attitude. You're not like her.

Richard reminded himself of the order of needs—get the emergency workers focused on Marco, join the search. He concentrated on his movements. He ran his fingers through his hair. "How many more questions do you have?" He looked from one officer to the other. "My daughter is distraught. My son is missing." His voice shook. He moved closer to the couch. Show concern. Show fear. Show distress.

Richard hoped he wouldn't have to kill Marco. He didn't want to, just like he didn't want to kill Katia. Just like he didn't want to kill Roger all those years ago. But he would. To save himself, he would.

While Katia went up to get a piece of Marco's clothing, Richard paced the room. He wasn't worried about a dog picking up his son's scent in the house. It was everywhere, and the room was hidden. He paced because it was the only way he had to release the anger that was building inside. Brent knew the rules. He had broken the most important rule of all: Follow my instructions specifically. Disobedience wouldn't be tolerated. He would take care of Brent when this was over. Brent would die. The only regret Richard had was that he would no longer have someone to take the women away.

Katia came back into the living room. She had Marco's favorite science T-shirt in her hand. Before she handed it over to the officer, she held it to her face. "Will we get this back?" Her voice was muffled by the material.

"Yes. Of course." The younger of the two officers touched her shoulder. The two were working acquaintances, and it was obvious he struggled with remaining calm.

The group moved toward the front door. As Richard passed the kitchen table, his whole body tensed. The pictures scattered there infuriated him. A son was supposed to honor his father. What kind of way was this to repay the person who allowed you into such a beautiful world? Richard killed during storms, plotted them on a board he kept in the workshop. When Marco was small, five or six, he had taken an interest in the board, studied it for hours, touched it lightly, head cocked in silence. Richard was afraid he would move a pin, add one where it didn't belong, maybe even figure out a pattern in his autistic brain. He couldn't afford that, so he got the boy his own board. The board and a subscription to a weather magazine. He taught Marco where to put the pins. It was their secret world. It made the betrayal he felt now more painful.

Richard wondered if he should move the pins around on both boards. Fuck it. None of these idiots are smart enough to connect the kills to the dots on the board.

He heard Katia tell the officers she would stay at the house. He didn't move away from the table. He stared at the picture of the door handle. His insides shook. The smells of the day his son pushed open the workshop door flooded his memory. Later that night, he sat on the edge of his son's bed and explained it all to him. He loved his family. He wanted to stop for them. And he did once. For several years, their love was enough. And then another woman hurt a child. And he needed to save him. And then another. Each time his love for his wife and family grew stronger. Richard was happy. He was happy in his heart and in his mind.

"Marco. I did this for you. You have to understand. I did it all for you." He repeated those words to Marco the day he came through the garage door and saw the woman bleeding in Brent's arms. And Richard told Marco the same words when he left him today, cross-legged and rocking, his thumb and inside palm tap-tap-tapping against his knee, on the mattress that still smelled like the blood and urine of Elizabeth Dahl.

Chapter Twenty-Two

Until a few hours ago, Katia didn't think things could get any worse. They had. A charred body was pulled from Brent's burned home. Elizabeth's lifeless body was dumped on the beach. Her mildly verbal teenaged brother went missing. And now Frankie was acting weird.

Katia moved from room to room. She looked at her phone constantly. Where was everyone? She knew, of course. Volunteers and firefighters were still on scene at the Grainger home. Dr. Webb and Zahra were analyzing the scene at the beach, after which Elizabeth would be taken to the morgue in Greenville to be with the others. Her father was combing the island with a small search party for Marco. Knowing didn't help. She felt as if she were crawling out of her own skin.

She wanted to be a part of the search party, but her father had vetoed that idea. "He probably went to find you," her father said. "His routine is off."

She agreed with the routine being off, but something didn't feel right. She checked Marco's ankle bracelet regularly. She tried to remember whether she'd noticed the tiny light on her brother's ankle earlier in the day.

Frankie's whine cut into her thoughts. He hadn't stopped for over an hour. Damn dog. No wonder Papi doesn't want one.

She looked Frankie's direction. "Come here, boy," she said. "What else do you want?" Katia had taken him outside to do his business, but that didn't satisfy him. She had put down fresh water. That didn't work, either. He had food. "Do you know I'm freaking the fuck out, little dude? I don't want us to be stuck in this fucking house, either." She reached down and scratched the pup's head.

Katia knew the dog was distraught. Marco and Frankie had bonded as soon as their eyes met, way back when Gina brought the pup home. She'd taken Marco over to play with him on multiple occasions. "Go lay down. Seriously, Frankie. What do you want?"

Sighing, she tapped the front of her phone for the hundredth time. No new messages. She moved from the living room to the hallway, from the hallway to the dining area. She tapped on Paige's name. The last text was twenty minutes prior. *Bob just got here with the dogs.*

Fuck. Only twenty minutes? Time was dragging. She needed to hear from someone about something. Where are you, Monkey Face?

She tapped the screen again. Tapped Zahra's name. The last two messages were time stamped ten and eleven minutes prior: *It is going to be a long night.* And: *I wish I was with you.*

Katia responded: *I wish you were, too.* She could no longer pretend that it wasn't true.

Katia made sure the volume was at its highest level and slid the phone into the pocket of her sweats. She stretched her arms high above her head until the stomach muscles begged to be released. The pull felt good. She needed something to shake herself away from the edge of the precipice where the tears and anger threatened to consume her. She pulled her outstretched body to one side, freeing a strip of skin from her T-shirt. The breeze from the open window tickled its way up to her armpit. She shuddered, released the stretch, and pushed her arms out in front of her and around in circles. She'd agreed to stay close to home in case Marco came back, but she wasn't doing well with keeping her word. She was an emergency worker by trade, and every ounce of her being wanted to be on the beach, at the Grainger house, or finding her brother.

She looked into the living room at Frankie. The dog was pawing at the door to the workshop, his little paws relentless against the carpet. "Come on, boy. Do you want a treat?" She made kissy sounds and patted her leg. No response. He continued to ignore her and scratch.

She moved toward him. "He didn't even mention you being here," she said, talking to the dog as well as herself. Katia examined the spot where he'd been digging, his nose practically shoved under the door. "That's how distraught he is." She squatted next to Frankie, ran her hand back and forth on the carpet. "There's nothing here, boy. Do you want to go out again?" Frankie stopped momentarily and looked up at her. "Come on. Let's go out the front."

Katia stood and walked to the chair. She grabbed the leash and moved back to her little ward. "I can't take you if you don't cooperate." She hooked the leash to its matching blue collar. Frankie continued to whine and scratch. "Fine. We'll go through the workshop." Katia reached for the handle and turned.

As soon as the door was opened wide enough for Frankie to fit through, he ran his lead completely taut. But he didn't run toward the door, instead, he bolted toward the workbench where her father sanded his beautiful pieces of wood.

"This way, boy. Come on." Katia pulled the leash and took a few steps toward the side door, but Frankie stood strong, tail down, nose against the wooden leg of the bench. There was a deep guttural sound coming from his throat. The goose bumps Katia felt earlier returned, but this time, they weren't from the breeze on her bare side. They were from fear.

Her gut tightened and butterflies fluttered faster and faster, as she realized Frankie was trying to tell her something. "What is it? There's nothing here but Papi's workbench, scattered tools, and wood chips and shavings."

It smelled like freshly carved childhood to Katia, a smell that brought back memories of laughing with her mother and father as they tracked a storm on the weather board and talked about someday being a family of storm chasers traveling the country measuring, reporting, and taking pictures.

"Until you died," she said into the wood-infused air. "Until you fucking died. And now I'm here. And something's wrong, and Papi's out looking for your son, and I'm here. And. Fuck, Mami. I'm here. And Marco's gone. And I don't know what to fucking do."

Frankie looked up at her. His eyes seemed to beg for understanding. Like Marco's eyes. Katia walked over to him, letting the leash recoil into its base as she moved. "Okay, Frankie. What do you see that I don't?" Kneeling next to the animal, she looked toward the area where Frankie was focused. Nothing was visible. "It's a wall, boy. A concrete, workshop wall."

Her phone buzzed in her pocket.

Nietzsche didn't pick up anything. Good news on that. Any word on Marco?

Katia was relieved, even though none of them thought there was another burial site where Elizabeth was dumped. Whoever was doing this was too smart for that. If there was another site, it wasn't there. She tapped out her response:

No word. Papi thinks he's hiding. Overstimulated. Still looking.

She thought about writing more, but Paige had her hands full at the beach. She didn't know what she would say anyway. I'm sitting on the floor staring at a concrete wall because Frankie is freaked out by the smell of wood?

She hit Send, slid the phone back in her pocket, and returned to Frankie and the wall. "Okay, mister. What are you trying to tell me?" Frankie licked her face and moved farther under the bench.

Katia got on all fours and crawled into the confined space. It took a second for her eyes to adjust to the change in light. She used her hand to compensate, running it along the smooth concrete. Nothing. She tried again to see what the dog was seeing.

Maybe it isn't sight. Maybe it's smell. She remembered Dr. Webb's speech about how many olfactory receptors a dog has in his nose—over 220 million—and she wished for one moment that she had as many. Katia closed her eyes. Breathed deeply through her nose. Wood. I smell wood. And oil. The air held a tinge of the lubricant her father used for hinges. And the slight scent of her father's aftershave. More childhood memories flooded in. She shook them away. Focus Katia. What else?

Katia spent a full minute or more on all fours, breathing in, her eyes closed. Frankie's guttural sounds were softer now as he waited next to her. Marco's pictures. He had one of a doorknob. It was the doorknob, the one to this workshop. And the weather board. Both his and Papi's boards. He took the same pictures over and over again. And there was part of the workbench. When she had reviewed the picture with Paige and Zahra, they thought it was just a piece of wood. Now she wasn't so sure.

Katia's head spun with new thoughts. Marco was trying to say something with his pictures. What? Her eyes flew open. The pictures. They're still on the table in the kitchen. Every part of her being reverberated with a new knowledge, a knowledge she understood had the power to change her life forever.

She left Frankie where he was and headed back into the house. Katia felt her heart beat faster with each breath. Anger welled inside as she walked through the doorway. And then—Darkness.

****

Richard watched through the lens on his phone as his daughter started to come to on the blood- and urine-stained mattress, her brother next to her, rocking, chanting. Most of his words were incoherent, but he made out a few: Slash. Fast. Katia. Bad.

Richard wondered if they made sense inside the boy's head.

Nothing was going according to plan, and Richard hated when things didn't go according to plan. It made him itch, literally itch, inside and out. Today, more than any other time since the day on the beach when he took control of his own life by taking the life of his aunt, he itched.

He looked first at the screen where Katia tried to make sense of what was happening and then to his arms where he had dug long lines of skin from their place between hand and elbow. The pain from digging deep felt good. It helped him focus. He never dug where people could see. Today it didn't matter.

"I'm sorry, son," Richard said, looking back to the screen. "I'll fix it. I will." He scratched the corner of his eye with his fingernail, where tears threatened to congregate. Not on my fucking watch. He scratched deeper. No time for weakness. Fix it, Richard. Don't let them win.

Marco was there because of Katia, because of Paige and Zahra and Elizabeth, because of Gina, because of the stupid little dog that somehow picked up Marco's scent through layers of soundproofing and concrete, and ultimately because of his aunt, the woman who had started all of this when he was a child.

Don't think about Marco right now. Marco will be okay. Get rid of Katia. Eradicate the cancer. Fix it. Until today, Richard thought the answer was to get Marco into a home where his needs could be met, where he would be monitored at all times, and where he wouldn't be able to tell Katia what he had seen.

Modern technology. Dr. Callum Abney. Katia.

His head was pounding. Nothing was right.

Fix it, Richard. Don't let them win.

Katia and Dr. Abney wanted to try a word-making device. He had vetoed it. If God had wanted him to talk, God would have given him the ability to form coherent sentences.

He and Katia had fought hard over that. I'm the father. This is my house.

Richard looked at the screen and moved his gaze to Katia. He talked to her picture on the screen. "Why did you have to love him too hard? Why did you have to find the pictures?"

Katia attempted to sit up. She shook her head from side to side as if trying to shake the drug from her system.

"Why did you bring the disgusting mutt into our home? We had everything we needed. If you had made a better choice, you would be helping me look for Marco. We would have grown closer. Instead, you ruined it."

Richard hated dogs, hated all animals, actually. When he saw Katia come through the door after her run, that thing in her arms, he almost went off. Almost. It was obvious it didn't belong to Paige. That was another lie. But he had to keep it together; the next minutes, hours, days, were crucial to his plan.

His gaze moved away from Katia and back to Marco. Don't be afraid, son. Richard thought about Marco in front of the television set when he came downstairs, sitting in what he knew was the exact spot his sister had left him. The idea was to eat one of the cinnamon rolls he knew would be sitting on a plate on the stove. She never made cinnamon rolls without making enough for her papi.

When he turned the corner from the hallway to the kitchen, his mind created a scene that was almost unbearable. He saw her there. His Rosario, teaching their daughter to sprinkle the cinnamon just so, the brown dust on their matching, white-and-pink aprons growing darker with each shake of Katia's hand. He heard Rosario's laughter. It was deep and real. When they cooked, Rosario's eyes sparkled with love for her daughter. He heard Katia's young voice. "Is that enough, Mami? Did I do it good?"

"Well, *chiquita*. Did you do it well? Yes." He watched his beautiful wife touch their daughter's chin and lift her face toward her own. "You did it well."

Her hand on Katia's chin. The look between them. It made him shiver, even now, after living without his wife, and without his aunt, for so many years.

This is your fault, Auntie. Richard remembered the feel of his aunt's fingers on his face, the feel of his hand on the knife as it slashed through her slick skin.

Rosario and Katia vanished as he reached the stove. The rolls were exactly where he knew they would be. He picked up the plate in one hand and a cinnamon roll in the other. Half of the first roll was gone before he reached the table.

"What the…" He looked at the pictures scattered across the flat surface. He glanced at Marco, oblivious to everything except the seventies cartoon characters on the screen, and then back at the table. "Why? Why couldn't you have left well enough alone, Katia? What have you done?" His voice was low, not meant for anyone. He put the plate on the table, the cinnamon rolls and the past that held a wife and little girl now gone.

The pictures told him all he needed to know: Yogi Bear and a picnic basket; the underneath corner of his workbench; crayons the color of blood, skin, and shoes; the weather boards, his and Marco's, the tacks telling the story of where women were abducted and which storm was brewing as they died.

Richard looked at Marco again. It saddened him. He loved his son, more than any other creature on the planet. But what if the boy found the words he was seeking? What if he took his sister's hand and led her to the bench in the workshop? Would she be smart enough to find the tiny latch built into the wood on the underside of the bench? It was way in the corner, covered by an additional piece of wood, noticeable by touch only. She won't find it—she can't.

His daughter was smart. Richard looked at the pictures again. He loved his children, both of his children. He wanted no harm to come to either of them. His plan formed quickly. He would lead Marco to the room, leave him there for a few days while the town searched for him, and then find him late at night and bring him home. Katia would forget the pictures for the moment. He would leave them on the table only long enough to have multiple people in and out. Then they would disappear.

Perfect. He felt pride as the plan came together in his mind. I am the parent. I don't give a shit how old either of you are. You'll learn I'm in charge in this house. He practiced the speech in his head as he moved to the living room and touched his son's shoulder.

****

The fog in her brain and the grunge in the room swirled together behind her eyes. Everything was blurry and seemed far away.

Marco? She blinked rapidly, trying to clear her vision. Where the fuck? Nothing made sense. Frankie. The voice in Katia's head was soft, full of pain, as pieces began to reformulate.

Frankie found something. What was it? The pictures. I was going to go look at the pictures. But why? Why was I going back to the table? Something Frankie did. He was sniffing, and whining, and digging. He was sniffing at the workbench. Marco had pictures of a workbench. Marco had pictures. He was trying to tell me something. Something about Papi? Papi, did you find something?

She remembered her father's face. Papi? Talk to me. He reached out. To hug me? No. What was he doing? A cloth. And that awful smell.

Katia wanted to fade back into the darkness where it was safe and warm, where she didn't know what was happening. She wanted to go back to a time and place where her family was safe and she wasn't here with her head in her brother's lap as he rocked back and forth. Marco stroked her hair. The movement pulled the stench from the soft floor beneath them and sent it wafting into her nostrils. "Marco. Stop. Stop."

The smell jostled the remnants of cinnamon rolls and coffee, which now moved up her esophagus.

"Marco, please," she whispered.

****

Paige tried another text and then another call. Until an hour ago, when she told her no other bodies were found on the beach, Katia was texting her every ten or fifteen minutes. Now, silence. She paced the sandy lawn of Brent Grainger's home with Nietzsche.

"Come on, sis," Bob said. "Let's get him home. Let's get us home." He motioned for her to join him at the edge of the property where several cars and emergency vehicles were now parked. "We're all tired."

Paige breathed in the smell of burned wood and wires. Soot filled her nasal passages. Her throat tightened. She moved slowly in his direction. Bob's look told her he thought she was way too involved. They trained cadaver dogs. They worked scenes with Nietzsche and Derrida and Voltaire without becoming attached to whomever they were searching for or with. Those were the rules.

But rules don't apply this time, do they? Some motherfucker is in our house, on our island, killing what we love. She thought about Voltaire lying just inside the door of the center where he had obviously died trying to defend his territory. What paperwork was important enough for you to be killed for, boy? What did we find that cost you your life?

Paige reached her brother.

"Are you ready, little sister?"

"I can't." It was all she could manage to say.

Bob lifted a clipboard from the hood of one of the cars. "Well, at least help me load up."

Andrew arrived just as Paige loaded Nietzsche into the truck. She waved him over and waved her brother away. "I'll be home later. Take care of the pups."

She walked toward Andrew, meeting him halfway between his Volkswagen and the empty spot where her brother had been. "Hey," she said. "You look exhausted."

Andrew skipped the small talk. "I know we don't have enough hands. Everyone's at the beach. Thought I'd come by to see if I could be of help here." He motioned toward the burned remains of Brent's home.

Paige knew the girls didn't trust him, but she found him sincere. Weird. Distant even in his attempt to fit in. But sincere. She fell in step with him, and together they walked back to the house.

"Nietzsche didn't find anything." Paige looked sideways to Andrew. Her voice was raspy from the smoke and soot.

"You think he had anything to do with the bodies?" Andrew stopped when they reached the front doorframe. He touched the charred wood with his index finger.

Paige stood several feet back.

They both understood the dangers beyond the opening, and they both respected the men and women who risked their lives, too much to disrespect the parameter.

Paige motioned toward the metal swing in the yard and moved in its direction. Her body ached from work and stress. After they both were seated, she said, "I do. I think it's all too coincidental. I do hope I'm just paranoid."

Andrew's eyes grew wide. "I happen to agree. Looks like those guys agree."

Several men and women in dark-blue jackets with big, gold letters moved about. Their gloved hands picked up unrecognizable items. They talked in low tones. They placed items in little baggies.

"Why do you think they're here instead of on the beach?" Paige asked.

"You've got me. All I can figure is someone higher up told them to check it out."

"Guess that makes sense." Paige wasn't so sure, but it didn't seem worth pursuing.

"Above my pay grade," Andrew said.

"I can't get hold of Katia." The words came out like they were punching the air. Paige looked up at Andrew. She wasn't sure why she shared with him, but her gut said it was safe.

"What? Since when?" His body visibly tensed. His intonation rose with each word.

"Over an hour now." Her insides were being wrung out like a dishrag by the fear of what that might mean. It seemed more real to say it out loud. She watched Andrew's reaction.

When Andrew didn't answer right away, she added, "Going to text Zahra. They've gotten really close. If anyone knows where she is, she does."

She took her phone out of her jacket pocket and placed her thumb over the tiny pad. Her screen jumped to life. She found the string of texts between herself and Zahra. They were a good representation of their relationship. Nothing. And then a flurry. All too fast to digest. She tapped out a message.

Any word from Katia? Worried about her.

Zahra's text was immediate: *Tried her forty minutes ago. Body in Grainger house too burnt to ID by sight. Elizabeth ID'ed. Both headed to Greenville*. Her text was accompanied by several emoticons—sad face, angry face, confused face.

And another text immediately after: *You?*

Paige typed: *Tried five or six times. Nothing.*

Paige watched her screen, waiting for a response. One minute. Two minutes. Three. She bit her nail while she waited. Her body tingled. Her stomach vibrated in a tickly sort of way, the way it always did when something was going to happen.

Andrew quietly waited while she typed. Paige looked up from the silent screen. "Nothing."

"Maybe they found Marco. Or he came home."

There's that tickly feeling again. She looked closely at Andrew's body language. His back was erect, his head turned methodically from side to side as he took in the scene. His eyes seemed to dart until they found something worth settling on, and then again and again, like an old typewriter. His eyes met the eyes of another man on the scene, and held, and communicated something silently. More tickles.

She thought back through scenes from the week. The man he made eye contact with looked familiar. He was FBI, obviously. Blue jacket. Gold letters. His name was something Wells. She changed her own posture a little, shook her hands out close to her sides, rolled her head slowly, pulling to one side and then the other so she could focus unnoticed on the blue-and-gold-clad man several hundred feet away.

Gerald Wells. That's it. The executive assistant director for one of the criminal branches of the FBI. She raised her shoulders, pushed them forward, and moved her gaze back to Andrew. Her phone buzzed. She and Andrew both looked at the device in her hand.

Overwhelmed. Doc, too. Can't leave. And another.

Elliot's here. He won't leave. Shock, I think.

Paige swallowed. "I'm finished here," she said to Andrew. She tried to keep her voice steady. She wanted to believe she was overreacting. "I'm going to bail."

Andrew nodded. "I'll see if they need my help. I was in the military in another life. I have a strong stomach for this kind of thing. Whatever I can do, you know?"

"Sure. I get it."

She didn't get it, didn't get any of it. Brent's house was in ashes. He was or would soon be lying on a steel table in a sterile room with the cold body of Elizabeth and Gina and others who all had some connection to Buxton Beach, North Carolina. Marco was missing. Katia wasn't answering her phone. She tapped out a response to Zahra, stood, and headed to her car.

Paige fought with herself as she slid behind the steering wheel. She needed to go home to deal with the papers and her brother and the animals and Voltaire. She also needed to know Katia was okay.

"Woof. Woof. Woof. Woof." The barking came out of nowhere. "That's not really an answer," she said out loud to no one. Her brain was obviously trying to offer a moment of levity.

The sound got closer. "Frankie? What the…"

The dog was in her lap before she could finish her sentence.

Chapter Twenty-Three

With every pin Richard touched, he felt a prick in another part of his body. The weather board was his, his and Marco's.

Marco. His son. His beautiful, autistic son. Richard wanted to share his world with him. It had always been his dream. He started to do just that through the wonderful twist of fate when one of the women woke up too quickly and Marco responded to her screams. He was furious at first. Marco knew to never open the workshop door.

He found the pin that marked the burial spot of the woman who brought Marco to him on that day. He touched it gently before he stepped back to admire the whole board. So many cruel women. So many wicked souls who walked the earth.

He thought about his daughter. He wanted her to be different. He wanted her to be clean. He touched the red pin next to the date of Elizabeth's death and then the purple pin. He looked at the workbench and felt his blood rise and beat in his temples. He had no storm to wash away the pain of this kill and no dune to house the hurt.

Richard's finger throbbed where the dog sunk his teeth into the flesh when he tried to grab him. Little piece of shit. Richard wished he would have held on. Should have taken him to the sink and slit his little furry throat. His agitation grew as he thought about his inability to follow through and take care of business. He needed the storm.

He hoped the little mutt was seriously hurt from the hard kick to the side he gave to send him flying out the door and off the back deck. He hoped he drowned in the ocean.

He put his left hand against his pants pocket and felt his phone solid between his palm and leg. He didn't need to open it again to know what was happening in the room behind the wall. He knew. And he knew she had to die.

****

It took Paige ten minutes to travel to Katia's house via the sand-encrusted highway that ran from one end of the islands to the other. Fucking storm. Normally Paige wasn't one to swear. Katia certainly rubbed off on her this week. Fuck was her favorite word. With the events of the past week, she'd come to learn that some situations demanded a one-word response. Fuck the storm. Fuck all of the bodies. Fuck the fire. First Gina, then Elizabeth, then Marco. Fuck. Fuck. Fuck.

Paige scratched the alert pup on the top of his head. She could feel his agitation. "I'm going as fast as I can, mister. What's up at the Billing's house, huh? How did you get out?"

Frankie's yips and wiggles slowed as Paige turned the car into the driveway. His body stiffened and his nose twitched.

Something was wrong. Paige felt it deep inside. But the house seemed exactly the same as it did early that morning when the women sat looking at pictures and eating cinnamon rolls. "Everything can change in an instant," she said, watching Frankie bounce from the rear seat to the front and back again. She gripped the handle and pushed open the door. "Show me what I need to see, boy."

Frankie headed behind the house. Paige considered calling him back and going to the front, but her instincts told her to quietly follow where he led—wherever he led. The back door was ajar, and Frankie nudged it with his front paw, looking up at Paige as the door moved inward.

Marco's pictures were scattered across the tabletop and on the floor. Paige pushed the door fully open and stepped inside. One foot in and one foot out, she paused. The house was too quiet. She opted to enter without a sound. Once inside, her eyes took in the scene. The television set was still on. Some cartoon she didn't recognize streamed into the room. That was weird and kind of eerie.

Frankie ran to the door of the workshop. Paige followed. She looked back at the TV. She wanted to turn it off, or at least mute the sound, but she couldn't. As long as seventies cartoons were alive, so was Marco. And if Marco was alive, so was Katia. And Katia had to be alive.

The door made no sound as Paige pushed it open and walked through. She'd never been down here. It felt strange to enter into such a private space. Katia's father was well-known, his work praised as some of the best in the business. The house she stood in now was his own work. She remembered the story of how he had made it for Katia's mom before they married. He wanted her to have a place to feel safe and loved, a place to raise a house filled with children. There's that "Everything changes in an instant" thing again. Katia's mom was killed by a drunk driver when Marco was a baby. According to Katia, she asked her father to build something smaller. That didn't go over well. Paige got it. This was his home, his space of memories. And his humongous workshop. She looked around it.

"Geesh," she said quietly. "What a layout."

Frankie had parked himself at the workbench that ran from midway of the far wall to the side door. Paige watched her own feet as she moved. One step, then two, three. Deeper into the cavernous space filled with the sweet smells of different wood shavings. Paige inhaled her own childhood memory of her grandpa, his hand on her shoulder. He loved to have her in his shop. She loved to be there.

****

"You act like her, you know," Richard said. "Your aunt. Not sure why it surprises me." He knew she could see the disgust in his face. He wanted her to see it. She sat there, now fully awake and aware of her surroundings. He hadn't planned to come back so soon. But when she took Marco's face in her hands, when she had kissed his forehead, he knew it was time. He had to save his son from her.

"Papi, what are you talking about? You're not making sense. Where are we? Why are we here?" Katia met his eyes as she spoke, still not understanding, still hovering between fear and relief that the three of them were here together.

"Marco," Richard said, his voice stern but loving. "Marco, look at me." Richard paused and waited as Marco moved his gaze from his sister and met his eyes.

Marco was shaking, and tears ran down his cheeks. "Come on, son. I need you to come to me."

Katia reached for Marco's hand, but he pulled it away. "That's it, son. You know who she is. What she's doing. She's just like those other women. She's bad, and bad girls have to pay for their sins."

Marco rocked. A low guttural sound moved through his lips and turned into words. “Sla. Sla. Slash. Fast. Slash. Fast.” His chant came more quickly. The words blurred together.

Katia looked at her brother.

Richard wondered what she thought. He could see the concern in her eyes for her brother. Marco’s words weren’t all clear, but enough of them were to know that he was chanting two words that told the world he knew what had to happen next. “Yes, Marco. That’s right. It’s your turn. Your sister is a bad girl. She’s given into the sins of others, and she’s trying to take you in, too.”

Richard glared at Katia. “I saw the way you touched him. You pretend to comfort him so you can take advantage of him.” Richard clenched his fists at his sides. “Just like her.”

He paused. He had to focus. He felt the red anger push up from his chest and into his face. “I love you. I do. From the moment we brought you home, I doted on you. I let your mom dote on you and your brother, and I didn’t hurt her. I never hurt her.”

“Papi. Why would I think you hurt her?” Tears welled in her eyes. “You’re not making any sense.”

Richard stood quietly. It was the only way he knew to regain control. He watched Katia’s face. She was starting to remember. He let her remember the pictures on the table, the reason she left the workshop and headed back upstairs.

“The pictures?” Katia pulled her brother toward her.

“Yes. Marco knew.” Richard turned toward his son. “You tried to tell your sister, didn’t you? What did we talk about, Marco? No one can ever know. And now she knows.” Richard pointed at Katia. “And now we have to do this together, son. And then we’ll hunt together during the storms and watch cartoons and mark our weather boards and build a hero’s life—together.”

“The picture of the corner of the workbench,” Katia said. “Your workbench.” Her words came out slowly. Her face contorted in what Richard thought to be something between anger and pain. “The purple shoe. We only found one at the crime scene.” The realization of what her father really was became apparent in her expression. “You have the other one. Marco has seen the other one, hasn’t he?”

“Marco’s old enough, now,” Richard said with pride. “He’s ready to work with me.” Katia’s scream filled the dingy space. Marco covered his ears and quickly moved toward his father.

Katia grabbed for her brother's hand, leg, foot. She couldn't get a good hold as he got farther from her. She screamed again and again.

Marco kept his hands over his ears. He started to chant.

"Slash. Fast. Slash. Fast." Marco's voice echoed.

Katia screamed.

Richard smiled. "No one can hear you."

Chapter Twenty-Four

What she thought was only the memory of her grandpa's hand on her shoulder turned out to be a real hand, the hand of Zahra. "What the hell?" Paige screeched and turned abruptly, forgetting to stay quiet.

"Sorry," Zahra said. "I tried to let you know I was here without scaring you and without warning anyone else in the house. You looked right at me."

"Fuck," Paige said. "I didn't see you." Paige motioned toward Frankie rather than waste any more words.

"What's he doing?" Zahra kept her voice barely above a whisper.

Paige matched her tone. "Not sure. He found me at the Grainger fire. Alone. I figured I needed to see what was going on. How'd you know?"

"What? That you're here?" Zahra furrowed her brow. "I didn't. I couldn't stand it anymore when Katia didn't answer. I told Dr. Webb I was going to take a quick break and swing by. The back door was open."

Paige's eye caught a glimmer of light at Zahra's side. Her gun was drawn. "Do you think you need that?" Paige was a pacifist. Guns made her nervous.

"Fuck, yeah," Zahra said. She held the gun tightly and rubbed it with the palm of her free hand.

"Why in the world would you… Never mind. Do you think the pup knows something we don't?"

"Did you search the house?" Zahra's voice was steady and low. Paige was glad she was here.

"Yes. And no. We came straight down here, so we didn't go upstairs, but there were no sounds. Nothing has happened since we came down here." Paige stood at the bench. She ran her fingers around the edges to feel for irregularities. "Something about the bench. Frankie refuses to move."

Zahra tucked the gun into the holster and got down on hands and knees. "What's down here, boy? What do you see? You smell something?" She looked up at Paige. "Too bad he can't tell us. There's nothing down here. It's a bench. Just wood and nails."

They moved back into an upright position away from the workbench. "We can stare at it all day," Zahra said. "It isn't going to change anything. I say we try calling and texting again, then we take a look around the house. There has to be something here to tell us what the fuck is going on."

"Did you see the pictures when you came in?" Paige asked.

"Yeah. Figured Katia was frustrated being alone and waiting for news. She was in the last text. Probably took a swipe at them. I would have."

Paige nodded slowly. "Probably, but what if—"

"Don't start, Paige," Zahra interrupted. "I can't. Katia's fine. She just couldn't wait any longer and headed out with Frankie and then he bolted. Now she's looking for her brother and you." Zahra looked over at Frankie, who was still under the workbench, a low growl in his throat.

Zahra pulled her phone out of her pocket. "Shitty reception down here. Come on. At least come up to the kitchen. Let's look at the photos again. Maybe we missed something."

"You go," Paige said. "I'm going to take one more look." She moved back toward Frankie, his tail thumping against the wood as she neared. "You want me to stay, don't you, boy?" Paige sat on her bottom and looked at the underneath of the bench. Nothing. She searched the corners and the seams. She ran her fingers along each grain of wood, hoping something would stand out. Nothing. Paige tapped, rubbed, looked over everything several times.

She was about to give up and join Zahra upstairs when something caught her eye. It was a hairline fracture in the wood, against the grain. It looked like two pieces of wood were linked together. She tapped the Flashlight icon on her phone and pointed the light on the crack. As she ran her finger across it, a piece of wood gave way and then popped back in place. She pushed again. This time, she held the wood and slid the finger of her other hand under the raised piece. She felt a button.

Paige moved her mouth to yell for Zahra as the whole bench moved outward. A section of thick, dark concrete moved as well. Beyond it was a doorway. Beyond that, a dingy light. It took what felt like an eternity for her eyes to adjust. There were two figures. One moved quickly toward the other. Marco?

Everything seemed to be happening at once. Sounds were everywhere. Paige couldn't tell where one started or where another ended. It seemed like everywhere and nowhere at the same time. She tried to concentrate on the shadow that looked like Marco. He appeared unmoving except for his right hand, which tapped out a rhythm against his leg.

There was more movement, another sound. Katia's father moved in slow motion. Something shiny was by his side. He raised it until it pointed forward from his chest.

"Marco," Richard said. "We have to go. Come here, son." Richard touched Marco's fingers and pulled his hand away from his side.

Just at the edge of Paige's sight, a new movement. She turned. Katia. The woman strained against something that held her in place. Her voice was austere. "A knife." She pulled harder against the restraints. "Marco. Get Marco."

Paige strained to understand the words, to sort through the sounds. She told her own body to react, but she was frozen. Not even her arm would raise to defend her face from harm.

Richard pulled Marco tight against his chest. A glint of silver pushed against Marco's neck.

And then Frankie was there. He jumped past Paige and straight up toward Richard's arm.

Richard jerked. The knife came away and found Frankie.

The dog yelped and fell to the ground. He got up and headed for Richard again.

Paige willed with all her might for her legs to move.

The sound of the chains clanked in her ears and mixed with Katia's scream and Marco's guttural noises.

Then she heard a shot and the sound of her own scream.

Richard slumped forward toward Katia. Blood streamed onto the floor.

Paige looked to where the knife touched Marco's tan skin. Marco. Marco stood still except for the fingers that tap, tap, tapped, and his mouth that formed two words over and over again: "Slash. Fast. Slash. Fast. Slash. Fast." Paige turned away. She needed to see Katia.

Katia stretched forward as far as she possibly could to reach Marco. The sound of her scream danced across the room to meet with his chant and with Paige's scream.

Paige stood motionless, still unsure of how to make her feet move.

Zahra appeared, weapon in hand. She pulled Paige away from the crude opening and sat her down against the opposite wall before she stepped through to assess the situation in the concrete room.

Richard Billings was alive. Her shot went through his leg. It was her only choice based on the way he held Marco. She kicked the knife away from his side and pointed her gun at his head. "You move, and I'll kill you."

Richard didn't move.

Frankie was okay. His cut was superficial. He now sat between Richard and Katia.

Katia's restraints were hinged, double-lock steel. Zahra said to Richard, "Where are the keys for these?" When he didn't answer, she moved her gun as if to strike him. "Where?"

"In the workshop," he muttered.

Zahra would worry about that later. More pressing things needed taken care of right now.

"Are you okay?" Her question was pointed at Katia, who stopped screaming and now sat perfectly still and stared at her father.

Katia nodded. Her voice was wooden. "Get Marco out of here. Get him somewhere safe." And she said to Marco in a more-normal tone, "Listen, Monkey Head. I need you to go with Zahra. You do exactly what she says, okay?"

"Slash. Fast. Slash. Fast. Katia was bad. Slash. Fast."

Zahra looked toward Paige. "The police will be here soon. I dialed 911 as soon as I heard you scream. I threw the phone on the workbench."

Paige's voice shook. "You are the police."

"Touché. You think you can take Marco up to watch cartoons and sit with him while I tend to Katia and Richard?"

Paige stood and gave a wan smile. "I think I can do that." She took Marco's hand and led him through the opening and up the stairs.

****

Zahra sat next to Katia on the stained mattress, her leg against Katia's, the gun pointed once more at Richard's head. "I'm going to wait with you. Help's on the way."

In a delayed reaction, Katia's entire body shook. Her teeth chattered when she tried to talk. "M-m-mar-m-marco."

"Marco's fine. Paige is with him."

"He, I, he, he thought I was doing something to Marco," Katia stuttered. "He said something about his aunt and him." Katia's words were broken, choked out of her mouth one at a time. "I don't understand. He wanted Marco to kill me. He wanted to kill me."

For a quick moment, Zahra wrapped her whole body around Katia, her eyes never leaving Richard. "I know. I'm here." She kept one arm around her and sat back at attention.

"What am I going to do?" Katia's gaze was on her father.

Zahra looked in the same direction. Richard didn't move. "We. What are we going to do? I am not going anywhere, Katia. When the other officers get here, they'll take your dad away. You and Marco—and Paige and Frankie—will be evaluated. And then, we'll start to rebuild. You and me. I've got you."

"I, I." Katia laid her head against Zahra's shoulder.

"Shhh." Zahra laid her head against Katia's. The sirens were close. They were safe.

Epilogue

Katia watched as her brother chose a series of pictures to form a sentence on his new communication aid. Marco refused to use it for the first two weeks after their father was pulled from the small room under the dune. Paige and Dr. Abney were tolerant and persistent, though, and by week three he was quite adept at this new method of interaction.

Katia hoped her brother's short bursts of words would eventually turn into full sentences. There was so much about their father that he had locked inside, so much that she needed to know.

She thought about her phone conversation with their father shortly after he was released from the hospital and taken to prison to await his trial.

"You should have died, Papi."

"Come see me, Katia. I'll tell you everything."

"Leave us alone, Papi. I can't. Do you know what you've done to us?"

"I'm going to be executed, Katia. I deserve to see my children."

She felt her body tense and her throat tighten. He didn't care that reporters stood outside their home, that they followed her everywhere, that there were death threats in her email every day. There was even an online discussion board about them where people claimed she must have known and that Marco probably helped.

"No. I'll not let you continue to hurt us, to hurt him."

She hung up on him. He didn't call back. Some days she wanted him to call. As much as she hated the Sandman, she missed Papi.

Katia turned her attention back to what was important.

Paige sat next to Marco. She made faces at his word choices. He chose something else equally as silly. She made another face. He doubled over in a fit of teenage laughter.

Mornings like this were becoming more regular as days turned into weeks and weeks into months. Four months, to be precise.

Katia looked out the window. Instead of the sand and ocean, she saw the fence that was built to keep them safer from harm. "Not safe," Zahra said after it was built. "Safer. You still have to be aware of your surroundings at all times."

Even on this chilly March morning, tourists crowded the sand outside the wooden barrier. Apparently, they hoped to get a glimpse of the daughter of one of the most horrific serial killers of all times.

There would be a trial. She would have to testify. There would be peaks and lulls in the number of reporters and gawkers and threats. But every day, people withdrew a little more. Every day the townspeople stared a little less.

Her one constant was Zahra. She listened to her now as she hummed an old Bruno Mars song in the kitchen. She didn't talk much about what she and Dr. Webb found over the months that followed the discovery of Gina's remains. She told Katia to let her know when she was ready. Katia wanted more facts. But not yet. Nothing else yet.

Bruno Mars's lyrics got closer as Katia looked at the crew assembled in her home.

When Zahra wrapped her arms around Katia's waist, the humming stopped. "Quite a motley crew you have here, my love."

Katia smiled a genuine, full-face grin. "Indeed, milady. A more unlikely crew you will rarely find."

Both women observed their friends who came together to celebrate Zahra's birthday. In addition to Marco and Paige, there were Elliot and Mrs. Ellington who stood together outside the big, dining room window. Elliot tended to the burgers on the grill, and the older woman hung on to his every word. Elliot's wife, Josephine, talked quietly with Bob in the living room. The two of them watched Elliot and Josephine's daughters roll around on the floor with Frankie. The house was filled with what Katia could only describe as a cloud of laughter.

Katia turned to briefly press her lips to Zahra's. She looked again at the assembly. "I actually kind of wish Andrew was here." Katia tilted her head back against Zahra's shoulder until Zahra's soft curls tickled her forehead.

"Oh you do, do you?" Zahra said. "I thought he creeped you out."

"He did. Does. Did. Fuck. Whatever. He was a part of this. I just hate to think we ran him off without giving him a chance."

"We can only go forward." Zahra pressed herself tightly against Katia's back.

Katia could feel the smile of this amazing woman, could feel the warm breath against her neck, as she let herself sink back into the comfortable contours of her soft body.

Zahra sighed. "I always want you by my side," she said.

"I kind of like being by your front, actually." Katia reached her arm up and back, cupped her partner's head and pulled it down toward her own.

Their lips touched. Zahra spoke softly. "Oh. There, too. And behind. And. And. And."

Katia looked back to Paige and Marco. The two were still lost in their world of jokes and laughter.

Somc days, Katia still saw horror and pain in his eyes. She wished she could wipe away the pain of knowing, of seeing. But only time could do that. Until then, they would live for days like today. Today, the sun was shining. Today, she was surrounded by friends. Today, love was winning. Today, that was enough.

THE END

About the Author

Tammy Bird lives in Wendell, North Carolina with her wife and two cats. She is an educator by day and a writer by night. Her greatest passion is storytelling with a purpose. As such, the most important part of the writing process for her is the development of characters who represent the under-represented.

Tammy's work is rarely defined as sweet or cozy, and that is okay. She is not here for sweet or cozy. She is here for psychologically hard and gritty and real.

You can connect with Tammy on Instagram @tammysbird or on Twitter @Tammy_Bird. You can also visit her website at https://tammybird.com.

Additional Titles From Flashpoint Publications

Our Happy Hours, LGBT Voices From the Gay Bars

Story Collectors Lee Lynch and S. Renée Bess

During the days and nights following the massacre at the Pulse Nightclub in Orlando, Florida, the world listened as various spokespersons attempted to explain to the general public exactly what the gay bar/club meant to LGBTQI people.

The words "safe place," "refuge," "free to be ourselves" flew through the air.

We queer writers grappled with the tragedy alongside our brothers and sisters. How could we express our feelings about the places where we could drop all pretense of conforming to the hetero-normative society's rules? What words could we gather to let the rest of the world know the pain we felt upon losing so many beautiful strangers on a night in June and in a place that had been one of our havens?

How and why does the gay bar intersect so many of our lives? The stories and poems living between the covers of this book attempt to answer those questions. Spend a few happy hours with us in our gay bars.

All profits will be donated to LGBTQI Youth Organizations

Gum for Gracie

By Ona Marae

In the summer of 1974, Bobbie Rossi's life is near perfect. She's twenty-eight, has a teaching position at a junior college, a new lesbian lover, and a family she adores. There is only one problem. Her twin sister and her nieces live on the other side of Kansas with a man who is abusive, a man who absolutely hates his wife's twin and will do anything to prove that hatred.

In trying to help her sister and nieces escape the abuse, Bobbie sets into motion an explosive emotional prairie fire, with Bobbie's young niece, Gracie, caught in its direct path.

Now, in the aftermath, will working through the abuse of a family, and the guilt spawned by the assault of young Gracie, destroy the life that Bobbie has created? Or will it weave three women and three young girls together in a new family as only love and fire can?

Finding Gracie's Glory
Book 1 in the Romance in the Yukon Series

By Patty Schramm

Gracie Kato survived years of abuse at the hands of her wife. While her body has healed, her heart and soul remain damaged. Gracie seeks solace at her grandfather's home in the Yukon Territory of Canada. There she'll be able to work at his gold mine, named for her grandmother, Gracie's Glory. It's the perfect place for her to start over again.

Liv Templeton's heart was crushed years ago and she doesn't see any chance of recovery. She's never alone unless she wants to be, but never seeks any commitments. Instead she puts all her energy and time into running the family mining business. From the moment they meet,

Gracie and Liv's connection, physical and emotional, is obvious to them both. Is Liv ready for a serious relationship? Even if she is, will she be able to convince Gracie to trust again? To let her soul heal? Will Gracie open herself up to Liv? Or will she close her heart forever?

Reflections of Fate

By Patty Schramm

Leoni Wolf lived and worked on the Qualla Boundry in Cherokee, North Carolina her entire life. It was her home and the place she belonged. Leoni once believed in fate and that everything happened for a reason. Until her wife, Tayanita, was killed in a tragic accident. What possible reason could there be for her death? The event shattered Leoni's world.

Each day Leoni awoke, gazed at her reflection in the old free-standing mirror and convinced herself she could get through one more day.
Nicola Daelis was tired of fate intervening in her life and wanted to throttle her. Before Nicola could act on the event that could change it all, fate landed a beautiful, dark-eyed woman in her lap and turned Nicola's world upside down.

Fighting for their lives, and often against each other, Nicola and Leoni must embark upon an adventure that could be the beginning of something new. Or the end of them both.

Better Together

By Patty Schramm

Mac Bradenton has never been south of the Mason Dixon Line or across a body of water wider than the Ohio River. But her best friend is sick and on a quest to complete her bucket list. First stop is Paris, France. Mac goes along expecting to enjoy the time with Kristy, never anticipating just how much her life will change.

They meet up with Kristy's friend, Lenie, who has promised to give them a guided tour of Paris and while there, romance blossoms between Mac and Lenie.

Once home, life takes some major turns for Mac. As she struggles to deal with the challenges thrown at her, will everything fall apart? Or will she be able to lean on Lenie knowing that, no matter what happens, they are better together?

Souls' Rescue

By Patty Schramm

Kelly McCoy is a firefighter and paramedic who's lived most of her adult life in New York. After 9-11, she relocates to Cincinnati, nursing a broken heart and looking for a new start. She takes one day at a time, trying not to let her losses overwhelm her.

Talia Stoddard is an insurance wiz who's always been smart on the job, but unlucky in love. After years of being told that she's too big, too tall, too black, too lesbian, and not a very snappy dresser, Talia has resigned herself to a life alone with only her dear gay friend Jacob for a diversion.

When Kelly and Talia's lives crash into one another, it's under the most stressful and threatening circumstances. Talia is in terrible danger, and it's up to Kelly to rescue her. In the horrendous situation they end up in, neither expects to find a friend, much less a soul mate.

Will they rescue one another and heal the wounds of their pasts? Or will they both continue to believe that they're not worthy of the kind of love the other might offer?

Souls' Rescue is the story of opening up to love, taking chances, and building a life that everyone dreams about, but few people ever find.

CPSIA information can be obtained
at www.ICGtesting.com
Printed in the USA
FFHW010748230319
51154766-56622FF